LEGACY OI

LEPRECHAUN

A VILLAGE MYSTERY

DAVID HUXLEY

- 0 -

HASLEMERE PUBLICATIONS

Second Edition - reprint.

Haslemere Publications. 16, Haslemere Drive, Cheadle Hulme, Cheadle, Cheshire. SK8 6JY.

ISBN 978- 0 – 9508727 – 1 - 1.

Cover Illustration – Cliff Murphy.

Cover design - Kwik Communications Limited, Stockport, Cheshire

Printed by - Deanprint Limited, Cheadle Heath Works, Stockport Road, Stockport SK3 0PR

With my grateful thanks to Barbara, Judy, Alan and Mike for editorial help and advice   and Jean for endless support and forbearance during writing and revision over many long hours.

oOo

HASLEMERE PUBLICATIONS

LEGACY OF THE LEPRECHAUN

CHAPTER ONE

"Georgina, are you busy at the moment, my love?" Mrs. Ponsonby was calling from the dining room.

"I be 'elpin' Jim to 'is seat by the winder, Mrs. Ponsonby," replied the young waitress in her soft, Devonshire accent, as she settled the old man into a wicker chair and plumped a cushion before placing it at his back. He dropped heavily onto the seat; the walk from the dining room where breakfast was still being served to this spot in the sun lounge was more than enough for limbs that were feeble now, after serving him well for some eighty-five years.

"Well, when you've done that, Georgina, please would you give Millie a hand in the kitchen? She's on her own, and getting terribly behind with the breakfasts. Ann's just phoned in to say she's sick again."

'Likely morning sickness' thought Georgina. 'Well I wouldn't put it past her'. "Yeh, right y'are, Mrs. Ponsonby, I've done in y'ere, now, anyway. 'E be fine.

I'll go and get things movin' a bit.   Yer can rely on me."

"I know that, my love, thank you."

"Now, you enjoy this 'ere sunshine, Jim.   It'll do 'ee good, it will.   You'll feel a lot better for it; you will, really."

"Aye, thanks, luv.   I'll be all reet 'ere a bit.   I'll be great.   You go on.   Boss wants yer – in't kitchen."

So Georgina left the old man sitting at the large wall of glass and taking in the picturesque view from the sun-lounge of the small sea-side hotel in South Devon. The secluded site was on a ledge, a little way up a red sand-stone cliff.   In front, outside the large window, a terrace ran the full length of the building and around one side to where the main hotel entrance was situated.   From here, a wide access drive led up to the entrance gates and then onto a lane that went a few hundred yards down to the small village with its one larger hotel, some guest houses, a post office, cafes, kiosks, and the obligatory car park.

At the other end of the terrace, a few stone steps, with guard hand-rails, led into a small garden, mostly of lawn with a few flower beds.   A shingle path then led further down to a slipway for small boats, and beyond that still, a sandy, gravelly beach, onto which there was the constant ebb and flow of the sea, the ceaseless swish and suck, swish and suck, as the waves lapped the sand. Sometimes the water would come with the fury of a raging storm, lashing the slipway and sending clouds of foam way up into the hotel garden or even onto the terrace itself; the spray pelting onto the glass of the sun lounge window with deafening sound. At other times, and this was such a time, the gentle splash at the shoreline could only just be heard in the lounge, even with the top and side windows wide open. Today the sea was calm; a blue almost cloudless sky was reflected in the smooth surfaces of the waters, while the hot, bright sun shone with a brilliance that illuminated the whole scene with a warm glow. And the sea just sparkled.

Behind the hotel, the red cliffs soared upwards for over a hundred feet and continued along the line of the coast, always fronted by the beach, for what might have been many miles. Gulls and many other sea birds nested there, and their cries could be heard constantly, as they whirled around, landing now and then to extract some morsel from the ground – or sometimes to pick up food thrown by walkers or other users of the beach and even by hotel staff with leftovers from meals.

As soon as Mrs. Ponsonby was satisfied that Georgina had gone into the kitchen to assist the cook, and that all was well in that quarter, she made her way back to the dining room. She was a tall, 'matronly' type of woman with greying hair tied neatly into a bun on the top of her head. Georgina was a very pleasant, obliging nineteen year old, willing to 'fit in' wherever she was needed, and as it was Mrs. Ponsonby's belief that happy staff equals efficient staff, the lady endeavoured to maintain both. Now, with Georgina speedily putting breakfasts onto plates and pushing them out to the two waitresses, all seemed to be well.

In the dining room, the latest arrival had just come down from her room, helped herself to the breakfast starters, orange juice and a small dish of cornflakes, and was seated at the table allotted to her. Mrs. Ponsonby crossed to greet her new guest. "Good morning, Mrs. Lomax," she said. "Did you sleep well, last night?"

"Very well, thank you." The reply was spoken after a sip of the orange juice, for Mrs. Ponsonby had taken

Mrs. Jane Lomax by surprise. Then the guest added, "I always sleep well even in a strange bed, and last night was no exception. I slept soundly."

"I'm so glad. I think you'll find it very restful here, and we try to maintain a relaxed atmosphere. You'll enjoy it."

"Yes, I'm sure I will. Thank you."

"Now, I won't disturb your breakfast any longer, Mrs. Lomax. The main course will be along any moment, and if you require anything more – anything at all –don't hesitate to ask. We're all very happy to help."

"Thank you, Mrs. Ponsonby. I'll remember that." Then Mrs. Ponsonby moved away.

The dining room was situated behind a sun lounge and there was a connecting doorway with a glass-paned door between the two. Once, before the sun lounge had been constructed, the dining room was the front room of the house. Now the view down to the garden and slipway could be seen from the room no longer, but a large side window looked along the line of the cliffs and down to the shore and the sea. The shore stretched quite a long way before it disappeared at a point where the cliff jutted out seaward and, except at very low tide, the waves lapped the rocks at its base. Then it was just the blue sea, ebbing and flowing, splashing and bubbling, stretching to the far horizon. The table allotted to Mrs. Lomax was not actually in the window because one which was set for three or four persons occupied that position, but she was still able to see over it and admire the expanse of seascape before her. Now, people were strolling along the expanse of sand, some with dogs that barked and scampered after the gulls – although the birds were much too fast and took to flight long before any predatory animal came close enough to pose even the slightest danger. Several children played at the water's edge, young boys threw stones and pebbles into the foaming surf, attempting to bounce the missiles on the wave crests. It was a pleasant scene.

By the time Mrs. Lomax had finished her breakfast, the room was empty; the other guests having left to return to their rooms, some to wander through the sun lounge, some to admire the view, and some to continue onto the terrace, into the garden, and even, as some chose to do, stroll down to the sandy beach. Others were preparing for the day's sightseeing, before going to the small car park at the rear of the building and driving away in their respective vehicles. So the lady rose from her seat and sauntered across to the door through which she entered the sun lounge. No one was there now, except for the old gentleman, slumped in the wicker chair and gazing out to sea. She could hardly tell whether or not he was awake and she was reluctant to disturb him. She crossed to another seat at the other end of the lounge and took in the sight once again. It really was lovely.

Jane Lomax had recently celebrated her fortieth birthday. She was a slender woman of reasonable height, with dark hair, now streaked with grey, which grew down to her neck and shoulders and was cut into a neat fringe. It covered her ears, and framed her delicate face. Her intelligent eyes darted incessantly from one thing to another, so there was very little that passed unnoticed.

In life, she had done well. From her childhood home, on the hillside of a north-country village, she had gained a scholarship to Manchester High School for Girls, and gone on to take a degree at Lancaster University. It was there that Simon Lomax came into her life, and never left it again. They both graduated, and when Simon joined the civil service with a posting to London, she followed quickly, and soon they were married. Barely two years later, she was the mother of two daughters, to whom she devoted the many years that followed, living in a comfortable, roomy house in suburban London, tending the substantial garden that became a credit to her, and doing the many tasks allotted to her as housewife, mother, and more recently, confidante and adviser on many matters of the heart that seemed to confront most people in the teenage years. She enjoyed the role and even thought of setting herself up as an 'agony aunt', with a regular column in the local newspaper.

Simon progressed in the civil service and gained promotion to the diplomatic corps. As a result, he often spent days – and nights – away from home, away from her, but always returned with an eager passion for her, and tender nights of re-union followed. She knew that Simon worshipped her just as much as she worshipped him, and the times apart were no more than the necessity of his career, to be endured, and compensated for afterwards. Each trusted the other implicitly and knew that they had no reason to do otherwise. Jane, perhaps naively, even flattered herself that Simon never looked at another woman.

On this occasion, though, it was she who had come away, alone. There was no problem; Simon had no further assignments for the immediate future and knew that this was something she wanted to do – had to do – for herself, and he was quite content. The girls were old enough now to look after themselves and, if necessary, their father as well. Jane also knew that if any of them had volunteered to accompany her, she would have had to decline, and if they had pressed the matter she would have closed the whole thing down, and forgotten it all for a while, although not for ever. But no one had suggested that she should have company – probably they would have found it boring anyway – and so she was alone, and now she found herself at this charming little hotel on the south coast of Devon, looking out to sea on this bright, sunny morning. For a while, she mused on the situation, and then a voice almost startled her. "Not goin' far this mornin' then?" It was the old man at the other side of the lounge.

"Er, no, well, I don't know, yet," she managed to blurt out, feeling so silly at making such a feeble, indecisive reply. The old chap came to her aid:

"Aye, well, 'appen there's time. Not been 'ere long enough to know, like. 'ave yer? "

"No, that's right. I'll have to start exploring. In fact, I think I'll wander down there now."

"Oh, don't go 'til yer ready, luv. I wasna suggestin..."

"Of course you weren't. But it is time I got moving. I want some sea air in these lungs of mine. I really need that."

"Aye, well, do yer good. Aye, it'll certainly d' that," the old man remarked. " 'Bye, then."

"Goodbye." And with that Jane wandered out onto the terrace, down the steps into the garden, and on further until she reached the sand. When she turned and looked back up to the hotel she saw that the old man was still seated there at the lounge window. She raised her hand in a polite wave, but there was no discernable movement from the man, and she concluded that he was either asleep, or else his age meant that his eyesight was worsening. So she turned away, determined not to look up there again.

It had been her intention to continue along the beach, below the cliffs for a while, but she soon noticed that, in the other direction, there was a flight of stone steps which were cut in the rock that formed a low promontory separating the beach from the village and this would inevitably take her over to the village, without the necessity of returning to the hotel and then going out of the main drive, and down the lane. So she climbed up onto the promontory, its flat top dissected with low fences to form two or three small gardens or allotments for village residents. The path cut through these until steps at the other side led down again and joined the lane almost at the point where the village began.

In the village there was quite a lot of activity by this time, as holiday-makers from a wide surrounding area started to congregate, as they did each morning. The post office-cum-newsagents was crammed with folk, jostling with as much politeness as they could manage, buying newspapers and magazines, post cards and gifts, and more essential items such as bread, milk, sweets and cigarettes.

A few doors along, a small café was doing very good trade already, and coffee was being served, even at the two small tables that spilled out onto the narrow pavement.   Across the road, people were congregating at the start of a guided walk, and a short distance further down, cars were queuing for parking spaces.   A luxury coach bearing the sign 'Torquay' blocked the narrow street for a few moments while it stopped to pick up a few passengers for the twenty-odd mile journey to its destination resort.

Jane managed to procure a daily newspaper at the shop, and then wandered on along the little street that ran parallel to the sea until she reached a less-crowded spot and a vacant public seat.   Beyond, the road turned somewhat and then headed northward along the open coast - the 'Torquay' coach had gone that way.   She sat down and felt the wooden seat, warmed by the strengthening sun, through her thin dress.   She felt the sun on her face, accentuated by the gentle breeze that also ruffled her hair, and she smelt the sea – the clean salty air.   What a joy! Settled on the seat for a while, she began to read snippets of news from the paper.   Then there was the sound of a jingle from the inside of her handbag.   Reaching into it, she extracted her mobile phone. Simon was calling: "Darling, where are you?" he asked

"At the seaside. In gorgeous weather. Where are you, my dearest?"

"In the bloody office. Cloud-covered London."

"Are you all right? Is everything…?"

"Everything's fine. Don't worry about a thing."

'The girls?'

"They're o.k. Emma went off to college just after eight, and I dropped Sally at her place well before nine. In fact, I was in early this morning. Beth made a cheeky comment about it." Beth was Simon's P.A.

"And yesterday? Did you get your meals properly?"

"Of course we did. All three of us can cook, you know. Sally made a smashing shepherd's pie."

"That sounds good, then."

"It is good. Stop worrying, Jane. Now how's it going? Your investigation? Got any positive….?"

"Darling, I've hardly been here a day, you know. So I can't expect results immediately. But I've made a start, and I know what I shall need to do next. I shall just need a little time.   It will come together, you'll see."

"Well, I wouldn't expect anything else, knowing you. Superwoman!"

"I'm not, you know.   But it's nice to have the vote of confidence."

"You deserve nothing less. Anyway, my dearest, I must go. E.U. meeting in ten minutes.   Just enjoy, and take care."

"Yes, I will. 'Bye, my love   Oh, tell Sally I'll ring her tonight."

"Ok. Will do. 'Bye, darling."   And he rang off.

Time had passed, and now Jane began thinking about lunch. On the end of the seaward-facing buildings, she had already noticed a sign advertising a restaurant. She decided to take a closer look.   A conglomerate of small buildings faced the sea, with their backs to the main street; most of them had been fishermen's cottages. Now much 'improved', they had become holiday cottages, small 'bed and breakfast' establishments and, right at this end, furthest from the village centre, one had become a restaurant. Black notice boards with writing in white chalk offered,

'Breakfasts, Lunches, Afternoon Teas and Evening Dinners – Open every day, 7.a.m. to 10.p.m.'

Jane went inside, climbed the polished wooden staircase to the upper floor and entered a medium-sized room containing about a dozen dark wooden tables, each set for two or four people. Table mats and cutlery had been placed on the bare wooden table tops and wooden chairs were in position. Everywhere was spotlessly clean, although the room was rather dark, being lit from only two small windows that overlooked the small promenade. Three tables were already occupied, but Jane was able to take a small one, set for two, near one of the windows. Promptly, a pleasant young man came to take her order – a baked potato with some filling or other, salad – always there was salad – and a glass of red wine. Ice cream and coffee afterwards. She lingered over the coffee, thinking about Simon – how much she loved him – and the girls, once so innocent, trusting, vulnerable, and now growing well, learning, working, full of happiness and joy, expectant of wonderful times in the future, and yet sufficiently practical to know that there would be bad times as well as good – and Sally could even make a good shepherd's pie.   She wondered if, and then who, they might choose to marry, and when they would have their own children   She knew that Sally was already 'going steady' with Rupe, her boyfriend - and she had the warm certainty that both her daughters would be excellent mothers.   She was still musing when she heard a voice behind her.   "Did you enjoy your meal, madam?   Was everything all right?"   The young man was ready to clear her table.

"Oh yes, lovely thank you.   I'll have the bill, now please."

"Certainly, madam."   The man hurried away, but returned a moment later with a small plate on which the bill was placed.   She took the slip of paper, paid the amount requested and called "Goodbye," as she descended the wooden staircase, and went out into the bright sunlight of the promenade.

The afternoon sun was quite strong and, by this time, many people had arrived on the beach – a stretch of fine sand that continued beyond the last buildings of the village and for an indefinable distance beside the open road which, she assumed, led finally to Torquay.   Almost by the minute, the beach became wider as the tide receded. Children were playing there now, building sand castles, trying to fly small kites, running, paddling in pools of water, some wearing bathing costumes and others preparing themselves for fun in the gentle, splashing waves. A young girl wearing a bikini was lying face downwards on a towel, allowing the sun to warm the soft skin of her back, and although she seemed oblivious as she read a book placed on the sand in front of her, she would have been well aware of the attention being paid to her by several young men as they passed by, whistling, coughing, or adopting other ways of expressing appreciation. A young boy, hardly old enough for school and clad only in swimming trunks, wandered right up to her and seemed to stare. She turned to look at him. "Hi," she said. But timidity got the better of the lad, and he turned and scampered away, back to where his mother was sitting in a hired deck chair with her eyes closed.

"Where've yer bin, Sammy? You awright?"

"Aye," said Sammy, as he squatted down on the sand and continued to play.

The tide had receded further now, and Jane noticed that the water's edge was beyond the end of the little promontory which separated the main village beach from the one that fronted her hotel, and so she was able to walk on the sand, around the rocky outcrop, and arrive on the stretch of beach from where she had started that morning. It only took a couple of minutes, rather than the five or ten it would have taken if she had returned to the village and used the steps and path past the little croft and allotment gardens or had climbed the hill with the surfaced road leading to the main entrance to the hotel grounds. Soon, she had climbed up to the hotel terrace, from where she entered the sun lounge once again. The room was deserted. She turned to look back at the view – the sunshine, the rocky cliffs, the much extended beach, more populated now, and the waves, further out, but still breaking into white foam, splashing, gurgling, sucking, as they reached the pebbles and soft white sand. A voice came from behind her. "Afternoon, ma'am, be ee all right?" It was a soft, gentle voice with a southern accent and belonged to Georgina. Jane turned to her.

"Oh, yes, thank you. I was just admiring the view."

"It's usely a good 'un from 'ere, ma'am. Even when weather's poor. Always summat to see."

"Yes, lovely." There was a pause and then Georgina asked: "Can I get ee summat, ma'am? A drink, mebbe?"

"Oh no, thank you. I'll go to my room and make something there a little later. I've only just had lunch."

"Right y'are, ma'am, as you wish." The girl turned away but after a moment, Jane called her back.

"Tell me," she said. "There was an old gentleman sitting here this morning?"

"Ole Jimmy, yer mean? E'll be in 'is room, I 'spect. Spends 'is time up there. Fast asleep till night time when the 'soaps' come on the telly. Then 'e stays awake half the night, watchin'. Watches films 'til the early hours. Well, there's nowt else 'e can do, is there, ma'am? Not that 'e sees much, mind. Not wiyis eyesight goin' an' all. But 'e sees a bit, and 'ears the rest. "

"Does he not go out? Take the air?" Jane asked.

"Not in 'is condition. Lost the use of 'is legs, y'see. Can't walk nowhere, now."

"That's a shame.   But you seem to know him very well?"

"Aye, ma'am. 'E comes for about ten days, two or three times a year.   'Is daughter brings 'im down from up Bristol   way.   And   she   fetches   'im   back   after. She's due down 'ere on Saturday."

Jane asked: "I wonder if he'd enjoy a trip out in the car.   I'd take him, and I'd enjoy the company.   What do you think?"

"Well,   yer   can   ask   'im,   ma'am.   'E   might   be thrilled, or 'e might not.   But there be no 'arm in askin'. An' it'd be right good of yer, really it would.   Yer can ask 'im tomorrer."

"I thought tonight, after dinner?"

"E 'as it in 'is room.   Doesn't come down.   We take it up. We don't mind."

"That's very kind of you," Jane said.   "Then I'll see him in the morning."   Then she went off to her own room, made her tea and enjoyed it with her favourite biscuits.

ooooooOooooo

CHAPTER TWO

Nobody saw the vehicle and its trailer as it careered, driverless, across the 'T' junction where Fell Lane meets the valley road and crashed into the sturdy stone wall that protects the steep river bank on its far side. Although the wall had recently undergone re-building with large stone slabs and layer upon layer of cement, it could not withstand the force of the impact. It crumbled, gradually at first, but inexorably, until its whole structure gave way, and the runaway vehicle, with its flat-bed trailer attached, slid down the almost vertical, rocky bank, and plunged into the deep, swirling, murky waters of the brook. The waters were swollen, following three days and nights of almost continuous rain. The intakes and rivulets on the high moorland, which normally sheltered the village at its top end, were saturated. The water flooded down, deepening the brook by many feet, and continued on its rushing way, along the valley, through woods and farmland, hemmed in here, flooded there, bridged and sometimes forced into culverts in the villages and towns lower down. Only the gurgling, splashing, roaring of the rushing waters far below the bank could be heard. The rest was silence.

Two young schoolgirls passed the spot on their way to school, but they were too busy with their own chatter to notice any difference in the wall structure. A lone cyclist passed by, and being, quite likely, a very infrequent visitor to the area, he was also unaware of any change. The silence went on.

Joe Hodge was the first to notice that something was different. Joe lived in the first cottage at the start of the village, just a little way up from the T junction; a small group of trees and a little croft separated his side fence from Fell Lane. When he peered out of his landing window, looking to see how the weather was, he saw the gaping hole in the wall where, only a few days ago, men from the Council had put the strengthening stonework, not only in the upper part, but right down, tie-ing it all to the rocky bank and well into the foundations. It was a 'proper job', they said: good enough to withstand a hurricane or worse. Well, what could be worse? Joe just stared. His wife, sitting in front of the fire in the living room, heard him calling: "Eh, Martha. Summat's 'appened," he shouted.

"Always 'as wi' you. What naar?" his wife asked.

"No, listen. Wall musta given way. Top o' river bank. Where Fell Lane End is."

"Nay! They only did it a few days ago. Proper good job. Yer said so, yersel'."

"Aye well, it's down I tell yer. Summat's given way," he yelled to her.

"Well, we 'eard nowt, did we? Any road, are yer goin' to 'ave a look?"

"Aye, p'raps I'd better go down. No one else is theer."

"Probly not noticed owt yet," said his wife.

"I was theer not long since. It were all reet then. I'll go an' see."

"Better let th' Council know an all. They'll need ta coom." Martha said. "Yer knaw, Council will 'ave ter…"

"Aye. We'll tell th' Council, soon enough. I'll pop down, then."

So Joe put his cap on, left the cottage, and walked the short distance down to the road junction. That the wall had given way seemed perfectly clear. But the mystery was, how? A perfectly sound wall, built on perfectly sound foundations? It seemed incredible. He peered down into the swirling torrent and at first that was all he saw: swirling rushing water. But soon his eyes became more accustomed to the murky darkness of the ravine, and he began to make out what seemed to be the rear end of a vehicle, a truck maybe, at least some kind of wagon. Almost as soon, he was able to spot the markings on a makeshift number plate and he knew he had seen the vehicle many times before: it was, unmistakably, the rear end of Farmer Gregson's flat-bed truck. Gregson pulled it behind his tractor and drove it all over the place, day in, day out. That was certainly Gregson's truck. Joe recoiled, his head spun. What the hell was he to do now?

A few moments passed, and then he came to his senses. This was a job for the police. Eric Brewer, the local constable, was based at the top end of the village and finding him there was always a problem Also, the nearest public telephone was in the centre of the village; even that was almost half a mile away, up the steep hill, and Joe's legs weren't as nimble as they once were   Time was important, Joe realised, and it would take him a while to walk to either location.   Then he remembered that the Halsteads had a phone at their house, only a few doors up from his. The Halsteads were a bit better off than most of the other folk in Clough Top and so they could afford a phone. At that time, less than twenty years after the Second World War, the majority of the village folk didn't want a phone and most wouldn't know how to use it properly if they had one.   So, as fast as he could, he hurried up to the Halsteads, and rang the door bell with an urgency that frightened poor Annie Halstead almost out of her wits. She hurried to the door, untying her apron as she did so.   She saw Joe there.   "Why Joe," she exclaimed. "You look terrible. What's the matter, lad?"   She always called him 'lad', even though he was probably as old, if not older, than she was.

"I think there's bin an accident, Annie. Can I use yer telephone? We must get the police, right away, I reckon."

"Why? What's happened? Where?"

"Summat's gone in th' river – at Fell Lane End. I think it's serious."

"Well, come in. If you think it's that bad – course, there's the phone." Annie indicated a telephone on a ledge in the hall. "Do you know what to do?"

"I don't know, rightly. Will yer show me, Annie?" requested Joe.

"Just lift the receiver and dial – 9 9 9."

"I ain't done that before," said Joe. "What happens then?"

"Well do it and see," urged Annie.

So Joe responded to her instructions, and soon he heard a voice saying in his ear, "Which service do you require?"

"The police," he managed to blurt out.

"I'm putting you through, now," he was informed. Somehow, something automatic seemed to take over Joe and he was able to tell the girl at the police station, wherever she was, that a vehicle had crashed through a stone wall at the Fell Lane End junction, Clough Top, and plunged into the river. He could still see the back end of it, sticking out of the waters. He described exactly where the location was – the girl didn't seem to know Clough Top –

and gave his name and the number of Annie's telephone. "We'll send someone immediately." she told him. "E.T.A. twenty minutes."

"Thank you, miss," said Joe, politely. He replaced the receiver. "They're sending someone, immediately," he told Annie.

That's all right, then," she said. "Are you going back?"

"Oh, aye,' he said. 'Well, I think I'd better, don't you?"

"Yes, of course you must. And I'd better come with you. I'd better see for myself what's happened."

"Nay. No need for you to bother yersel. An' I'm all reet, Annie, thanks all t' same"

"Yes, I know, Joe. But I still think I'd like to know."

As Joe knew very well that Annie Halstead had to know about everything that went on in the village, he realised that there was no point in arguing with her. So he just said "Aye." Then he asked her, "But eh, what does E.T.A. mean? 'E.T.A. twenty minutes', the young woman said on th' telephone."

"I don't know, perhaps - extra time allowed", she mused.

"Aye. P'raps she thought it'd be nearer thirty. If traffic's bad. Any road, we'd better get back down, Annie. So come on, if you're comin'" So they made their way back towards the Fell Lane End junction. They passed the front of his own cottage and Joe was tempted to drop in to tell Martha what had happened, but he thought better of it and continued with Annie to the junction. Just as they were about to peer down into the murky depths, Joe heard the sound of a car engine approaching from the village. It was a police vehicle. 'That was quick', Joe thought, until he spotted that it was local man, Eric Brewer, in a new patrol car. Brewer parked at the side of the road across from the river wall and emerged from the car.

"Hello, Eric," Joe greeted him.

"Since when have you had that vehicle?" asked Annie Halstead.

"Last Friday," the constable replied.

"Nobody thought to tell me, then," remarked Annie, emphasizing yet again her self proclaimed right to be told everything that went on in Clough Top.

"No," was Brewer's deliberately curt reply. "It's a lot better than the bike, anyway."

"I'll bet," said Joe. "Nice 'un."

"I'm hoping it's a sign of better things to come. Like promotion. Can't wait."

"Nowt like ambition, I s'pose," said Joe, who'd never done anything ambitious in his life.

Eric Brewer was in his late twenties. He wasn't very tall and was quite stocky. His hair was jet black. He turned to look towards the gap in the wall.

"So what've we got here, then?"

"Summat's gone int't river. I phoned '999' from Halsteads. Thought it quicker than tryin' to find you, Eric."

"I was in my office, Joe.. They've just radio'd me from H.Q. Someone's coming over from Macclesfield. Be here before long."

" 'E.T.A. twenty minutes', the girl said on th' telephone."

"Right."

"What does that mean, any road? E. T.A.?"

"Estimated time of arrival," the constable told him.

"Oh," said Joe. "Should be here soon, then."

Constable Brewer walked across to the gap in the wall, and peered down to the river. At first, he too only saw the rushing water, far below, but in a few moments he was able to distinguish the rear end of the truck and the home-made number plate that he also knew so well. He'd spoken to the farmer, Jim Gregson, about it on several occasions. It was hardly legal, but tolerable here in the farming area, but there was no mistaking it, it was Jim Gregson's truck all right. Without a word he walked back to the car, and Joe could see him speaking into a radio microphone.

Now, there was the sound of another vehicle coming the other way, up from the lower part of the valley. But it was only a van from the quarry, some ten miles away. It slowed and then stopped at the junction. Steve Dinnet emerged, as he was being dropped off after his night shift. He saw the police car, saw Joe, and then noticed the gap in the wall. "Bloody 'ell!" he exclaimed. "What's....?" But the police constable had seen him too, and came to him hastily.

"All right, Mr. Dinnet," he said. "The wall's just given way.   I'm getting a gang up from the Council. They'll make it safe for a day or two."

"Only just been done, that 'as.   Bloody poor workmanship if yer ask me."

"Well, the water's been high after the storms, you know. Probably undermined it all. But we can look into that, later on."

"They should know what force the river is 'ere. They should put extra strength in.   Bet they bloody forgot that."

Constable Brewer knew Steve Dinnet very well. He was the biggest loudmouth in Clough Top, and it was important that he shouldn't know anything about the vehicle yet.   That would be disastrous   So he put a gentle arm on the man, and tried to steer him away from the wall and up towards the village and his home. He also signalled to Joe to keep quiet.   Joe did.   Dinnet made to look over the edge, but Constable Brewer stood in front of him now. Come on, Mr. Dinnet, it's very dangerous just there, and I don't want any casualties. You've got a home and a wife to go to, so I'd get on there if I were you."   Dinnet smelt a rat, there was more in this than Brewer was saying, but he'd been on the wrong side of the Law too many times to try anything now.

He just said, "Yeah, right," and wandered off up the road towards his home.

A police squad car came down the fell road and stopped behind Brewer's car.   Two officers emerged and went to meet Brewer.   "What's up, Eric?" one of them asked.

"Looks as if a vehicle's gone through the wall. The drop's about thirty feet."

"Lord! How long ago?"

"Dunno. An hour may be," Brewer speculated.

"Any one see it?"

"Not at the time. The chap there lives at the first cottage. He saw the gap in the wall and raised the alarm. But it might not have been noticed for a while."

"Call came through to Barbara.   Anything else?"

"You can just see the back of the trailer sticking out.   There's a number plate, home-made job.   I know whose it is."

"Go on."

"Local farmer. Jim Gregson. Usually pulls it behind a tractor."

"So you think...? We'd better get something moving."

"I already have," said Brewer. "Macclesfield are sending lifting gear and some more blokes up p. d. q."

"Come on, then, let's have a look." So the three policemen crossed to the gap and peered over the edge. The sight was still the same, with the gushing water bubbling around the back end of the trailer, and the number place just visible under a few inches of foam.

"Going to be a job getting that out," one policeman remarked. "This could be a long day."

"Possibly a night as well," said his colleague. "They could do with a rocket, coming over from Macc. Are they using sirens?"

"I dunno," said Brewer.

"Well they'd better be. And we need that gear – now. Might need the fire brigade as well. Ladders and things. I'll radio back." The man ran back to use the radio in his police car.

The other one asked Brewer: "This farmer, Gregson. Does he live here?"

"Farmhouse, beyond the top of the village. Took over from his old man. Been there years."

"Family?"

"Wife and daughter."

"We'd better have young Sara up, then. When we need to call."

"If we need to call." Brewer interjected. "We're not sure, are we?"

"No, but best be prepared," the policeman suggested. Sara Dawson was a W.P.C. whose training and sympathetic approach enabled her to comfort families when bad news had to be conveyed. This might turn out to be such an incident. "And the chap who raised the alarm? And the woman with him? Can we get them away? Gently like, but it'd be better."

"I'll speak to them," said Brewer.

By this time, Steve Dinnet had raised his own alarm. As he walked up towards his home, he met two or three villagers and told them about the wall. Others were hearing it, and quite a few men, women, boys and girls were coming down the road now. There'd be a crowd in no time. Brewer went to meet them, at the same time taking Joe by the arm. "Better keep this lot back, Joe," he said. "Can you help a bit?" So Brewer and Joe intercepted the advancing group of people just near Joe's own cottage. "Would you all mind not going any further at the moment, please? They'll need some space down there very soon. Please keep back." One young lad tried to pass, but Brewer spotted him. "Hey, Ronnie, back. I don't want you down there. Come back here, now."

"Why, Mr. Brewer? I'm only goin' to 'ave a look. Can't I 'ave a look?"

"No, you can't. For one thing, it's not safe down there. The road might give way. We don't know how stable it is."

"What's happened, Eric?" someone shouted.

"The wall's caved in."

"It was only done, last week," Annie Halstead said. 'Couldn't 've been a very good job."

"Well what d'yer expect with this Council? Doesn't surprise me a bit," a man said.

A moment later there was the sound of emergency vehicles. Sirens and hooters blaring out, as more police cars came over the fell and a fire engine came up the valley road. Everything arrived almost simultaneously and the scene changed rapidly. Uniformed men were going to the gap and peering down, pointing, gesticulating, discussing the situation. A Council lorry arrived with a small gang of workmen, and there was an ambulance as well.

"What's that for?' someone else shouted. "Nobody's hurt, are they?"

"Just a precaution," said Brewer. "There's a nasty drop on the other side you know."

The crowd, even bigger now, tried to surge forward. Brewer was struggling to hold them back. Another young constable emerged from one of the police cars, and came to his aid. "Get back, please," he shouted. "There's nothing to see here." But anxious to find out what was happening, people were craning their necks and pushing and shoving. "We'll get a cordon up in a few minutes, mate," he told Brewer. "Hey, you, back." It was another young lad, trying to get by, unnoticed. But he obeyed the policeman, and stayed back in the crowd.

"Who's taking charge? Do you know?" Brewer asked.

"Tozer, I think," his colleague told him.

"Tozer! Blimey, top brass, eh?"

"The reports sounded more serious than we thought at first. Anyway, if it's Tozer, Tozer it is. Give him something to do."

Chief Superintendent Tozer was well known in the Cheshire force. Basically a traffic cop, he'd come up through the ranks, and had a reputation for getting things done. He understood machinery, and what equipment would be required for the most complicated incidents. He was a tall, lean man, whose greying hair made him quite distinguished, and gave him an air of authority. The last quip of his subordinate was way off the mark. Alec Tozer was a very busy man.

Now, men were preparing ropes and ladders, obviously getting ready to descend into the river, and the time came when two of them, suitably attired, climbed over the edge and down long ladders taken from a fire engine. Safety ropes were attached to one of the vehicles, and played out as the men lowered themselves to the water.

After spending some time making inspections, looking, feeling, examining, they indicated that they were ready to ascend, and climbed back to the road. Tozer was waiting for them. He had arrived only moments before, driving a huge police car.

"There's certainly a trailer there, sir," one reported. "Seems to be jammed tight in the river bed. We couldn't get beyond it. But it is probably attached to a vehicle. That's a make-shift registration plate."

The other man was carrying the plate, wrenched away from the trailer. He handed it to Tozer. "I think Constable Brewer knows something about this, sir," he said.

'That the local chap?" asked Tozer.

"Yes, sir."

"Send him over to me, then. I'll see what he can tell me."

"Sir," the policeman said, and hurried away to Brewer. Two other policemen soon relieved Brewer of his task in holding the crowd back. Brewer went down to Superintendent Tozer.

Tozer showed him the number plate, a strip of white metal with black letters and numbers painted by hand. 'BRT 612', it read. "Know anything about this?" he asked. Brewer told him that it belonged to a local farmer, Jim Gregson, who displayed it at the rear of a trailer that he towed behind his tractor. "So the chances are that both the tractor and the trailer went through the wall and finished up in the river."

"I've never seen one vehicle without the other, if that's what you mean, sir. He always keeps them together, sir."

"Then there's every likelihood that he was driving the tractor, and...?"

Eric Brewer recoiled. "The thought is unbearable, sir" he said. "I've known Jim Gregson for years."

"I'm getting some more lifting gear sent up. We need to pull that lot out as soon as we can. It might take hours, though, and with the darker nights still upon us, I've asked for arc lights. We could be here well into the night. Meantime, get rid of that blasted crowd and we'll cordon the whole area. And hide that bloody thing in a vehicle. We don't want any local seeing that."

"Certainly not, sir" said Brewer. "I'll stow it now."

"Right. Oh, constable. This farmer. Any family?"

"Wife and daughter. Live beyond the top end of the village."

"W.P.C. Dawson is on her way over. When she turns up, you'd better take her to visit the wife. I think she ought to be prepared."

"Right, sir. It won't be easy, but we'll do the best we can."

"Aye. Difficulties come to us all, remember. And the W.P.C. knows how to handle matters better than most.. Leave as much as you can to her."

"Very good, sir." said Brewer. "Now I'll see to this thing." And he walked across to a police car, wrapped the number plate in a cloth that he found in the boot, and hid it from view.

Joe Hodge thought it was high time that he went back to Martha. In any case, he more than fancied a cup of tea. So he went into his own cottage and put the kettle on. Martha was sleeping in her chair by the fire, but she woke when he came in.

"What's up?" she asked as soon as she saw Joe. "Ya've bin ages."

"No, ya've been asleep, that's all, luv."

"Well?" she pressed her question.

"Yon wall's caved in, where I said. There's a torrent coming down and it must've dislodged the foundations."

"But wall were only done last week, you know that. Couldn't have made a good job of it, could they?"

"No. But likely the cement hadn't had enough time to set properly. It does 'appen. And after the rain we've just had."

"Well, p'raps they'll learn, next time."

"P'raps they will," said Joe. "I'm makin' a cup a tea. D'ya want one?"

ooooooOooooo

CHAPTER THREE

Moorside Farm is beyond the top end of the village. The house nestles in the hollow of a hill, a little way off the main road from the village itself, and is reached by a stony, rough shale track that leads from the roadside entrance, where once there were gates, but now only stone pillars with projecting iron hinge brackets remain. Beyond the farm, the hilly road becomes quite narrow as it climbs over into the next valley, through rough, open fell country, criss-crossed with dry stone walling, and filled with boggy land, heather moor and grassy patches. It is bleak in winter, when even the most hardy of sheep find welcome shelter in the lee of the walls, or in specially-built pens, which are constructed in the field corners. In summer, it is paradise, with the springy, mossy turf, warm under the sun, smelling fresh and sweet, and shimmering with an abundance of wild flowers, where butterflies and bees hover, and birds fly and swoop, start up and dip in flight, constantly filling the air with song, twittering, calling. The landscape is dotted with walkers carrying rucksacks, or bags, cameras and binoculars, some keeping to roads and footpaths, others wandering freely; some even daring trespass to enjoy the environment even more.

That afternoon, Edith Gregson was busy in the farmhouse kitchen. She was preparing pastry, and there was complete silence, broken only by the occasional sound as she placed bottle, bag, or box back in its place on the shelf, or took another to the work table for use. Sometimes a sheep would bleat out on the pasture, or 'Brack', the dog, would bark in the yard. For Edith, life was pleasant enough. Jim, whom she had married about fifteen years ago, was making a reasonable job with the farm – they'd never make a fortune, but money wasn't as important as the pleasures of the unhurried, uncluttered way of country life that she had now. Edith was content. She was a thin woman with hair already going grey, and she looked rather frail and under-nourished even though she ate as well as she could and enjoyed her food. She wore a white blouse, buttoned right up to her skinny neck, a cardigan, thick skirt and equally thick stockings with black shoes. She put on the same clothing each and every day, except on special occasions and on Sundays, when she always went to morning service or evening prayer, and quite often to both.

Then she brought out the same frock, silk scarf, and a little hat that she had purchased soon after she came home from her honeymoon, for which they had gone to London for the first and only time in their lives. She thought about that time; the Horse Guards, Buckingham Palace, Downing Street, Parliament, St. Paul's and Westminster Abbey. She remembered their cruise along the Thames to Hampton Court, and the walks with Jim, their arms around each other, in Hyde Park. Young and foolish then, she – they – wouldn't do that now!

Just then she heard a light step on the gravel path and the rattling of the latch on the outside door. A moment later, there was the familiar call, "Mum!" It was her daughter, Jenny.

"Yer're early for once, Jen," said Edith.

"The bar suddenly emptied and Malcolm said I could go when I'd finished cleaning up. He'd manage the rest."

"Aye well, that's nowt. All t' time yer put in theer, extra, and theer's never any overtime, is theer? I reckon Malcolm knows when 'e's on to a good thing."

"I enjoy it there, Mum," Jenny said. "It's good experience for when I get my own pub.   I will, one day, you know."

"Yer won't on what 'e's paying yer."

"I'm saving a bit, Mum. So, one day......!"

"Well, I 'ope yer reet," Edith said. "But yer'll 'ave to save a lot 'arder for a pub of yer own, yer knaw."

"Dad said he'd help me, when the time came."

"Aye, I suppose 'e will. I don't doubt 'e'll do what 'e can. Eh, you say th' 'Untsman bar emptied quick. Why was that, then?"

"Something going on down at Fell Lane End. An accident or something.   Everybody wanted to go and gawk, I suppose. Didn't interest me."

"That's right, luv. Any road, yer better coomin' 'ome. Why don't yer sit out in the gardin for a bit? It'll be nice out theer, just now."

"Going to have a wash and change, first, Mum." Jenny told her.

"Right o' then, yer do that." Edith replied.

Jenny moved away, and then hesitated and turned back. "Mum?"

"Aye, luv, what is eet?" said Edith.

"How would a girl be sure if she's pregnant?"

"Well she'll tell soon enough by 'er periods. Then I 'ear now she can buy a kit or summat from the ...Yer're not thinkin'...?"

"No, not me. Don't be daft, Mum."

"Oo then?"

"Karen Dinnet. She asked me to ask you."

"Oh. Too scared to ask 'er own ma, then?"

"It's her dad. If he knew, he'd kill her on the spot."

"Nay, I don't think 'e'd do that, luv," said Edith. "But she shouldn't talk to ya abart things like that. Dirty little devil."

"It's not dirty, Mum. It's natural," said Jenny.

"Natural! At 'er age? Filthy little monkey. She's no right to ...Does she say oo t' father is?"

"She doesn't know she is, yet, Mum."

"Well, she must 'ave bin with some lad."

"She thinks it might be William."

"Nay," exclaimed Edith firmly. "She's not going to blame William. William might 'ave some funny ways, but 'e wouldn't do nowt like that."

"He's a lad, Mum, and just because he's a bit 'different' doesn't mean he isn't natural." Jenny said.

"Of course 'e's natural. But I know William very well. I've talked to 'im. 'E's a good lad. He'd run a mile from owt like that."

"You mean having sex?" said Jenny.

"Now yer can just stop using words like that an' all. Yer don't proply know what it means. An' yer can stop talkin' abart William in that way, too. If something like that got spread around, the poor lad could be in a lot of bother."

"It's only what Karen said."

"Well don't say anything more abart it. It in't true. Yer mark my words, Jenny. That one'd blame William and she thinks 'e wouldn't be able to defend 'iself. And that's not fair So never repeat such a thing again. D'ya 'ear me, Jenny?"

"Yes, Mum," said Jenny. "I'll go and have my wash." And she went off to the bathroom.

Ever since she gave birth to her daughter, Edith had dreaded the day when she would have to explain certain facts to her. One didn't talk about such things because in Edith's eyes they were dirty and shameful. She married Jim only because, well, yes, she loved him, and she wanted to have a child – one, but not really any more. And soon after the birth she began to arrange things in a way that indicated to him that certain activities were no longer a good idea. He seemed to accept the situation, and together they focused on the home, the farm, and bringing up their daughter who, they hoped, would be a credit to them one day.

But this latest allegation against the boy, William, troubled her greatly. He was about nineteen and had come to lodge in the village two or three years ago. Although he had no regular employment, he did odd jobs, and did them well. Jim often gave him work on the farm and always paid him fair wages, at least that's what Jim told her. He was strange, she acknowledged that, and in times past he would probably have been commonly called the 'village idiot.' Nevertheless, he had received some education; he could read simple things and at least write his own name –

he had demonstrated both to her – but that was about all. He had a happy disposition, always laughing – though this again undermined him, because people assumed that he was simple. He sang tunes aloud, regularly, and often could be heard having conversations with himself. But Edith was quite sure that there wasn't an ounce of badness in him and there could simply be no truth at all in the rumour she had just heard from her daughter. Whatever Karen Dinnet's motives were, such talk was wicked, and the lad could end up being accused falsely - she had no doubt that it was false - of something that she preferred not to put a name to. By the time Edith had finished her preparations and put her pastries in the oven to cook, Jenny had changed, washed, and gone into the garden, where she sat in a deck chair, enjoying the short periods of early spring sunshine, and reading a little book. So Edith put the kettle on, brewed a pot of tea, and took a tray, tea pot, milk, sugar, cups and saucers, spoons and a small plate of biscuits out to her daughter.

The rear garden of the farmhouse was very pleasant. There was a large lawn, with a small flower bed in the centre, surrounded on three sides by borders containing well chosen herbaceous plants and bushes. Beyond the lawn was a small area where Edith enjoyed growing vegetables, and beyond that still, was an orchard, surrounded by a high stone wall. At one corner of the lawn, Jim had erected a trellis at an angle to a small tool shed, and this was so positioned as to form a windbreak, essential when the winds swept across the high moorland, as they did many times each year, and a sun trap for the days of summer when the sun could become quite hot. Jenny had chosen to sit in the arbor, taking one of the deck chairs stored in the little shed. There she was, reading 'Pride and Prejudice', when her mother arrived with the tea tray. "I thought as yer'd be ready for a cuppa," Ethel said.

"Oh, thanks, Mum," said Jenny. "I'll fetch another deck chair and that small table from the shed." She did so, and they sat together, enjoying the refreshment as well as the sun. It wasn't hot, but warm enough not to warrant a coat. Edith even undid her cardigan, although she decided not to take it off. Jenny wore a sleeveless summer top, and jeans.

As she loaded the used crockery, the tea pot and the milk jug back onto the tray, Edith heard footsteps on the gravel path at the side of the house; and now Brack was barking, too. "That'll be your father," she said to Jenny. But Jenny was facing the house and was able to see the uniforms of two policemen as they approached the kitchen door.

"Mum, it's not Dad," she said. "It's the police. Mr. Brewer, it looks like."

"Oh, right. I'll see what 'e wants then. I'll bet it's a cup o' tea," said Edith, and she called, "I'm 'ere, Eric, I'll coom up, now." And Edith went to meet Constable Eric Brewer and the young policewoman who accompanied him. "What can I do yer for, Eric? Or p'raps that should be, what do yer want to do me for?"

"Nay, I wouldn't want to do you for anything, Eedie love, ever," Brewer replied reassuringly.

"Well, then?" she asked him.

"Can we go inside?" he asked. "Oh, and this is Constable Sara Dawson, from Divisional H.Q."

"Hello, Mrs. Gregson," said the policewoman.

" 'Ello, love. Aye, coom inside. What's this abaart, then, Eric?" They went into the kitchen. "Jenny's in th' gardin. D'you want 'er as well?"

"No, not just now. Let her enjoy the sunshine, while she can," said Brewer. Then he went on: "Eedie, there's been an accident down at Fell Lane End."

"I 'eard summat abart that, well, at least Jenny did." Edith told them, "She was able to come 'ome early for once. There was nothing' for her to do, like, in th' bar at th'Untsman."

Then Eric Brewer told her exactly what had happened, and how, at that moment, every effort was being made to lift the wrecked vehicle the thirty odd feet from the swirling waters. He told her also that there was little doubt that the rear number plate was from Jim's trailer. Ethel asked: "Well, where's th' tractor? That' use'ly be in front o'th' trailer. Yer know yoursel, Jim never undoes it, well, not unless he's got to. Bein' lazy, like 'e always is. Where is eet?"

"I can't answer that, yet, love. But it would certainly complicate things if it's down there as well." Brewer turned to the woman police officer. "Better radio that down, right away. They might need even more gear." He went outside to get a clearer reception on his radio.

The policewoman, Sara Dawson, was an attractive young lady of twenty-three. Unlike many, in fact most, of her female colleagues who were physically strong and well-built almost on a par with the men, she was of reasonable height, slim and lithesome and had a pleasing figure, with adequate curves showing beneath her uniform. Requisite dark stockings covered her otherwise shapely legs, and her dark hair, tied into a pony tail at the back, blended perfectly with her make-up, red lips and the dark highlights in her eyebrows. She was a caring, friendly, sympathetic girl, who showed great concern for all those with whom her duties brought her into contact.   She was ambitious, too, and hoped that her efforts, as well as her personality and increasing qualifications, would stand her in good stead for promotion when the opportunities came along.

Sara went to put her hand on Edith's arm. Very quietly, she asked, "Are you going to sit down a while, Mrs. Gregson?" But Edith froze as she stood near the table. "Come on, love," said Sara. "Just sit for a few minutes. Can I get you some tea?"

"I've just 'ad some, thank yer, lass," said Edith. "In the gardin wi' me daughter."

"That'll be Jenny?"

"Aye."

"How old is she?"

"Goin' on fifteen." Edith told her.

"Still at school, then?"

"Aye. But she 'elps out like, at the local pub. part-time, as well. Wants to own one 'erself someday. She thinks of this as a bit of 'esperence', like."

"Best way to learn, I suppose. Good for her," said Sara.

"She likes it, any road. Can't serve behind the bar, yet, thaw. Strict rules abart that, yer knaw."

"Yes." said Sara. "Do you want to tell her about any of this, yet?"

Edith considered. "I think she ought to knaw," she said at last. And at that moment Jenny came into the house. Brewer followed her in.

"What's going on, Mum?" the girl asked.

"It's the accident down at Fell Lane End, luv...." Edith broke off, but Sara continued,

"We think it's possible that your dad is involved, Jenny."

"Me dad? How? Is he hurt?" Instinctively, Jenny went to her mother.

"We can't be sure about anything yet, Jenny, but his tractor and trailer have gone through the wall and into the river. It's going to take time to get them out again," Brewer told her.

"But where's me dad?" Jenny asked frantically.

"We don't know, love."

"He'll not be dead," said the young girl, irrationally. Her mother hugged her.

"No, love, don't think about that. You know your dad. Got out of many scrapes in his time," said Brewer. Mother and daughter stood with arms around each other, and they were crying.

Sara crossed to them. "Come on now," she said gently. "You must try to be positive. Perhaps are right. Perhaps…"

"I want to go down there. I want to see what's happening. Mum, we must go down, now," Jenny said.

Edith's eyes were filling with tears as she looked at the two representatives of the Law.

Brewer said, "If you want to come down, Eedie, we can't stop you. We'll take you both in the car. But it might be best if you weren't seen or recognised. News, even inaccurate news, soon gets about. We don't want that at the moment."

"We'll put blankets over our heads, Mr. Brewer. We can, can't we, Mum? Will that be all right, Mr. Brewer?"

"That will be fine, young lady." Brewer told her. "Incognito. I reckon you'll enjoy that."

Some fifteen minutes later, the little police car arrived at Fell Lane End. Constable Brewer was driving and was accompanied by W.P.C. Sara Dawson. Although there was quite a crowd in the roadway, all the onlookers had been pushed even further away from the accident site to where the hill down from the village began to level out, well beyond Joe Hodges' cottage. Policemen controlled the cordon and parted the crowd to allow Brewer's car through. Similar cordons had been set up on the other side, blocking the road up from the valley, and on the end of

Fell Lane itself. Vehicles were being allowed to proceed through the junction, but on the strict instruction to keep moving and not to slow down within the area that had been cordoned off. Brewer's car stopped in a secluded area of the road, and eventually Edith and Jenny emerged from beneath blankets. Brewer left them with Sara Dawson while he went to inform a senior officer of their presence.

The scene that met Edith's and Jenny's gaze seemed to them to be one of utter confusion. Men, some in uniform, others not, were darting everywhere, and many of them were peering through the gap, or over the part of the wall that was still standing, shouting down to others below, gesticulating, listening, calculating. A lorry with a crane upon it was being manoeuvred into position near to the gap. "Right 'and down a bit, Andy. That'll do, steady, woe!" And the lorry halted, its rear end almost through the gap itself. Lights were being switched on, tested, focused. The crane was positioned.

A senior police officer came over to Edith and Jenny. "Mrs. Gregson and Miss Gregson, I understand," he said.

"Aye, that's reet, sir," replied Edith   Jenny just nodded her head. The policeman turned to Sara, whispered a few words and pointed to a vehicle parked nearby.

"I'm sorry that we can't be more positive about anything at the moment, madam," he said to Edith. "But there's a vehicle registration plate we'd like you do look at, please, if you will. It's in the van just there. W.P.C. Dawson will show it to you"

"Well...aye.... I'll 'ave a look, then. Certainly, aye" Edith said hesitantly.... .

"Do you want to stay here, Jenny?" Sara asked.

"No, I'll come with Mum. I can, can't I?"

"Of course you can. Follow me, please."

They crossed to the van, where Sara extracted the number plate that was wrapped in a cloth. As soon as she unwrapped it, both mother and daughter knew where it came from. There was no doubt. "That's from my dad's trailer," Jenny said. Edith stood motionless and without expression. Sara put an arm around her.

At the same moment, a loud grinding and cracking sound came from the crane and the women saw the gantry buckle and the lorry on which it stood shake and rattle and rear up and down. Men were running, shouting, swearing. Then everything stopped, the crane could not take the weight. It would not move the vehicles which were stuck fast between rocks and boulders in the river. Better equipment, more effort, perhaps an attempt to un-couple the tractor from the trailer, would be required, and nothing more might be possible until the following day. For a time, everybody seemed to be standing around, discussing problems, alternatives, situations The gang of workmen gathered together in a huddle.

"They'll need to get shut of this bugger for a start," one man said. "Get somethin' better down."

"Termorrer now," said another. "So they might as well send us 'ome. It's getting' cold, now, and I'm bloody starvin'."

After a few more minutes, a message was shouted from the river below. The man receiving it walked across to a group of senior police officers and conveyed it to them. There was another wait, and then the senior man, who had spoken to them before, came across to Edith and Jenny. He said, "As you see, ladies, we've got quite a problem, and there's nothing more that we can do until daybreak, tomorrow. More equipment will need to be brought in. But it has been possible to physically locate the tractor, beyond the trailer. The seat is empty; there is no one on it."

"No body, yer mean?" asked Edith.

"That's right, there's nothing."

"So the force of th' water would 'ave...?"

"I can't say that, madam. It's too soon to even speculate."

"It's pretty obvious, thaw, in't it?" Edith said, tearfully.

Sara took Edith's hand. "Don't jump to conclusions, love. Please don't.," she said. Then she saw Jenny's little face. She was crying. "Come on. Let's get you both into the car and take you home. At the moment, there's nothing more for you here." Darkness was falling, and in the gloom the three women walked across to the police car. Neither Edith nor Jenny bothered to cover themselves this time. What was the point? The news would be out in no time Jim Gregson was involved in whatever had taken place there – his family had been brought to the scene. So the police car was soon speeding up the hill, through the village, and towards Moorside Farm. In fact, no-one noticed that they were in the car, most of the crowd had dispersed anyway, and the remainder saw nothing.

Sara turned the car off the road and drove up to the farmhouse. She went along its side and parked in the little yard at the back. "Would you like me to come in with you?" she asked.

"That's reet kind. Thank yer, Sara," Edith replied. The three women got out and moved towards the rear door of the house. Brack could be heard barking.

"I didn't know you'd left the kitchen light on, Mum," said Jenny.

"I didna, luv,." Edith replied.

"Well, it's on now, look," Jenny pointed out.

Sara held them back with a hand on each shoulder. "Are you sure about that, love?" she asked.

"Certin. It was daylight when we left, remember. An' I don't believe in wasting electric. It costs the earth as it is." The three moved cautiously to the outside door. Sara opened it, and they went into the empty kitchen, and, yes, the light was on. Edith wondered whether she had put it on, perhaps earlier, and then forgotten and not noticed it when they left. 'I mun be losin' me brains. More waste of money,' she thought. When they went through to the living room, the light was on there, as well, and Jim Gregson was sitting in his usual armchair, drinking a mug of hot tea.

oooooOooooo

CHAPTER FOUR

"Dad" Jenny cried, as she rushed across the room to him. Edith stood by the door, motionless, but her face bore a look of some astonishment.

"What's up, Jen?" her father asked as he glanced across at his wife.

"There's been an accident, Dad, down at Fell Lane End. Your tractor's gone into the river, and we thought....."

"My tractor? In th' river, d'ya say?' He stood up, still holding Jenny near to him. He noticed Sara, now, and looked from Edith to her, and then again to Edith.

"It's through th' wall, Jim. Ya knaw, where t' Council repaired it only last week. It's in th' river – trailer an' all," Edith told him.

"How d'ya know it's my tractor?" he asked.

"That number plate, ya knaw, the one ya made up yersel, was on the back. We've seen it. They've brought it out and put in a police car." Edith crossed to him and held his arm.

Momentarily, the three stood clasped together, as if unable to move. Jim swayed a little, and sat down as the women released him. "Bloody 'ell!" was all he could utter. Sara realised then that it was right to join the conversation at that point.. She moved towards them.

"Mr. Gregson," she said.

"Aye, hello, miss." Jim said.

"Oh, Jim," said Edith, hastily. "This 'ere is W.P.C. Dawson. She's bin very kind."

"Sara Dawson. Mr. Gregson. I'm a sort of part-time liaison officer. I'm here to help in any way I can."

"Oh, right." said Jim. "Aye, an' I'm sorry for swearin' like. But, me tractor!"

"That's all right. I'm used to that," Sara said. "But I'll need to talk to you, shortly. First I'd better go out to the car and radio my superior officer. Your appearance here makes quite a difference to the situation. I need further instructions."

"Aye, well I suppose it does." said Jim. "We'll see ya soon, then, miss?" Sara went out to her car. Edith sat down, staring blankly in front of her.

Jim Gregson was a tall, lanky man, now in his forties. From the chair where he sat, his legs seemed to stretch right across the hearth rug, covering the whole width of the fireplace. He wore a cloth cap, even in the house and even at meals, and Edith thought he'd wear it in bed if she hadn't objected right at the start. "Nay, lad, you're not coomin' ter bed wi' that on yer 'ead. Gerrit off, now, d'ya 'ear." And Jim had removed the cap and thrown it in a corner of the bedroom, only to put it on again in the morning. As a result of being out in the countryside and in the fresh air most of the time, Jim had a tanned complexion; he had brown hair under his cap, although it was thinning now and showing signs of going grey. He had been at the same village school as Edith and had fancied her, even then. Lately he had often asked himself had he done the right thing. The only real joy in his marriage these days was Jenny, whom he adored. He had begun to look upon her as something of a consolation. He loved Edith, yes, and he knew she loved him in her own way, but – anyway, he'd got the farm to run, the family to support, and Jenny certainly needed him around. He was, he supposed, happy with that.

"We thought tha were dead, Jim," Edith said at length.

"No, love, I'm not. I'm all reet, I'm 'ere." He put an arm around her. Then he said to his daughter: "Jen, make some tea, will yer, love? Yer mum needs one, and I expect you do as well."

"Yes, Dad. Right away." And Jenny went out to the kitchen.

"Your, well 'our', tractor is in th' river, Jim. D'yer understand that?" Edith asked.

"Aye, course. But 'ow the devil…?"

"Where did ya leave it? And where've ya bin, all day?"

"I left it on th' croft at Fell Lane End. You know, where I always leave it. And I've been up yonder, on Far Moor – seeing th' walls. Some have been down for months, like I told ya. I said I were goin' up theer. 'Bin on my mind for weeks."

"Aye, I knaw." Edith said. "But why didn't ya go up on th' tractor?"

"Never make it. Too boggy, especially after the rain we've 'ad. Tractor'd get stuck in no time. I could soon see that."

"Ya could've gone part on th' road. Save walking all that way."

"I chose to walk it, that's all. Stretch me legs a bit. Do me good. Anyway, I went over th' backs and up Long Acre. Much quicker than coming round th' road. A good day for walkin', too."

"Take William with yer?"

"Nay. 'E 'ad other things to do. Went off somewhere – I dunno."

"William? Other things ta do? That's a likely story," said Edith.

"Well, you know what 'e's like. Casual labour. I can't force 'im."

"No, I know." Edith said. The events of the last few hours had completely blotted from her mind the accusation that young Karen Dinnet had made against William but, even if she had remembered, this was hardly the time to speak of it. She went to stand in front of the fire – she was cold. "There's pande-mononium goin' off, down at Fell Lane End," she told Jim. "That vehicle's stuck on th' river bed. They've already broke one crane, tryin' to pull it aart."

"I'd better get down there, then," Jim said. "See if I can 'elp."

"Best wait till young woman cooms back. She might 'ave some orders. Where did ya leave it?"

"On the croft at the junction. You know, side of Joe Hodge's place. Where 'is orchard is. I always leave it there. Safe as 'ouses."

"Not this time, though," Edith said.

"Two large stones for chocks in front o' th' wheels, in gear, brake full on. What more could I do?"

"So what 'as 'appened, then, do yer think, Jim?"

"God knows. I only 'ope I'll know, soon enough." Sara came back from the yard. They both looked at her.

"I've got instructions to take you down to the scene, Mr. Gregson. My superiors would like you to confirm something right away. Is that all right?"

"Course. I'll get me coat." Jenny came in with mugs of tea on a tray.

"I've done one for you, Miss Dawson.. Have you time?"

"Yes, Jenny, I've time," said Sara, as she helped herself to a mug. "Oh, that's hot," she exclaimed, and put it down again quickly on a convenient ledge. Jenny gave another mug to her mother and began to sip from one herself. Very soon, Jim came back, wearing an anorak and his large working boots. He looked at the three women. "Right then," he said, and there was a glint in his eye that he could not disguise. "You lead on, miss. I'll follow you."

Sara finished drinking her tea – it cooled quite quickly – and she moved to the door, "Yes, come on, Mr. Gregson. Thanks for the tea, Jenny. I was ready for that. And by the way, you can call me 'Sara', I don't mind. I'll be in touch, later." Jim had taken his mug of tea from Jenny, gulped a couple of mouthfuls, and put the mug down again. Then he went out, following Sara Dawson with the same eagerness that Brack often showed when the dog followed him.

There was silence in the room for a little while; both Edith and Jenny were still sipping their mugs of tea.

At last, Jenny spoke. "What do you think will happen now, Mum?" she asked.

"I just don't rightly knaw, luv," replied Edith. "But I reckon there'll be some bother for yer father. Yer never knaw where it could lead to"

"He's done nothing wrong, has he?"

" 'E ses he 'asn't, but police might 'ave other ideas."

"Like what?" Jenny persisted.

"I don't knaw, luv. But when th' police get bees in their bonnets, they never give up. They might accuse yer dad of leavin' th' tractor unattended, or sumat. I reckon they could easly coom up wi' summat like that t' charge 'im wi'. "

"But he always leaves it there unattended. It's always been safe, before."

"'E might think that but, like I say, police might think different."

"Dad'll think of something to say," said Jenny, comfortingly.

"I reckon 'e'd be better sayin' nowt.. That way might save bother."

"Well, he'll have to say something. It's our tractor and trailer in the river." Then Edith replaced the empty mugs on the tray and took them back to the kitchen.

* * * * *

Sara Dawson's car drove through the village and down the hill to Fell Lane End. The village itself was quite deserted now, and although the cordon at the junction was still in place – as it would be for some time - the crowd had dispersed and the car was allowed through without even having to slow down. Sara parked near the junction, at the corner of Hodge's garden wall. Most of the police personnel and all the workmen had departed, leaving a wooden barrier across the gap and a policeman standing on guard. It was growing dark, light was fading and the scene was lit by two or three floodlights. Sara told Jim to stay in the car for a few moments. She got out and crossed to the policeman on guard. After a short conversation with him, she went to the only other vehicle still parked there: the one that contained the makeshift number plate. She extracted it from the rear and crossed back to her own car. She showed the plate to Jim. He confirmed that it belonged to him. Then she returned to the other vehicle, replaced the number plate and got into the driving seat of the vehicle. After a few moments, Jim could just make out that she was using a radio there. When Sara came back to him, she said, "There's no need for you to stay down here at this time, after all, Mr. Gregson. They're bringing heavy lifting gear over in the morning, soon after first light, and you'll be needed then. In the meantime, best to go back home and get a good night's sleep. I'll take you, and pick you up again after breakfast."

"So what about...?" Gregson began to ask, indicating the gap in the wall and the police guard.

"Don't worry. Everything's under control. Someone will be here all night – not the same man, they'll change over every hour or two."

"Sounds like Buckingham Palace," Jim quipped without thinking about how serious the situation was. "Sorry, I didn't think....."

"No, that's all right." Sara realised that a little light relief could be helpful. She re-started her car and drove him back to the farm.

* * * * *

Something woke Edith in the night. It was about half past three. She turned herself over in bed and saw that Jim was not there. Normally, Jim never needed to get up in the night. She listened and couldn't hear him in the bathroom. She got out of the bed and went onto the landing. On seeing a light showing downstairs, she went down. Jim was sitting at the kitchen table, another mug of tea before him. "I was thirsty. I needed a cup. Want one?"

"If one's goin'," said Edith. Jim went to the stove and made another cup. He handed it to her. "Couldn't sleep, then?"

There was a long silence before Jim remarked: "That police woman, you know, Sara, isn't it?"

"What abart 'er?"

"She seems nice."

"Nice enough. S'pose that's part of 'er job, to be nice. Liaison officer, or summat."

"Very suited to it, I should think."

"As suited as any, I s'pose."

"When ya thawt I'd drowned, gone in th' river, what were yer main worries, love?" Jim asked.

"You, fer t' start. What an 'orrible death? In the deep water, drownin', unable to fend fer yersel, alone; no-one t' rescue yer, Jim; I couldn't bear the thawt, the agony of it.," Edith told him. She sat near him, crying, sobbing. He put am arm around her.

"There, love," he said. "It's all reet. I'm 'ere. I 'aven't drowned."

"And then I thawt abart our Jen. 'Er little world, shattered. Only this afternoon she reminded me of 'er ambition, to own a pub. She said you were going to 'elp 'er – you'd promised 'er some money."

"There's already somethin' in th' bank," he said. "She would 'ave got that when the time came – not a lot, but enough to start out with." There was a long silence, and then Edith asked him:

"What do ya think will 'appen, Jim?"

"What? About tractor? I'll be asked a lot of questions, I 'spect, like 'Where did you leave it? Was it safe? Why there?' And I can only tell 'em what I know."

"The Council won't be too pleased. Just re-built that wall. Couldn't't've bin very strong," Edith remarked.

"Poor workmanship, I reckon. It should've withstood some impact."

"Aye. Any road, it's cold down 'ere, Jim. I'm goin' back to bed. Are ya coomin'?"

"Presently," Jim said. "I couldn't sleep before, so I thought I might as well do summat useful. I could tidy that junk cupboard."

"Tidy that.....ya've been goin' to do that for t' last three years!"

"Well, I could do it now."

"Coom back up and get warm, yer daft aporth, she said. 'Cupboard'll keep a bit longer, I reckon. Coom on, naar, luv. I reckon ya could do wi' a cuddle."

"Ay? It's a long time since we...."

"Well....An' try not to get bothered. Tha'll need some sleep. Tomorrow could be a busy 'un." So Jim followed her up to their bedroom. Edith was soon asleep, but he only had a few fleeting moments before waking again and remaining so for what seemed like hours. Jenny slept soundly in her own bedroom, the whole night through.

oooooOooooo

CHAPTER FIVE

When the hand on dressing table clock turned six, Jim had really had enough and couldn't lie in bed any longer. The alarm was set go off at half-past, but instead of allowing it to wake Edith, he cancelled it. He got out of bed and went through to take his usually stripped wash in cold water – they didn't have a shower then – and shave with foam and a razor. He dressed, went down and made a mug of tea and took one up to Edith. She woke up, took the tea, thanked him and even kissed him.. Then he went out to find the dog, go down to feed the pigs and inspect two of them that were in need of extra care.

It was better out there, in the fresh morning air, striding lustily across the green pasture and through the barred gate that was fastened to its post with thick string – the latch and padlock had broken months ago and there'd not been any time to mend it. He worked with Brack, the dog, and soon he was satisfied that all was well with the pigs. Afterwards he and Brack made inspections of other parts of the farm and then returned across the pasture, where he tied the gate once more. That was the moment when he felt a strong inclination to wander off, away again, over the hill onto Far Moor and beyond. For no-one would reach him there, and if they came looking, he'd know where to hide. Instead, he knew that he'd be stuck in some office, some interview room, with all the bloody forms, and papers, questions, telephones going off. 'Bugger that!' he thought. But he was just about to call Brack, and run for it, when a voice from behind him said gently, "Dad."

He turned to see his young daughter, Jenny, dressed in her school uniform, fresh, clean, with the breeze ruffling just the ends of her hair that touched her shoulders and covered the lily white skin of her neck. She was smiling at him with big blue eyes and lips parted allowing her white teeth to glisten in the morning air. He moved towards her, to hug her, to kiss her little cheek. "Mum's got your breakfast done. I've had mine already."

He took her hand, then, and called, "Brack, coom on." Together they walked back to the farmhouse where he had his usual cooked breakfast. Jenny set off to catch the school bus, which came through the village before turning round at a wider area of road just below the farm.

This diversion was not for Jenny's personal benefit, but because there was only one spot where the turn round was possible, although it was also very convenient during the four years that had almost passed since she had first gone to the secondary school at Broadlea, a few miles down the valley. On those days when she wasn't required to be in school, she helped out at the Huntsman, in preparation for a future career as an hotelier upon which she had already set her mind. Because she had lessons on this particular day, she was on the bus which went through the village and past Fell Lane End, where there was quite a lot of activity already. Most of the other children on the bus craned necks to see it all as the bus slowed, before being beckoned through by a police officer.

Just before nine o'clock, Jim looked from the farm window and saw a small police panda car coming down the track. He recognised it immediately as Eric Brewer's, but hoped that Sara Dawson was driving. The car stopped in the yard, and Brack began to bark. Jim went out and saw Eric standing near the dog, calming it down, and scruffing its neck. "Mornin, Jim," he said, letting go of Brack.

"Mornin' Eric," answered Jim. "Nice one, an' all. Down, Brack. Get out of th' way, will yer." But with the dog still jumping up his legs and barking, Brewer crossed the yard to Jim.

"Be good out on the tops today, I reckon," said the policeman.

"Aye, but chance 'ud be a fine thing," Jim remarked, as he grabbed Brack's collar and held him. "Stop it, Brack, d'yer 'ear?" Brewer stood in front of Jim and the two men looked at each other for a few moments. They had been friends for many years, and often Brewer had helped Jim with small problems on the farm – trespassers, licences, minor matters – and they regularly had a pint or two with the other men in the village, down at the Huntsman. But somehow this was different. Jim might be responsible for what turns out to be a nasty occurrence – whether criminal or not could not be said at this stage. Eric Brewer had to uphold the Law, and answer to his superiors, and hardly anyone was more superior than Chief Superintendent Tozer. Brewer allowed Jim to take the dog back and tie it with a rope to a little post at one side of the yard. Jim made the rope safe and gave the dog just enough length to move a few feet in either direction. Then he turned to Brewer. "Yer've come for me, then?"

"They're trying to lift your trailer out, this morning. We thought it best if you came down."

"The policewoman said she'd come for me. I was waitin..."

"Well, if you'd rather have a bit of skirt, Jim..."

"Nay, Eric. I just wondered, that's all."

"Wouldn't blame you if you did fancy it. There're quite a few blokes in the force, and out of it, who wouldn't mind knowing her better. But she's a police officer, Jim, not a fetch and carry girl. She's got other work to do, you know, school kids' crossing patrols, neighbourhood disputes, all sorts. Still, she'll likely pop up to see Edith later on."

"Aye. Right then. So, you're taking me down to Fell Lane End now?"

"When you're ready, Jim."

Jim was ready, and after a word with Edith, who had come from the house by this time, the two men got into the panda car and drove away.

The scene at Fell Lane End was chaotic. Several police vehicles were parked at the roadside, two small lorries were at the end of Fell Lane, a Land Rover was on the croft, near to Joe Hodge's garden wall, and there was a very large crane being manoeuvred into a position near the gap in the river wall. Men seemed to be dashing everywhere, and of course, the cordon had been re-instated, even though there were not any onlookers now and traffic both through the village, and on Fell Lane, was very light. Eric Brewer and Jim got out of the car and walked over to the wall, near to the gap. At that moment, Jim realised what the impact must have been. He saw several men down on the river side; safety ropes attached them to suitable points higher on the banks and they were indicating how they wanted the chain of the crane to be lowered. The morning sun was now giving extra illumination, and Jim could make out the rear end of the trailer just beneath the swirling water. Somebody shouted, "Will you get back, please, chaps? Out of the way, if you don't mind." And both men retreated across the road to a safe distance.

Clamps were placed in front of the crane, and so too were several railway sleepers. A strong chain went from its rear to a concrete peg, driven well into the ground at the far side of the road, making the road which went up to the village itself temporarily impassible for vehicles. Suitable notices had been put up at strategic points throughout the whole area. There was a long delay before everything was ready for the lift to begin. When the moment came, a large police car came down from the direction of the village and stopped just inside the cordon. The large frame of Chief Superintendent Tozer emerged. He was acknowledged by one or two of his junior officers standing by, including Eric Brewer, who half saluted and said, "Sir!" Then all was ready.

Several attempts were made to lift the vehicle and trailer, but without success. Every time more pressure was exerted, the crane shuddered and shook, rocked to and fro, the engines revving even more loudly, but still nothing moved in the waters below. Finally, Jim said to Brewer; "It'd be a lot easier if th' tractor and trailer were uncoupled and dragged out separately, yer know."

"But I can't see how, Jim. The coupling must be under at least two feet of water."

"Aye. But it's a very simple mechanism, Eric," said Jim. "I reckon I'd 'ave it unfastened in no time."

"You? Like how?"

"Let me go down, walk along th' trailer; it can't be more than a foot or so deep, Eric. I could just get me 'ands under th' water, and unfasten it. I know what to do. I know how it's fastened, like, don't I? Bin doin' that for years."

"Might be deeper than you think, Jim. The trailer is at an angle, much deeper at the far end, where the coupling is."

"But it's worth a try, Eric. I'd be roped up, wouldn't I? Quite safe? And I'd not do owt stupid. I'm not trying to be a bloody 'ero."

"No, I know. Well, I'll get a word to the Super. He'll have the final say." Eric Brewer walked across to a group of senior officers and spoke to them, indicating back towards Jim. Soon heads were shaking; there was some arguing and some laughter. Two or three officers peered over the wall and surveyed the problem. More words were spoken, and then, at last, Brewer returned to Jim. "He thinks it might be worth a go. But he'll have a word with you first. Hang on a bit. He'll come over."

At that moment two more cars arrived and parked as directed by a police officer, before several men in suits and mackintoshes emerged. They were officials from the Highways Department of the County Council. They began surveying the scene. Tozer talked to a senior man, who was making notes as he looked down into the river and then back across the road. At one moment, he pointed up Fell Lane and brought his hand down to the gap in the wall. There was shaking of heads, more indicating, and an inspection of the remaining section of the wall that was still standing. At last, the group began to drift back towards their vehicles, although one even then turned, retraced his steps, and looked over the wall and at the gap once more, before walking swiftly to rejoin his colleagues. As they passed near to Jim, he was just able to hear the remark, "Must have been doin' a hell of a rate of knots." Then they all got into the cars and drove away down the valley. Jim felt inside his pockets, searching for a cigarette, but none was there. He'd left his packet at home.

"Oh 'ell," he said. "I've left me fags behind. I'll 'ave to nip up t' Alice's for some more. Should be time, shouldn't there?"

"I dunno, Jim. But here you are, have one of mine." Brewer offered a cigarette. Jim took it.

"Thanks, Eric," he said, as the policeman also produced matches and lit the cigarette. Jim pulled on it, gratefully, before exhaling the smoke.

"Not good for you, you know." Brewer said, as he wryly lit one for himself.

"Yer mean lung cancer? Eeeh!" Jim exclaimed dismissively.

"That's what they reckon, anyhow," said Brewer. "I'm trying to cut down, but, well...!." Just then, another police officer came over to them. He spoke to Brewer.

"He's talking about getting an under-water team up now. Take them an hour or two to get here. I wouldn't expect much action before then."

"So they won't need me, then?" Jim asked.

The officer replied abruptly. "If you're needed when the time comes, sir, we'll let you know. Meantime, if I were you, I'd carry on with normal work. You must have something to do."

"Oh, aye," said Jim. "A farmer's always got plenty t' do. I'll go back to me farm, then."

"I'll run you up, if you like, Jim," offered Brewer.

"No, I'll walk, thanks Eric. An' I can call at Alice's on th' way up. Get some more fags."

"Aye, well, say nothing about this, if you're asked," instructed Brewer. "We don't know much ourselves yet, and we don't want any nosey buggers putting two and two together and making five."

"I'll say nowt to anyone, Eric. Yer can bank on me." And so Jim strode back up towards the village.

Clough Top could hardly call itself a village; it was little more than a collection of houses. From the end of the narrow road that led over the fell to Macclesfield, a point that had become known as Fell Lane End, the road from the valley bottom continued upwards, with the river bank and protective stone wall on one side and half a dozen stone-built cottages on the other side. The first of these was Joe Hodges', and each house had a stone garden wall and its own front garden. In the summer months, some of the gardens had quite a show of flowers and bushes and hanging baskets - a welcoming sight. At the top end of the cottages, at a point where the road begins to turn a little, a larger house, surrounded by its own garden, was Halsteads' After Halsteads', the road turned more abruptly and levelled out to form the main street, actually known as Spring Street. Once upon a time, a spring ran along one side of the road before cascading down to the river itself, but some years ago it had been fed into a culvert to avoid accidents. Spring Street then continued on a level, with more small cottages, some terraced, on both sides. Mixed in with the residential properties was Alice's 'stores' where you could buy almost anything, the pub – the Huntsman – and small trades premises: Arty, the cobbler; Ken and Ron, joiners; a wheelwright where the blacksmith used to be; and Ruth Teal, who made clothes. There was a small doctor's surgery, only open mornings, and a dentist's as well. Eric Brewer's 'police house' was there, and a District Bank using one room, open three mornings a week.

Almost opposite to Halsteads', a small road branched off at a V shaped corner, and then crossed the river by a very ancient and sturdy stone bridge, which was once used by pack horses on the track that came across the moor to the north, before passing through the village and out again towards the south. Beyond the bridge was the Parish Church, surrounded by its graveyard, and then there were a few better-quality houses, after which the road became a cobbled track , perhaps the original, that now led to Benson's farm, a larger, more successful one than Gregson's , although this never prevented Jim from being on quite good terms with Arthur Benson. Benson's had a good herd of cows; they stabled horses, which provided an attraction for a few teenage girls, and part of their land was cultivated.

Returning along Spring Street, there was a mixture of terraced cottages, which were fronted by a rough gravel path, but had good-sized rear gardens, at least one or more of which always had a line of washing on display. Almost at the end of the road was the Methodist Chapel, the only other church in the village, and that relied on visiting preachers to take services Beyond the last building there was the large open area that was used for turning the buses, and then the road climbed again, passed Moorside Farm, and then went out across the open moorland. Eventually, it led down into the next valley, but it was a difficult route for motorists, and more the domain of walkers and hardy, proficient cyclists.

Alice served Jim with a packet of cigarettes. She made no mention of the events at Fell Lane End. She made her usual comment about it being a nice day, and that was all. Jim left the shop. But he had only gone a few yards further along the street when he heard a woman's voice calling from a cottage door. " 'Ay, Jim!" It was Betty Marsh, a middle-aged woman who was the mainstay of St. Luke's Church. St. Luke's was the 'Parish' Church now, although it was formerly just a Chapel of Ease to the much larger St. Benedict's at Furness Bridge, lower down the valley. " 'Ave yer seen William? 'E didn't come home last night." Betty called out when Jim turned to her.

" 'Aven't set eyes on 'im, Betty. Not since yesterday," replied Jim.

"E said 'e was going to help you, after 'is breakfast, yesterday. Said you 'ad some work for 'im," Betty said.

"I saw 'im in the morning. 'E did some jobs with me, like, and then just wandered off. You know what 'e's like, yourself."

"Aye, but 'e's never stayed out all night before."

"Always a first time, you know, Betty. 'Appen 'e's found 'imself a lass."

"A lass? William? Aw, come off it, Jim. Any road, 'e likes our 'ome comforts too much to stay away long. An' 'e weren't dressed for goin' very far. An' 'e's not like some lads, you know. 'E wants some extra lookin' after."

Jim tried to re-assure her. "I wouldn't bother too much yet though, Betty. I reckon 'e'll turn up when 'e's ready. An' if 'e's shacked up wi' a lass..."

"Nay, 'e's not like that, Jim. I'm worried. Summat might 've... Do ya think I should tell P.C. Brewer abart it?"

"No. Eric's got enough to bother about at present, I reckon," said Jim.

.   "This accident down th' road, yer mean?"

"Well, that's one thing, aye," said Jim.

"What've yer 'eard about that, then? Summat's gone inter th' river, 'asn't it?"

"They say so. Any road, I reckon Eric's pretty tied up for a bit. That's for sure."

"That'll be a change, then? Not much else 'appens round 'ere, for 'im, does it?" she said.

"No, but...well, wait a bit longer. The lad might be back later. Just wait a bit, an' see."

"Well, if yer think...but I'm still worried, Jim. Any road, see yer."

"Aye." And Jim wandered on up Spring Street and then out into the open area, before climbing the hill that continued up to his farm.

Edith was in the kitchen when he walked in. She made a pot of tea and filled his usual mug. He lit a cigarette and while he enjoyed his smoke and his drink, he told her what was happening at Fell Lane End. "I'll need to go back in a bit. When this underwater team comes. They'll need me to 'elp."

"I 'ope you're not thinking of goin' down into any water," said Edith.

"Might 'ave to, love," he said, "I know 'ow the trailer's fastened, yer see."

"But tha'll get wet through, Jim. Catch yer death o' cold, man. Be sensible."

"It's my tractor, though, isn't it? My responsibility."

"Still, there's no need for ya to risk yer life fer it. Let them do that. They're trained up. They're used to that sorta thing."

"I'll be all right,' he said. 'I'll 'ave waterproofs and wellies, and be roped up for safety. And I wouldn't do anything daft."

"Well, be careful, Jim, please," she begged. "I thawt as I'd lost yer once, so I don't wanta lose yer now." Just then, a vehicle came down the track and into the yard. It was Eric Brewer. He came to the back door. "Fancy a cup of tea, Eric? There's one 'ere if yer want eet," Edith called. Eric Brewer was never one to refuse tea.

"Aye, that'd be smashing, Eedie. Thanks. Two sugars, please," he said. She prepared the tea and handed it to him. "They want you back down, Jim," he said. "The underwater blokes have arrived."

"Don't let 'im go down into th' water, Eric, please," said Edith. "I don't want 'im injured."

"Don't worry, Eedie. Jim'll be all right. It might not be necessary for him to go down, but they need his knowledge of the vehicles, that's all. And I'll see he doesn't get in harm's way."

"Well, if yer sure," Edith said reluctantly. "But take care, both of yer."

As soon as Brewer had finished the cup of tea, the two men went out to the police car and drove down to Fell Lane End once more. Two or three additional vehicles were parked there now, and a group of men stood around chatting and weighing up the problem that existed in the waters below. Because it hadn't rained for two days, the water level was starting to recede and the torrent was less severe, but most of the trailer and the whole of the tractor were still submerged. Jim was introduced to the team and soon he was explaining to them the unique manner by which the trailer and tractor were fastened together. They decided that, initially, they would try to uncouple the vehicles themselves, and only take him down to assist if it really became necessary. In the event, they did manage to separate the vehicles but, once free from the trailer, the tractor moved forward with the flowing waters for several yards, much to the annoyance of everyone. The movement was accompanied by shouts and groans, and a fear of what Tozer's reaction might be.

"Why didn't you think to make the bloody thing fast, first? You should've roped it back to the bank." The officer in charge of the operation was furious, although the men under his command whispered that he should have thought of that himself. After all, they reckoned, that's what his bloody big salary was for! A short time elapsed while the crane was re-activated, and this time there was no difficulty in lifting the trailer out of the river and winching it up and out onto the road. However, it was clear that it was completely smashed, with pieces of wood and steel bars hanging from it and its wheels buckled. It was placed on a clear part of the road, near the Hodge's garden wall.

Chief Superintendent Tozer had said already that he wanted the tractor to be brought out without any further damage, so that it could undergo the essential mechanical tests and inspections necessary to ascertain its state prior to the impact with the wall. This would not be easy, especially now that it had moved further down the watercourse, and extreme care was required. Men working in the river in waterproofs eventually attached the chain to the rear of the tractor, and this time, put more ropes around it, so that it could not slip further forward. They also hoped to use the ropes to ease the tractor manually, as the crane began its pull. The operation took the biggest part of an hour, and Jim was left to stand around, watch and be ignored by every member of the police force on site. After all, they were his vehicles, and his stupidity had resulted in the chaos. He would have a lot of explaining to do. Finally, the tractor was moved with much heaving and shouting and shoving, and lifted by the crane up and over the river wall. A flat-bed lorry was then reversed into position, the tractor placed upon it, secured with ropes, and then driven off down the valley, to take a long route to the nearest police testing compound.

"After lunch, can you pop in to my place for a chat?" Eric Brewer asked Jim.

"If you want, Eric, aye," said Jim.

"Nothing official, you understand, but the Super thinks it's time we got a few details down, that's all. He's anxious to know what you think happened," said Brewer.

"You're not going to arrest me then?"

"No, course not," Brewer re-assured him. "I hope I never have to do that, Jim. Anyway, want me to run you home?'

"No thanks. I want to see to summat up Fell Lane. And then I'll wander across the backs." Jim said. 'The backs' was a shortcut footpath behind the village.

"All right," said Brewer. "See you later."

"Aye, about two'ish?"

"Fine, when you're ready, Jim." The two men parted. Brewer went to his house, which had a small office attached to it, and Jim, as he had preferred, wandered off up Fell Lane, leaving the police officers to depart in their own time, and Council workmen to replace the temporary safety barrier across the gap in the wall Although he tried to ignore them, Jim was well aware of the glances of disdain, mutterings and gestures that all parties aimed his way for most of the time that he was around.

*   *   *   *   *

At just after two o'clock, Jim was sitting alone in the very tiny office, attached to Eric Brewer's police house, which was situated half way along Spring Street. He sat in front of Brewer's little desk on which there was a small writing pad, a telephone and a pen and ink stand. Eric's wooden armchair was on the other side of the desk, where also there was a little filing cabinet, which actually doubled as a safe, and a rack of stationery and various forms. Pinned to the wall behind the chair was a map of the area, one or two small charts and an 'official' notice about police duties. At the side of the desk was the small window that gave light to the office, even though the glass was opaque. On the wall behind Jim's chair were other notices about things such as pest control – the Death Watch Beatle – and an out-of-date Notice of Poll for the local elections. On one small ledge beneath the window, Jim noticed a framed photograph of Mabel, Eric's wife. After several minutes, Eric Brewer came in and had to squeeze past Jim in order to get to his own chair. "Sorry about that, Jim. I needed another word with Mabel and she'd popped to the smallest room."

"I thought this might be th' smallest," Jim quipped.

"Not much in it, actually," said Brewer. "No one would notice if we swapped them over."

Eric Brewer had been a copper for about eight years, and Clough Top was his first solo job. He hoped it was not his last, for, like Sara Dawson, he was very ambitious and needed to move on   He hoped to attain the rank of Superintendent within only a year or two.   His five-year marriage to Mabel had been good, although there was no sign of the start of a family yet.

He sat down, opened a desk drawer and found a pencil. He also found a clean sheet in his notepad.   "Now then, Jim," he began. "Can you tell me what you think has happened to your tractor?   I mean, where did you leave it last?"

"Yer know, where I allus leave it, Eric.   On th' croft, side of Hodges' garden wall" Jim said.

"And did you plan to leave it long?"

"Most of th' day, I s'pose.   I was going up onto Far Moor.   Some of me walls needed repair, like.   As it 'appened it took me all day, and I 'aven't finished, either. There's bloody miles to do, still"

"You didn't go up on the tractor, then?   I thought you usually went everywhere on…"

"The ground were a bloody quagmire, Eric, after th' 'eavy rain. Tractor'd get bogged down in no time."

"So you left it on the croft?"

"Aye. Well, we went up Fell Lane on it, first thing, like."

"We?"

"Me and William. Yer know, the lad often comes with me. 'E's 'elpful, and it puts a few bob in 'is pockets, you see."

"So William was with you?"

"First thing, aye. We went up to th' gate at th' end o' track across the fell. Then I could see we'd not get no further on th' bugger, not with the trailer attached as well. So I thought to bring it down again, park it on the croft, and go back up on foot. It'd be much easier."

"Well, why didn't you leave the tractor by the gate? You were half way up there, you know. Why bring it back, Jim?"

"I didn't want to leave it up there." said Jim. "Might get damaged, or summat."

"That's not very likely, is it, Jim? I mean, you've been leaving it all over the place for years. Nothing's ever happened to it before."

"I know, but yer never can tell, Eric"

"Anyhow," said Brewer. "You left it down on the croft. Was it secure?"

"Course it were. As always. Engine off, 'ere's the ignition key." He produced a key from his pocket. " 'Andbrake full on, and those two large stones that I use for chocks, one in front of each wheel."

"So there was no possibility of movement forward?"

"None at all, by accident, Eric. But if it were tampered wi'…"

"I'm coming to that," said Brewer.

"Well, it could've bin kids messin' about," Jim suggested.

"Yes, but children couldn't shift those stones, could they? They're a ton weight, you know, Jim. Bloody big rocks."

"Two or three of them might, Eric."

"Except that it was a school day. And very few children here stay off unless they're poorly. The odd one, perhaps, but not many."

"Some young idiots must've come up from the valley, Eric. It doesn't 'ave to be any from Clough Top."

Just then, the phone on the desk rang. Brewer lifted the receiver. "Brewer, Clough Top Police," he said, and the conversation continued. "Sir....Yes...I see.....Where, sir?...There now. Right, I'll get down straight away...ten, fifteen minutes at the most. Yes, see you then, sir. Bye." After replacing the receiver, he asked Jim Gregson. "Jim, was the young lad, William, with you all day, yesterday?"

"Nay, as a matter of fact 'e didn't come back with me at all."

"Why was that, then?"

"I dunno," said Jim. "'E just decided 'e didn't want to carry on. That's 'ow 'e is, yer know. Very enthusiastic one minute, and the next, 'e's lost it. Wants to do summat different. I'm used to it."

"But you could have done with his help?"

"Well aye. But I don't bother about it. And any road, I don't 'ave to pay 'im."

"Do you think he'd prefer to ride on the tractor? Is that the attraction?"

"I 'ardly think so. 'E's never said…."

"They've seen a body in the river, just below the weir at Furness Bridge. They think it's a young male." Jim sat silently for a few moments, taking in the news. Then he said, "It mightn't be William."

"They don't know who it is, yet, Jim," Brewer said. "But they want me down there, smartish. I'm going now. Perhaps you'd better come, as well."

ooooocOooooo

CHAPTER SIX

Only one police car stood on the river bank, above the weir at Furness Bridge, when P.C. Eric Brewer and farmer Jim Gregson arrived on the scene, although other unidentifiable vehicles were parked nearby. Several men were working down by the weir, watched by a little group of curious onlookers, whose number increased almost minute by minute. Very soon the sound of a siren heralded the arrival of an ambulance. It parked as close to the river bank as it could get and its crew began the tasks necessary to assist in this emergency.

During the drive down from Clough Top, Jim told Brewer of his conversation with Betty Marsh about her lodger, William. "I told 'er yer were busy, like. Not to bother yer."

"I'm never too busy to talk to Betty, Jim. But I understand your reasoning." But Brewer preferred not to remark any further, at that moment. He completed the drive and parked near to the other police vehicle. Both men got out just in time to witness a body being pulled to the bank, lifted out of the water and laid on a patch of grass at the water's edge. It was motionless. They covered it with a blanket.

The body was taken to the ambulance, but before it was driven away, Brewer went to the police officer in charge. The officer nodded his head. Brewer turned to Jim Gregson. "Stay here, Jim. I'll have a look," he said A few moments later he emerged from the vehicle, and nodded to Jim. "William" was all he said in affirmation. He made some comments to the officer in charge, and then wandered away, back to his own car. Jim followed and both men lit cigarettes and sat silently smoking in the vehicle for a few minutes. Finally, Eric Brewer broke the silence. "Not a pretty sight," he said.

"I s'pose not," said Jim.

"Poor little bugger." Brewer started the car engine and began the drive back to Clough Top, but it was not until they reached Fell Lane End, where Council workmen were now doing some temporary repairs to the shattered wall and blocking up the gap, that he continued, "Do you know if William had any family, Jim? Mother? Father?"

"'E's spoken about 'is mother, now and again," replied Jim. "I 'ave an idea she's over Yorksheer way, somewhere."

"There was no identification on him, you see. Actually, I gave the lad a nickname – 'The Leprechaun.' - I don't think I know his proper surname. Do you, Jim?"

"Tudge." Jim told him.

"William Tudge," mused Brewer. "Now it'll be down to me to call on Betty Marsh."

"Will yer be takin' Sara with yer?"

"Can't take your mind off her, can you? Does Eedie know?"

"I were only askin'. Will yer take 'er along? Nowt wrong in.... "

"Probably. I'll give her a call on the radio. Ask her to come up. Oh, no need. She's here already." As they turned into the track that led to Moorside Farm, he could see her car parked in the yard. He parked beside it.

Sara and Edith were sitting in the living room. Sara had tried to comfort Edith, saying that it was unlikely that Jim would be in serious trouble, especially if he had taken every precaution to ensure that the tractor was safe.

A mechanical examination would be necessary, but unless it proved that the vehicle was not roadworthy, Jim could not be blamed for what had happened. Jim and Brewer came into the room. "Some sad news, Eedie, love," Jim began, as he went to her.

"Let me, Jim," interrupted Brewer. "Eedie, we've found a body in the river, just below the weir at Furness Bridge. It's William Tudge."

Edith gasped. "Nay!" she blurted out.

"Jim and I have just been down. I've seen the body and I've identified it." Tears began to well up in Edith's eyes. She looked pleadingly at her husband, but he just nodded and looked away.

"But I don't understand. William? William Tudge?" She began to weep. Sara went to her and put an arm around her, and then glanced at Brewer.

"Who is William Tudge?" She asked.

Brewer told her. "He's a lad who lives here in the village. He helps Jim on the farm sometimes."

"And 'e's a reet good lad, is William. Not a bit like folk think," said Edith. "Ave they told Betty Marsh?"

"I'm on the way to see her now. Can you come with me please, Sara?"

"Certainly, Eric. Is she a relative?"

"No The lad just has lodgings with her. But she treats him like he was a son. Come on, I'll tell you more as we go. We'll use my car, and I'll run you back here for yours later."

When the two police officers had left, Jim Gregson sat quietly for a while. Edith went upstairs for something and didn't return immediately. It was quiet. He felt that he had just been through a whirlwind, and now it was the calm. He thought he should go to check on the pigs again, find Brack and go down there, but he just couldn't. For one thing, he didn't know what to expect, what would come of it all. He was certain that he could not be held responsible for any of this, even though the tractor and trailer belonged to him and William had been with him that morning. Could they say that he was responsible for William? No, William was a free agent, he did as much, or as little, as he wanted and Jim paid him accordingly – there was no other way with William. There was no formal arrangement, or for that matter, not even an informal one, and nothing on paper. Mind you, should there have been? Should he have had proper insurance cover? No, the boy wasn't working for him at the time; he had gone off on his own. There was insurance for the vehicles, of course, and that would cover their damage or more likely, their destruction, but he couldn't work out if, or how, it would cover what would amount to 'unauthorized use'. He was pondering it all when Edith came back.

"I dunna understand this, Jim," she said.

"Nor do I, love. I don't rightly know what to think"

"I mean, what could 'ave 'appened? 'Ow did tractor and trailer get in'th river for a start? That poor boy couldn't 've moved it, could 'e? Not by 'isself, any road. And now this. Drowned! 'Ow's that 'appen, eh?"

"Beats me, Eedie," said Jim.

"Where did yer leave tractor?"

"I told yer. On th' croft. Where I always..."

"Safely? Were it safe, Jim?'

" 'Course it were, love. I 'ad keys wi' me, still 'ave, 'ere, look." He produced the ignition keys. "The other set is still on th' board in th' kitchen."

"I thawt tha were going out wi' it, yesterday?"

"We did, for a start. But th' ground were so wet, I could see we'd get bogged down right away. Like a bloody big sponge it were."

"Well, yer needn't swear, Jim."

"I only said – aaah, sorry!"

"Well, I don't like eet. You knaw that. What'd Vicar say? So, any road, yer went back down wi' it?"

"Aye, that's right," he told her.

"An' what did William do?"

"Suddenly decided to stay down. Walked away," said Jim.

"Nay, that's not like 'im," said Edith. "I can't think what Betty Marsh'll say."

" 'Appen she'll know by now. They'll 've told 'er."

"I'll go down to 'er, presently. She'll need company, that's for sure." Edith said.

"Sara will 'elp. She seems a good lass."

"Aye, she's nice enough. But ... mind yer, people from the church will 'elp to comfort 'er, an' pr'aps Vicar'll coom. I s'pect she'll get on to him, first."

"'Ow about 'is mother?"

" 'Oose?'

"William's?"

"Aye, well. She'll need to be told. But from what I 'eard she'll not be bothered. She kicked im out at 'ome. That's why 'e came 'ere."

"That might not be reet, though, Eedie. I'd be careful about sayin' anythin' like that. Where does she live any road? Yorksheer, isn't it?"

"Somewhere that direction, I think. Betty Marsh'll know."

Through the window, just then, Jim caught sight of his daughter coming down the track from the road.

" 'Ere's our Jen. D' yer think we should say owt?"

"She'll 'ave ter knaw sooner or later," said Edith. They heard the back door open – Brack was barking in the yard – and then Jenny's customary call - "Mum!"

"We're in 'ere, luv, the sittin' room."

*   *   *   *   *

Driving back into the village in his police car, Eric Brewer told Sara Dawson all that he knew about young William Tudge. He was certainly odd, often to be heard singing and laughing to himself, and subject to erratic behaviour. Brewer had encountered him on one occasion sitting alone at the side of the lane, focusing attention on some invisible object. Brewer had stopped his cycle and gone over to the lad. "Everything all right, William?" he had asked.

"Shshsh! Mr. Brewer" the lad had said. "Tha'll frighten 'im off."

"Frighten, who, William?"

"'Im, 'im theer. See? A lepercorn!"

"Where? In the hedge?"

"Aye, 'e's theer, look!"

But, although Eric Brewer had seen nothing, he had just said "Well, you be careful, lad, or he might get you."

"Quite a vivid imagination, then," Sara remarked.

"Too vivid for a lad of his age," said Brewer.

"But that was harmless, though, wasn't it, Eric? I can think of much worse things..."

"Oh, yes, love, so can I. I'm only telling you what he's like."

"Was like," Sara corrected him.

"Yes. Ok."

"But I wonder where he got the 'Leprechaun' idea from? It's Irish folk lore, isn't it?"

"Is it?" Brewer hadn't given it much thought at the time. "I must admit I thought it was a bit strange, but, well…"

They pulled up outside Betty Marsh's little cottage in Spring Street, just a few doors from the Huntsman, and went to the front door. They rang the bell, and soon Betty appeared. She was a small, slender woman, her dark hair now streaked with grey. She wore a pinafore over skirt and blouse, thick stockings and black shoes.

"Oh, Mr. Brewer," she said. "Am I glad to see yer. William's gone missin'. 'E didn't come 'ome last night, and 'e's never done that before. I know 'e seems a bit strange sometimes, but …I asked Jim Gregson earlier, but 'e 'asn't seen 'im either. I'm gettin' quite worried, yer knaw. It's not like William at all. It really isn't, Eric."

"Hang on, Betty," Brewer said. "We'd like a word, please."

Betty began to suspect that there was something wrong. She realised, too, that Eric Brewer would normally call to see her by himself, but this time he had a 'lady policeman' with him. She stood back and looked from one to the other

"Won't you sit down, love?" asked Sara, kindly.

"Oh lor'," she exclaimed. "What's 'appened, Mr. Brewer?"

"There's been an accident, Betty," began Brewer. "We've found William's body in the river, below the weir at Furness Bridge. I'm afraid he's drowned." Betty dropped into an armchair. A look of horror came to her face, tears to her eyes. Sara held her hand.

Then Betty shrieked, "William, drowned? Never!"

"I've seen the body, Betty," said Brewer "There can be no doubt."

"But 'ow, Mr. Brewer? 'Ow did it 'appen?" "I wish we knew, Betty, love. But we don't, just yet. Jim Gregson's tractor and trailer crashed through the wall at Fell Lane End, yesterday. But what has actually caused that, and this with William, we can't tell. It's a mystery, love."

Betty began to cry again, and Sara held her close. Betty said "William were a good lad. 'E'd never do owt bad."

"No, of course not, Mrs. Marsh. We think it was an accident." Sara told her.

"I asked Jim Gregson not long since about William, but; 'e never said owt about no accident. Just said yer were busy, Mr. Brewer, an' not to bother yer."

"He'd just be thinking about his vehicles, Betty. He didn't know about William, then."

"Then 'ow...?

"We don't know, Betty, honest. I'm sorry to impose this on you now, love, but do you know where his parents live?" Brewer asked.

"I don't know nowt about 'is father, never 'eard about 'im at all. 'Is mother lives somewhere in 'Alifax, in Yorksheer. Not that she'll be much bothered. Couldn't get rid of 'im fast enough, from what William told me. That's why 'e came 'ere."

"Have you got an address in Halifax, Betty?"

"Nay, I 'aven't, Mr. Brewer," she replied.

"Then we'll have to search his room. I expect there'll be something there."

"I'll show yer up, then, Mr. Brewer. It's the room at the back. Very small, but 'e was 'appy wir it." Betty took them up the narrow, steep staircase, and opened the back bedroom door. Brewer went in, while Sara stood in the doorway, still with her hand on Betty, who stood on the tiny landing.

As Betty Marsh had said, the room was very small, and the equally small window, thinly curtained, gave only a little light. Brewer switched the electric light on, and noticed that even that was just a bulb, without a shade. Most of the room was taken up by a single bed, and there was a small wardrobe beside the window. A card table, folded, leaned against the wall, between the door and the wardrobe, and near the head of the bed there was a small wooden chair with a few pieces of a man's clothing hanging from it, and a Bible lying on the seat. An old coat hung on a nail at the back of the door. The floor had linoleum covering, but there was a warm rug beside the bed. "I let 'im keep 'is shaving kit and stuff like that in the bathroom. Well, there's only me, an' I'm not going to touch that, am I?" Betty said.

Brewer opened the wardrobe. Apart from two old jackets and a 'better' suit hanging from hooks, the lower part contained three cardboard boxes. Brewer took each one out with care and placed them on the bed.   Pieces of newspaper, an old school exercise book, half-filled with incomprehensible texts in almost illegible handwriting, some old postcards – none of them addressed to anyone – bus and train tickets, some leaflets bearing religious texts, a tennis ball, some old rags.   In addition, there was a small album of photographs, possibly of his family, and another envelope, quite a large one, bearing the words 'TOP SECRET'.   It contained a birth certificate for 'William Tudge'…   date   of   birth…..at   Halifax   General Hospital…..mother Fiona Tudge….father Patrick Tudge – Bricklayer.   There was also a small sheet of paper with an address in Halifax for "F. Wallace"   Brewer suspected that this was a relative, possibly William's mother, if she had left Mr. Tudge and married again.   In the event, this turned out to be correct.   "I've got an address here, Sara," Brewer called out.   "You might be taking a trip to Halifax."

With the envelope in his hand, Brewer closed the wardrobe and came out of the room.   "Better keep that door closed for the time being, Betty. Is that all right?"

"Of course, if you say so, Mr. Brewer. I'll not open it 'till you tell me," agreed Betty. "Ee, but poor lad. What will 'appen now, Mr. Brewer?"

"Dunno yet, Betty. But I expect there'll have to be an inquest," Brewer told her.

"An inquest? What will….will I 'ave to go to it?"

"Probably. But you'll see. And it won't be as bad as you think, love."

"Oh 'eck! I don't like them things. I 'ad to go when my Trevor passed away. Yer remember 'im, Mr. Brewer? Never 'ad an illness in 'is life, 'an 'e just dropped dead in the back gardin – just out there." Betty pointed to the back of the cottage. "That were enough of inquests fer me."

Sara tried to comfort her. "It might not be that bad, Mrs. Marsh. Try not to worry. Now, can we do anything to help?"

"Not really, luv, thank you. I'll pop down to the box and 'phone the Vicar in a while. 'E needs to know, and I 'spect' 'e'll coom up when 'e can."

"I'm sure he will," said Brewer. "Reverend Nuttall will be very kind. We'll leave you for now, Betty, but we'll be in touch as soon as we know more. Ok?"

"Yes, Mr. Brewer, thank yer."

"All right, love. You take care." Then Brewer and Sara left her

* * * * *

When she had dumped her school bag on the kitchen floor, Jenny came into the room. "Hi Mum, Dad. Everything all right? Any tea?

"I'll make a fresh pot, fer yer, luv. That one's cold and stewed," said Edith She went out to the kitchen.. After a few moments, Jenny said, "The kids at school are getting to know about the accident at Fell Lane End. They keep asking me about it, Dad."

"And what 'ave you said, love? What 'ave you told 'em?"

"Not much. Well, I don't know much, do I?"

"No, sweetie, you don't. An' we don't neither. But they've found a body in th' river, today," Jim told her.

"A body! Who? Dad, tell me, who?"

"William. I may as well tell yer, 'e's drowned."

Jenny began to cry. "No, oh Dad, no!"

"Found 'im down at Furness Bridge. Below th' weir there. Mr. Brewer's identified 'im," said Jim.

"That's awful, Dad," Jenny sobbed. "Poor William!"

"Yes, love, it's a terrible shame."

"Did you see his body, Dad?" Jenny asked.

"No, love. Mr. Brewer did everythin'. I left it to 'im. 'E seemed to want it that way, but 'e said it weren't very nice."

Jenny gasped and cried a little more. Speaking through her tears, she said, "What do you think has happened, Dad?"

"I wish I knew, love," said Jim. "But 'appen it'll all be sorted out in time. Try not to bother yourself too much. I know yer thought of William as a friend, but yer mustn't let this upset yer. Come on now, sweetie, there's my girl." He took her into his arms and held her. She sobbed into his embrace, clinging on to him.

"Dad," she cried, "Oh, Dad!"

Jim thought that this was something to do with a release of tension. The last two days had been emotional.

She had thought that her father had been killed in the accident at Fell Lane End, and his re-appearance last night, fit and well, must have been a shock just as much as a relief. That the family were involved, however tenuously, was obvious, and probably the little girl had worried about it inside herself. Now, she had to deal with some degree of inquisitive chatter from her school friends. Probably this was a very large issue for her, and she needed to break the tension somehow. He let her sob for a while, until Edith returned with a fresh pot of tea. "There now," she said. "Oo's for a fresh cup?"

"Pour one for Jen, love. She needs one right away," said Jim. Edith had realised immediately that Jenny was upset, but she thought it wiser to ignore the fact at that moment. She poured her daughter a cup of tea and handed it to her

"Thanks, Mum," said Jenny, as she took the tea and drank it. At that moment, they heard Brack barking outside and the slam of a car door. Eric Brewer and Sara Dawson had returned from Betty Marsh's.

Jim went to the back door and asked if Sara would mind having a word with Jenny. "She's upset. She might want a talk," he said. Eric Brewer made genuine excuses about having work to catch up on and drove back to the village, but Sara agreed to see the young girl. She followed Jim into the sitting room.

"Hello, Jenny," she said. "Your dad tells me you're unhappy. What's the matter, love? Want to tell be about it?"

"I'm all right, really," said Jenny. "It's just this about William. He was a nice lad."

"I'm sure he was. But it was an accident, my dear, and accidents do happen in life. Even to the best of us, you know."

"But he's dead, Sara. He's not just in hospital being treated for something and be out again, soon. He's dead. Gone for ever!" Jenny argued.

"Yes. And I know that's hard, very hard."

Jenny said, "I know he was a bit daft sometimes and people, unkind people, used to laugh at him. But he was kind, and was always helping people. He was a good lad, and it isn't fair." She began to weep again, and both Sara and Edith tried to console her. After a time, the weeping stopped and Jenny brightened. Sara could see that the nervous tension was ebbing away.

"That's good," she said. "You've got that behind you and you'll feel better now."

"Yes," Jenny said, as she finished drinking the tea. "I'd like to go and change now, Mum."

"Aye, do that, Jen," Edith said. "Likely tha'll be more cheery after."

"Thanks, Sara. Thanks, Mum." Then she looked at her watch and exclaimed, "Oh, I'm on duty at the Huntsman in half-an-hour. 'Bye for now." And Jenny went off to her room.

"She'll be all reet now, Sara. Thank yer very much," said Edith.

"Don't thank me, Edith. That's what I'm here for. This is all a bit too much for the poor child, that's all. Bless her. When she gets to the pub, she'll feel a lot better. Take her mind off things. Well, I must be off, too. I've much to do before I go off duty. But I'll pop in again tomorrow."

"Thank ya. That's very kind," said Edith. Jim rose from his chair.

"I'll see yer to yer car, miss," he said.

"There's really no need," said Sara.

But Jim insisted. "It's the dog, Brack. Gets a bit excited."

"I'm sure I can cope," said Sara, "But if you really think…"

"Aye, I'll come," said Jim, and Sara, having said goodbye to Edith, followed him into the yard. Edith thought rather a long time passed before she heard the door slam and Sara's car drive away. Brack was still barking when Jim returned.

"I'll take Brack down the field. And I must have a look at them pigs. 'Igh time I did. D'you think Jenny's ok.?"

"Aye, 'course she is," Edith assured him. "But what d'yer want ter bother takin' 'er t' car fer?

"Showin' a bit o' courtesy, that's all, love."

" 'Appen it weren't necessary, thaw. An' it took yer long enough."

"Meanin'?"

"Well, 'ow it might look. Yer married, yer knaw. I'm yer wife. An' after last night …."

"That's nowt ter do with it. Eedie, 'onestly!"

"Well, just think on. Any road, Jim, I forgot to tell yer summat else, as might be important."

"Aye, what's that then?"

"Summat Jen said, yesterday. She said that Karen Dinnet thinks she's in th' family way. An' she's blamin' William!"

With great difficulty, Jim prevented a smile from crossing his face. But he just said "Well, Eedie, stupid little lasses say stupid little things, sometimes. An' for that matter, so do their ma's. But I reckon that beats the lot. Don't you?" And he went out to find Brack, and out of the yard to inspect the pigs.

oooooOooooo

CHAPTER SEVEN

In a small meeting room in the Macclesfield Divisional Headquarters at Wilmslow Police Station, a group of senior people had gathered for a conference. Chief Superintendent Tozer was the Chairman, and he was flanked by two assistant inspectors, two men of lesser rank, and Sara Dawson was there as well. Across the table was an Assistant County Surveyor for Cheshire, three technical officers and a young male clerk, who was taking notes. As was usual at such meetings in those days, the air was, filled with cigarette smoke - even Sara smoked. Something akin to a fog descended over the table. As soon as anyone stubbed a cigarette into an ashtray, another one was offered, and almost without exception, it was taken and lit up automatically. The meeting was taking place on day following the discovery of William Tudge's body.

"Whatever rubbish we might be told," said Tozer, "I simply cannot accept that one young man like William Tudge – is that the right name?" he consulted some papers before him, "Yes, William Tudge, could possibly have shifted that tractor an inch from where we are supposed to believe it was parked. The owner, Gregson, says that he left it with handbrake full on, engine off and the ignition keys were in his possession. Two very large stones were in front of the wheels, the ground was very soft after heavy rain – in fact the tyre tracks in the mud are four inches deep. The ground slopes upward to the edge of the road tarmac, and there is a camber on the road itself. It would have taken ten men to shift it from that position, let alone cause it to career across the road and completely demolish that wall at the top of the river bank"

"There was also the fact, sir, that the tractor was tethered to the trailer, which itself must have been almost up to its chassis in the mud," another officer pointed out.

"Yes, absolutely," Tozer agreed.

"And then there's the wall itself, Chief Superintendent", said the Assistant Surveyor. "It had only just been strengthened considerably – ten days ago. The way the work was done, and the strength of the material used, would have made it impossible to cause so much damage with the minor impact that the vehicles could have made."

"We'll need more certainty about that, though, Mr. Cornhill, especially in the light of the preceding nights' rains. The foundations could well have been undermined, couldn't they?"

"Not a chance. The stress factors were very high." The Surveyor was quite indignant at the suggestion.

"Proof of that might be necessary at any inquest," said Tozer.

"Proof can be provided, sir," replied the Surveyor.

"Anyhow, that's rather getting away from the main question, which is how the hell did both tractor and trailer get from where he says they were parked, and through that bloody stone wall and into the bloody river? And to my mind, the answer is far from what we are being told."

"Have you your own theory as to what might have occurred, Chief Superintendent?" asked the Surveyor.

"No." replied Tozer. "Except that I don't believe the rubbish we have in this report." He indicated a paper in front of him. "This came from P.C. Brewer, the local bobby at Clough Top."

"Surely you believe him, sir," said another officer.

"Oh, yes. I believe that he's reporting what he's

been told. But I also observe that he's very chummy with Gregson, and not prepared to question him too much. Anyway, I've taken him off the case, as of this morning. John Harvey will be taking over down there. Brewer is being transferred here for a while."

"He won't like that, very much," whispered Sara, who thought that she could only be heard by the colleague sitting beside her, but Tozer heard her.

"It's not for P.C. Brewer to like or dislike anything, W.P.C. Dawson. He's off the case. All right?"

"Yes, sir, I'm sorry." It was all that Sara could say.

"We're waiting for the technical report on the condition of the vehicle, and I expect the Coroner will want an inquest. But I don't think we'll get much from either. The tractor will have so many defects now, that it will be nigh impossible to tell how many were caused by the accident or how many existed before. And the lad, well, he drowned in the water, but why, or how? God knows, but we might never know." After Tozer had spoken, it was the Surveyor's turn.

"I haven't come to this meeting today, Chief Superintendent, to play at being a detective. That's your job. But I am here to tell you that the wall had been strengthened, secured, cemented to the rock face of the ravine, very recently, and would have withstood a considerable impact. If the tractor with its trailer had only been moved from the position you say, and I agree that that in itself is very implausible, it would not have demolished the wall."

"So, have you any theory, Mr. Cornhill?" asked Tozer.

"Oh, none, Chief Superintendent. You're the detective," the Surveyor said.

"Then we'll have to make a lot more enquiries," said Tozer, as he glanced at his watch.. "And as there appears to be no further business at the moment, and it's getting towards lunchtime, I'll close the meeting. Thank you, gentlemen." Then with a glance at Sara, he added, "And lady." Sara blushed, but said nothing more, although she knew his reputation as a male chauvinist pig. But the closure of the meeting was a signal for a further round of cigarette offers and lightings as people relaxed. Tozer, however, gathered the papers in front of him and hurried away, followed by one of his officers who carried a file. After a few moments, the young note-taker edged his way around to near Sara, and after a short hesitation, he confronted her. "Excuse me," he said. Sara smiled at him. "I wonder...you see, I'm new here...and I didn't quite catch one or two names...of the policemen. I thought you might..."

"Which ones have you missed?" asked Sara. "The Chief Superintendent's name is 'Tozer'."

"Oh yes, I've got him. But his assistants?"

"Em, Superintendent Leather, and Inspector Rod Bygraves. And don't ever call him 'Max'. He doesn't like it."

"I'll remember that," said the young man.

"And I'm W.P.C. Sara Dawson – part-time liaison officer."

"Yes, I've got that, already....Well, he, the Chief Superintendent, called you by name, and it confirmed what I thought I heard you say at the start. But the other two..."

"Some people do mumble," Sara remarked. Anyway, have you got everyone now?"

"Yes, thanks. Thanks a lot."

"Glad to help," Sara said, as she began to move away. The note-taker moved to detain her.

"Oh, by the way, I'm Alan, Alan Hardisty."

"Well, hello, Mr. Hardisty."

"I've only been in this job a fortnight. I came down from Westmorland, Windermere U.D.C. The Lakes, you know." Sara let the unnecessary explanation pass.

"That's a very lovely area," she said. "Whatever made you leave?"

"Money. This job pays a lot more."

"I could say that money isn't everything, Mr. Hardisty, but I don't usually go in for clichés, and probably, you wouldn't agree."

"I would say that it's a large part of everything. But I know what you mean," said Hardisty. "To be honest, though, I'm missing home already. Can't wait to go back. I'll have a long week-end coming in a few weeks' time."

"Well, at least you'll have that to look forward to. Now, if you'll excuse me, Mr. Hardisty, I've got some calls to make. So I'll pop into the canteen for a sandwich and get on my way," Sara said.

"Yes, of course. But, actually, I thought…"

"It's been nice meeting you, and I'm pleased to have been able to help, Mr. Hardisty, but I'll say 'goodbye' now." Sara was very definite, that this was to be the end of the conversation. She began to walk away.

"Yes, anyway, thanks," said Hardisty. Then he, too, gathered his papers and went out in another direction. Sara did want to grab a sandwich and a drink in the canteen, she did have calls to make, and she was quite sure that she didn't want to exchange further small talk with Alan Hardisty.

After her lunch, while she was driving to check on a lady whose husband was to appear in court the next morning, she received a message on the car radio. It was Eric Brewer. Sara said, "Oh, hello, Eric. I hear you're on the move."

"Yes, that's right," Brewer's voice came back. "But look, Sara, that's not important at the moment and anyway, it's only temporary, and I agree with his reasoning. Honestly, I do. But something a bit delicate has cropped up that I think you ought to know."

"I think I'd better phone you, Eric. Are you still in Clough Top?" Sara didn't trust the police radio waves - anyone could overhear anything..

"Yes, I'm just tidying up in the office before the new bloke arrives. I'll be here an hour, at least," Brewer said.

"Right, I'll ring you in a few minutes. Bye." Sara closed the radio. As soon as she could find a phone box, she parked nearby and phoned Eric Brewer. He told her that Jim Gregson had informed him about Karen Dinnet and her possible pregnancy allegation against William Tudge.

"It could be significant, Sara," said Brewer.

"I'll say," said Sara. "If the lad knew what he was being accused of, true or false, he'd be pretty scared."

"Suicidal?" asked Brewer.

"The problem is, though, Eric, that we don't know what sort of a boy he was." Sara said.

"He was a churchgoer, and, as you already know, not...very bright, if you know what I'm getting at."

"Yes, you've told me that there were mental problems. The 'leprechaun' incident made that clear. So something like this could have dire consequences. I'm not a psychiatrist, but it's pretty clear to me that he'd be very frightened."

"That's presuming, Sara," said Brewer. "That he knew about the accusation? He heard what the girl was saying? And, more importantly, understood the implications."

"We might never know that, might we, Eric?"

"I reckon she would know. The kid might've told him, herself," he said.

"You think I should have a word?" Sara asked.

"Well, you're the one to do it. Tact, charm...."

"Oh, come off that, Eric. But yes, obviously it's a job for a woman. I'll get on to it," said Sara.

"Better report it and get authorisation first, though. And I'd better tell John Harvey, when he arrives. He ought to know, right away. He should be here quite soon," said Brewer

"Right. I'll sort something out with the powerful ones and, hopefully, get to see this young lady. That could be interesting."

"You'll keep me informed?" asked Brewer.

"Certainly, Eric. But how? Where will you be?"

"Not far away. I'm still living here, love, but not working in Clough Top."

"Oh, don't worry, I'll find you," said Sara. "I'll be in touch. Bye for now."

"Bye, Sara," Brewer replied. They rang off.

As she continued with her other duties, calls on people whose families or in some instances whose friends, were to appear in court, or who had suffered the effects of some criminal activity or other, Sara had time to think about the situation at Clough Top. To confront this girl, Karen Dinnet, directly, with the accusation she had made, might not be a wise move, initially. Better that she should skirt around the matter at first, perhaps hear if there was any general gossip, perhaps at Broadlea School. Maybe she should chat with Jenny Gregson – a very sensible, level-headed little girl – and discover if the rumour had got any further than schoolgirl gossip. This approach, she thought, need not really require authorisation. She knew that some of the senior men would go in with all guns blazing – even Tozer could do that. Instead, she would play it her own way for a while. The necessary authorisation could wait.

By late afternoon she had finished her scheduled visits for the day, and so she drove across the six or seven miles of open hill country to Clough Top, where she arrived at Moorside Farm. Brack, tethered by the long rope, barked and came as close to her as he could manage before being restrained. The back door opened, and Edith Gregson stood there. She smiled as Sara approached her. " 'Ello, luv. I never thawt ta see yer back as quick as this," she said.

Sara detected some anxiety in her voice. "Hello, Edith. It's nothing to worry about. I just wanted a word, that's all."

"Aye?"

"Can we go inside? Is Jenny about?" Sara asked.

"Aye, coom in, lass. Jenny's up in 'er room. Doin' 'omework, I think. 'Ave I to call 'er?"

"No, perhaps not yet, Edith. I'll ask you first." They went into the sitting room and Edith indicated a seat. Sara sat down.

"Can I get yer some tea, luv? Kettle's on," said Edith.

"No thanks, Edith. I've been offered tea all day. And I hope I shall be getting home after this visit. My mum will have dinner ready."

"Dinner?" exclaimed Edith, and then she realised that Sara would be referring to the evening meal. "Oh, aye," she said, and then she also sat down.

Sara began, "Edith, your husband has told us about the allegation made against this young man, William Tudge, by a young girl in the village."

"Ay, well, there's nowt in that, luv," said Edith. "The girl's a little liar, and a dirty one at that!"

"No, Edith, the point isn't whether the accusation is true or false at the moment, but rather, whether William Tudge knew about it."

"Yer think 'e might've 'eard about it, and...?"

"He would have been frightened, wouldn't he?"

"Aye, I s'pose, but....suicide? In th' river?" Edith realised the possibility. "So Jenny might know if 'e knew what the girl said?"

"That's right. So I wondered...?"

"I'll call 'er down, luv." And Edith went out to the hallway and called to her daughter.

Jenny came down and was pleased to see Sara, but she was unable to help with the question put to her. She said she could ask Karen at school tomorrow, but, even then, she could not be sure if anyone would know, or be willing to tell the truth.

Sara, on the other hand, did not like the idea of the girl making enquiries on her behalf – or, for that matter, on behalf of the police. "Thanks, Jenny, but no," she said. "It would be best if you said nothing. By all means, listen to anything that might be said, but don't ask, love. I'll do the asking. All right?"

"Yes, Sara," Jenny replied.

"Good girl, thank you," said Sara. Then she left the farmhouse and headed for home and the evening meal that her mother had prepared.

* * * * *

That afternoon, at the County Surveyor's offices, near Chester, Alan Hardisty typed up the minutes of the meeting that had taken place at Wilmslow earlier in the day. A top copy and three carbons would be enough for the boss to approve or amend, as he usually did, before re-typing on stencil for the duplicator. It seemed very important to stress the Technical Officer's and the Surveyor's insistence that the wall on the river bank had been strengthened considerably, only in the last few days, and would certainly have withstood being struck by a slow-moving vehicle, as had been postulated. On the other hand, he thought, a bit of faulty workmanship, together with the exceptional amount of water in the river at the time, might well have caused a problem – the bank and the wall might have collapsed prior to the accident with the vehicle, providing no safety barrier for the vehicle, which would then have careered straight over the edge. And the young lad could have simply fallen in as well, as he was trying to assess the situation. However, these considerations were unthinkable so far as his boss, the County Surveyor, was concerned, and Hardisty knew well that he must keep them to himself.

But he had another matter on his mind. The young Woman Police Constable, Sara Dawson, was someone he would like to know a lot more intimately. That she was beautiful, he had no doubt. She was intelligent, caring, kind and thoughtful - he was certain of that, too. Conversation with her was a pleasure, a friendship would be delightful, and love! He couldn't bear the imagining. But then, too, there were so many things he did not know. Was she married? If not, was she engaged? If not, was there a boy friend? Surely one of these was certain. These were overwhelming thoughts.

Just then, Mark Manion, one of the technical officers, entered the office. "Got those minutes ready yet, Alan?" he asked.

"Almost. Won't be long."

"Well, give them a bit of a push. His nibs is waiting."

"I'm doing my best, Mark. I said they won't be long. Did you hear?"

"Right." In contrast to Alan, who was quite small, thin and with brown wavy hair, Manion was a large man with jet black, oily hair and he had a slight squint in his right eye that made him rather intimidating at first glance. Oh, I say," he said. "You noticed that bird in the police team? I'm going to see what I can fix up with her, mate."

"She seemed a pleasant woman."

"Pleasant! God, man, she's a stunner. I'd soon have that uniform off her. Did you see those whats-its?" He made a gesture with his hands indicating her bosom.

"That's disgusting, Mark," said Hardisty.

"And we noticed you chatting her up after the meeting, Alan. Fancy your chances there, do you, old son?"

"I needed to confirm some names of the police team members. I thought she would know."

"Good one, that," said Manion. "Very original, I must say."

"I've only been here a fortnight. I don't know anyone much, yet. Not by name, anyway."

"Hasn't taken you long to notice the local talent, though, has it? But you'd better hurry up if you want to beat me to it. I'm not waiting for any starting pistol."

"What if she's already taken?" asked Hardisty.

"Depends what you mean by that, mate. Mind you, I wouldn't be put off too much if she was married." Hardisty finished typing, pulled the copies from the machine, extracted the sheets of carbon paper, and handed three of the four draft copies to Manion. "Here," he said. "You'd better get these to the Chief."

* * * * *

When she reached home, Sara Dawson, went to her room, changed from her uniform into comfortable slacks and a chunky jumper. She enjoyed the evening meal with her mother and father and relaxed for a short time. Then she went back to her room and continued her studies for an imminent police promotion examination. Men, and particularly Alan Hardisty, were far from her mind.

ooooooOooooo

CHAPTER EIGHT

'Yesterday, I walked across the Common – that area of flat, open grassland that stretches from behind my bungalow until, on the far side of a low wall of dry stone, the land rises to the higher hills and the fell country beyond. The ground is firmer now, the squelchy, slippery quagmire left by the melting snow and then the recent heavy storms that produced rain in torrents, has dried considerably. The chill has gone from the wind, the sun shines brightly from a blue sky, only speckled with the tufts of fleeting clouds, and the air feels warmer. Green shoots of fresh grass show beneath a swathe of the greying tufts of last year's crop, and just here and there spots of yellow mark the first sprouting signs of Celandine – Ranunculus Ficaria. If we only have a few more similar days, large patches of yellow will brighten these open acres. Sparrows, starlings and common tits chatter and chirp in the air, where, in just a few more weeks, we shall see wrens and wood pigeons, and hear lapwings – pee wit, pee wit, - and then the distant call of the faithful cuckoo – never once has he failed us. Only

*now we must wait a little longer and just know that soon
it will be spring.'*

This was the contribution to a national daily
paper, sent in from Clough Top for the week following
the death of William Tudge. Although, for the purposes
of the series she had been commissioned to write, she
used the nom-de-plume "Country Girl", the author's
name was Bella Warrington, a thirty-two year old
woman. Her home was a wooden bungalow built around
the time of the First World War, one of five originally let
as 'holiday homes' and used by less well-off families
from the cities – Manchester or Sheffield mainly – who
preferred to come out into the countryside for one week
in the year – rather than visit the more popular delights of
the seaside resorts on the Lancashire coast. Sometimes,
however, the choice was dictated by the considerations of
finance, rather than preference. Only three of the
buildings remained, built on a terrace on the hillside at
the back of the village. An un-surfaced track leading
from Fell Lane gave access to the properties, and Bella
lived in the first of them. From the front verandah, it
was possible to look across a small, grassy meadow,

walled and gated, and then to the rear of the cottages, the first of which was Joe and Martha Hodges' From this vantage point, you could look beyond the cottages with their slated roofs and plumes of grey smoke coming from one or more of the chimneys, across the road that goes up to the village, across the ravine with the gushing waters far below, to the open land on the far side; hilly, grassy land on which there were patches of scrub, bushes, a small copse, and where, a little later in the year, there would be bluebells and broom, and then purple patches of heather. But the road junction at Fell Lane End was out of sight, hidden by a clump of bushes and trees on the top side of what had always been known as 'The Croft', even though it was only a little wider than the grass verge that bounded the road for a long way up past the end of the track to the bungalows and onto the side of the Common.

As had become her routine, Bella Warrington wrote her article directly onto her typewriter, an upright, Underwood machine, which could be heard click-clacking away for hours on end in her little 'office' at the back corner of the bungalow, where she had a view onto her little side garden and then onto the side wall of the bungalow next door. Each Monday afternoon she would walk to the village via the footpath across the 'backs' passing the other two bungalows and then skirting the Common and coming out in Spring Street, almost opposite Constable Brewer's police house. She posted her mail in the box outside Alice's shop - Clough Top didn't even have a proper post office, the nearest being in Furness Bridge. Her article would appear in the paper each Wednesday and be read avidly by many country-loving admirers, some of whom would write appreciative letters to her, always sent on from the London office. On Friday, a very useful cheque would arrive for her in the morning post.

Bella was born in a suburb of Manchester and educated at the Girls' High School. She became interested in writing – and particularly journalism – and rather than go on to University, for which she was highly qualified, she accepted a job in a city newspaper office, much to the displeasure of her teachers, and particularly her headmistress, who never spoke to her again after the day she left. A few years later, Bella had to admit that her decision had probably been a mistake, for a university background would have meant immediate acceptance and 'open sesame' for her in places and situations where now, so often, she had to struggle and fight for recognition.   On the other hand, she knew that the grounding in the newspaper office, and the years at the 'coal face' of journalism, were the best foundations for her chosen career, and she had the satisfaction of knowing that she was admired and highly respected as a quality writer.

Bella was a tall woman with a comely figure, but rather than display any attractiveness, at least in public, she preferred to wear long, loose fitting frocks, thick stockings and plain shoes or even boots, often essential footwear in any case for traipsing around farms and fields in all weathers as she often had to do. She rarely wore make-up, and she allowed her long, bushy hair to hang loosely around her shoulders.   A girl from a nearby village came over about every ten days to cut or trim her hair as necessary, but apart from regular washing with shampoo, she never had anything resembling a 'perm', or any real styling.

Bella had also come to prefer, 'country village' life to the hustle and bustle of any city and, after three years at the bungalow in Clough Top, she found that she could enjoy the peace and quiet, the clean, pure air, and the ever-changing delights of the seasons, months, weeks and even days of the year, which left her with the uncluttered and undisturbed clarity of mind to produce writing of sufficient standard to earn her a decent living. She had a small car and travelled the area seeking out stories, situations and incidents upon which she could write for appropriate magazines, only rarely receiving rejections and always being paid well. She talked to farmers about produce and livestock and markets. She wrote and reported on other matters, such as domestic 'abuse', local authority activities, minor crimes, a scandal involving members at a local sports club, and theatre, especially amateur dramatics. She had also tried her hand at writing a play.

There was, however, one aspect of her life that set her on a collision course with a good number of the village ladies. She was sceptical of any form of religion!

She certainly had problems with the Christian faith. To her, the concept of sin and then forgiveness by the grace of some indefinable, unseen, omnipotent being, who understands and forgives all human frailty, seemed utter nonsense. She had already had arguments with local clergy, and her views – although never ever mentioned by any 'reverend' in person – had got around, with the result that she was shunned by many of the ladies. It was suggested that she might be practising witchcraft, and when it was observed that she was having regular visits from a young woman, who came by car, suspicions about her morality were rampant. The visitor, of course, was only her hairdresser – the girl operated a 'mobile' business, which Bella found more convenient for her routines.

Romance had not entirely eluded Bella. In her final years at the High School, where there were only girls, opportunities for meeting boys were somewhat restricted, even though most of her contemporaries found ways of getting around the problem, and at least one had been expelled for 'inappropriate sexual behaviour', though no one ever knew what the 'behaviour' had been.

But Bella was more concerned with her work, her studies and her prospects as a writer, to worry about having or not having a boy friend.   Nevertheless, after only a few months in the newspaper office, she found herself becoming on friendly terms with a boy called David, and her first ever 'date' was when she went with him to a cinema in Manchester.   As their attachment grew, they kissed a little, held hands, became close.   Then one day, when she went into the office earlier than usual, David suddenly appeared from a small filing room that adjoined the main newsroom.   Observing that he was flustered, Bella walked across and into the filing room where a young typist was trying hurriedly to fasten her dress.

Months passed before she felt remotely interested in friendship with another man.   She felt horribly betrayed, used and crushed.   Some of her confidence had gone.   Her parents, with whom she still lived, began to worry about her because she was hardly eating, behaving irrationally and having mood swings.   Eventually, she told her mother what had happened: "Oh, my dear, you don't know how lucky you are.   You found him out in time," said her mother.

"I know Mum, but it might have been my fault. Perhaps he wanted me to unfasten my…"

"No!" said her mother very forcibly. "No. You will only do that when YOU are ready, and you are with the right man, the man you want to do it for."

"I thought he loved me, Mum."

"Well he didn't, Bella. He wasn't right for you, I always thought that. I was always suspicious." Actually, her mother had hardly met David, but as Bella knew well, she liked to give the impression of having a great insight into character even after the slightest acquaintance. "Good riddance, that's what I say," she added.

For a while, Bella still moped, blamed herself, felt rejected, lonely, abandoned. Then she began to return to her work and rekindle her enthusiasm. Finally she thought to herself: 'Damn the man. I'm getting on with my life.' She laughed again, began to eat well, and found joy once more in the work she was doing. David did try to apologise, explain, resume the friendship, but Bella was firm: she didn't want any more contact with him, and even when they had to communicate or consult over work matters, she remained cool, distant and aloof.

She went out with other men, enjoyed companions at films and the theatre, and even went with one to several football matches. She also found, one day, a little shop, in a suburban area, that sold second hand and antiquarian books. It was pleasant, easily accessible from her home, and stocked many titles of interest to her, and at very reasonable prices. She enjoyed browsing and began spending more and more of her time there. She made numerous purchases, much to the delight of the shop owner, with whom she had many interesting conversations. He certainly knew his authors – "Dickens, spent a lot of time in Manchester, you know. You've read 'Hard Times', of course. Elizabeth Gaskell, Isabella Banks, local women authors both, but unfortunately dwarfed by the Brontes and George Eliot, nationally at least." And the anecdotes went on: – H.G. Wells and his 'affair' with Rebecca West; Priestley coming to Manchester only recently and giving an inspiring lecture at the University. "Pity you missed it."

Bella listened and was enthralled. He knew so much, even though he was barely thirty.

Oliver Grant was of middle height, quite thin and agile, clean-looking and with a crop of brown hair, cut short and groomed well. He spoke intelligently, was kindly, considerate and charming. As the weeks went by, Bella continued her regular visits to the shop. Then one day Oliver said to her, "I shall be going up to Burnley at the weekend, to a book sale. Seems a good lot from the catalogue. You might find it interesting, Bella," - by now they were on first name terms. "Would you like to come?" Bella was delighted, she would be very interested.

"Oh, Oliver, yes, I'd be thrilled. Thank you very much."

"Sunday. I'll have to take a van, but the spare seat is quite comfortable. I'll pick you up. Nine o'clock?"

"Yes, lovely. I'll be ready." Bella's excitement was obvious.

The trip to Burnley was one of many. Bella went

along and more than paid for the 'outing' with the help she gave, by packing books in boxes and carrying them to the van – even though Oliver stressed that she must not strain herself, She learned so much, and was able to write many saleable articles on her experiences and the things that he told her. By now, they were holding hands, kissing frequently, falling in love. Then he told her one day, "There's a good sale in Cambridge next week – might be two or three days. Good stuff, though, I can't miss it. Coming?"

"Yes, if you want me to," said Bella. "I can book a few days holiday from work."

"We'll go then, girl," Oliver said. Then he added: "Just one thing though. Staying overnight? Would you mind if we shared a room?"

"No."

"It'll be cheaper, you see. Bed and breakfast."

"That's all right, Oliver," Bella said.

At first, Bella's mother was horrified, even though Bella didn't tell her directly what the overnight arrangements were. But she realised that her daughter had long passed her twenty-first birthday, was a grown woman and made her own decisions.   She had no objection to Oliver Grant; she thought he was a fine young man, very suited to Bella, but she just wished, hoped, that the pair would not do anything foolish, but get married first. All she could say was, "It sounds very nice, dear, but don't let him do anything to upset you." The day came.   Bella, with suitcase packed, wearing a smart overcoat with a fur collar, a pretty dress beneath, stockings and shoes, waited patiently.   Oliver arrived, put her case in the van, kissed her as she got into her seat, and then the pair drove away.   Both her parents waved 'goodbye', but there was more than one tear in her mother's eye as she returned with her husband to the lounge of their house.

"Don't worry, my dear," her husband said. "Bella's old enough now.   She knows what she's doing."

"Does she?" queried her mother They're not married, you know.   Just think of the consequences if there was a child, Walter.   The scandal!"

"A child?   But they wouldn't....!"

"You don't think they'll do anything like that on

this trip?"

"Of course they won't. You've just said they're not married. And he's a pretty decent sort of a chap."

"That doesn't make the slightest difference, Walter. Not these days."

But her husband was getting old: too old to care. "Well," he said. "There's nothing we can do about it now. And I'm sure nothing like that will happen at all."

Bella and Oliver arrived at Cambridge late in the day and booked into a hotel close to the city centre. They were given a room on the top floor, at the back, with a window from which they looked over roof tops, and could see two or three towers and spires of the university and the churches. The room was sparse, but clean towels had been provided and there was a wash basin with hot and cold running water, a small wardrobe, cupboard and drawers, and a double bed; the bathroom and the toilet were along the corridor. Bella thought it all seemed quite bohemian, 'This could be Paris', she imagined.

Oliver then gave her a gold ring. "Wear it on your marriage finger at breakfast," he told her. There was a knock on the door and Oliver opened it to a little man in waiter's uniform.

"Excuse me, sir," he said. "If you require dinner, it's almost over. Do you wish to come now?" They realised how late it was, but decided against an expensive evening meal at the hotel, and instead, went out into the town, where they bought fish and chips and then visited a local bar and had beer.

Oliver bought well on the following day. Everything was top quality, he told Bella, and he was delighted. As usual, she helped to pack the books into boxes – always flat and never stood on ends which might cause them to become damaged and buckled with pressure from boxes on top – and then the boxes were loaded into the van. The final morning saw the van so crammed that Bella would need to have a small box on her lap in the passenger seat. By mid-morning of that final day, they were ready and Oliver began the long drive home.

They chatted for a time, especially while they were navigating the route out of Cambridge, but once they were on the open road, travelling well, though at a restricted speed because of the weight in the van, Bella fell silent. At first, Oliver thought she was tired. After all, she had worked very hard and had two late nights and two early mornings. But after a while, he asked, "Everything all right, Bell?"

"Yes, Oliver, I think so," she replied.

"Is that box a nuisance? We can cram it in the back somehow, if you...."

"No, it's fine," said Bella.

"Well, what then?"

"Nothing.

"Nothing? You think so? Come on."

"I'm just wondering. Have we done something wicked? Should we be ashamed?" she asked.

"Oh, don't start thinking like that, love. It's what life is all about."

"But if we'd been married..?"

"Would you have preferred that?"

"We could have waited."

"Why? It makes no difference. And if you're really worried, there's always confession."

"Confession?   In a church, with a priest, you mean?"

"Yes. You might be given some kind of penance, but ..."

"Oliver, you mean that we, I, should tell a priest we've been to .... everything?"

"If that makes you feel better about it, yes, why not?"

"But what we've done is between you and me. Secret, sacred. No-one should know about that."

"I shall go to mass on Sunday. Confession is part of the ritual."

"Yes, general confession.   But nothing very personal, very private."

"That depends."

"On what?"

"We'll see."

"We will not see, Oliver. Private matters are private. Church or no church!"

"Well, if you feel like that about it."

"I do. I'm not having my name spoken...."

"Names are not spoken, never, ever!"

"No. So I'm just a little tart you took away for a couple of nights."

"No, Bell, I'd never think of you like that. Never."

"Well, I feel like that. I feel betrayed."

He pulled the van into a suitable spot at the side of the road, stopped the engine and reached to put an arm around her. "Come on, Bell," he said. "I can see what it is. You're overtired." Yes, she was tired, and over wrought, but she was also upset, and worried. This man with whom she thought she was in love, was beginning to show a side that she had not seen before, and now doubts were creeping into her mind. Obviously he was a Catholic, at least nominally, something of which, previously, she had been completely unaware, and that in itself posed large, probably insurmountable, problems for her. Although she did not want to put too fine a point on it, there and then, she knew she couldn't embrace wholeheartedly the teachings of his church. Her parents were protestant and she supposed she was as well. Her father was a stalwart of their local parish church and held offices on the parochial church council. She had little doubt that the prospect of the marriage of his daughter to a Catholic man could have grave consequences for him. She admired Oliver for his encyclopaedic knowledge of literature and more his than a fleeting interest in many of the arts, but now there was something else, and she did not feel able to cope with it.

Nevertheless, she decided that a long journey home in an overloaded van was not the best time in which to cause unnecessary difficulties. "Yes, Oliver," she said. "Perhaps I am tired. And I'm sorry. Let's get on, there's still a long way to go." Later, when they stopped for a meal at a rather seedy transport café, she brightened up, held his hand, allowed him to caress her, and on returning to the van, kissed him passionately before the journey continued, but she was very glad when, hours later, the van reached her parents' house, and she got out, took her little suitcase, and waved 'goodbye' to him as he drove away.

As the weeks passed, she saw Oliver less and less. She did still visit the shop on a regular basis, and the two friends always met and parted with kisses. To give Oliver his due, he didn't attempt to pressurise Bella, although he was surprised when she refused to go with him to another sale, locally, which would not even involve any overnight stay. Nor would she agree to any further love-making with him. Then Bella became aware that her mother had started to observe her closely and increasingly, looking any signs of a pregnancy. Fortunately, there were none, although Bella, too, wanted to be certain, having heard girls at the office sometimes talk of an 'unexpected' baby. She even went as far as having a test, which proved negative. Finally, she was able to take a courageous decision and broke the relationship completely. She would not visit Oliver's bookshop again.

After some months, Bella began to feel restless and decided that she wanted to move away. She was not frightened of meeting Oliver; in fact, she did meet him casually on several occasions, but she was still living at home, under her parents' protection as well as their scrutiny, a scrutiny that had noticeably increased since the time of her outing with Oliver, even though there had not been any repercussions. "Where are you off to now, Bella?" her father would ask, just out of interest, or a concern for her safety, and although she realised this very well, and always gave him a truthful and polite answer, she often wanted to say 'Dad, mind your own bloody business, please,' although she never ever did so. Finally, Bella did find a small flat to rent, about two miles from her parents, and her move was organised. Her mother seemed to understand completely her daughter's need to make the move, but this time it was her father who was less compliant. "You've got a perfectly good, comfortable home here, with us, my dear. Why on earth you want to leave us just baffles me."

"I want to stand on my own feet, Dad." Bella said. "I'm twenty-six now, you know. It's high time I did. And it's only two miles away. It's not Timbuktu!" The old gentleman didn't argue any further and Bella moved into the flat.

She was very happy at the flat and stayed there for two years. She continued working for the newspaper and a promotion saw her become assistant editor, with a good salary to match. She also did free-lance work, increasing her income further, and so, when she saw the bungalow at Clough Top for sale, she decided that she could buy it, move there, and then consider her job.   In the event, she was able to negotiate her departure from the newspaper's staff, while remaining as a free-lance contributor on very good terms   So, at the age of twenty-eight, she began a new life: living in the country, with complete freedom of action, able to work well and be paid well, a situation so ideal that she often wondered if it was true.

* * * * *

On the day that she wrote the latest 'Country Girl' article and went across to the post box in Spring Street with it, as well as her other mail, she also called into Alice's for a few small provisions.   Alice served her with her usual friendliness.   Betty Marsh was also there with another woman whose name Bella did not know.   Betty Marsh was upset.   "I can't gerit out of me mind," she was saying.   "The poor lad, 'e must've bin terrified.   Scared stiff, I reckon."

"Come on, neir, Betty, luv.   We dunno what 'as 'appened, yet, do we?" said the other woman.   "An' any road, William might 'ave known little abart it.   Don't upset yersel."   Alice looked at Bella and raised her eyebrows.

"William Tudge," she whispered. "The accident."

"Yes, I know," said Bella. "Dreadful. You have my sympathy, Mrs. Marsh." But Betty Marsh didn't want sympathy from the likes of Bella Warrington.

"It's not me yer ought to say that ta, Miss Warrington," she said. "It's 'is mother. She's coomin over from Yorksheer, termorrer. Not that she'll be too bothered, I reckon. She'll prob'ly do what she 'as ta, tak 'is stuff, an' be off back, before she can turn round."

"She'll need some comforting, nevertheless," said Bella "And she'll need to stay at least one night. Is there somewhere…?"

"Oh, aye. There's a room booked for 'er at th' 'Untsman. Police 'ave done that. One night, that's all, mind yer. They're payin' fer it, though. Constable Brewer told me."

"Well, I hope she's comfortable and welcome. It will be a great loss, whatever the circumstances."

"Aye," was all that Betty Marsh said on the matter. "Well, must be off," she added. "Vicar's coomin' up ter see me. 'E'll be 'ere in a minute. 'Bye, Alice. Are yer walkin' my way. Mary?"

"I am, Betty. I'm coomin' now." The two ladies left the shop.

Bella made her purchases. Alice said, "Bit of a mystery, this about William. Don't you think so, Miss Warrington?"

"I don't know much about it, really. But the poor lad drowned. That's a tragedy," said Bella.

"Well, one thing's solved, anyway" Alice said. "Young Karen Dinnet's a little liar. She's never been near him, and she's made out that he's put her in the family way."

"No!" Bella really wanted to laugh at the very suggestion.

"It's all nonsense, of course. The kid's imagination. She's admitted it now. Mind you, I believe her father said that what's happened to William was probably for the best. Because otherwise he would have killed the lad himself."

"But if Karen has been lying?"

"Daughters don't lie so far as their fathers are concerned. And with a man like Mr. Dinnet - if he thought that William had even touched her."

"There's probably more in the whole business than meets the eye, Alice," said Bella. "More to come out yet, I expect."

"Well, the police aren't satisfied, that's for sure. And then there'll probably be an inquest."

"Yes. Anyway, Alice, we'll have to wait and see." And Bella took her purchases, left the shop, and made her way across the 'backs' to her bungalow

oooooOooooo

CHAPTER NINE

Where women were concerned, Mark Manion always considered himself to be a man of action. He wasted no time. On the same Monday that Bella posted her article, he told his colleagues that he needed to inspect progress in the wall rebuilding work at Clough Top, and set off in the morning. His need to inspect the work was legitimate because he was the Technical Officer and he would be required to certify that the rebuilding was as good as, if not better than, the original construction. He arrived at Fell Lane End, and spent some time there. A small gang of workmen were busy reconstructing part of the banking and retrieving as many of the original stones as possible from the water in the brook, which was much less deep now, as the surrounding lands were drying and there had been very little rain since the heavy storms of almost a week ago. He had a few words with the foreman on the job. "How's it going?" he asked.

"Difficult, but we'll cope." the man replied.

"We'll have to, my friend."

"I didn't think we'd 'ave to do this bugger again, as soon as this, though," the man said.

"No," Manion agreed. "I can't believe what they're saying, you know. They say the bloody thing just trickled across the road, there, at hardly any speed, and went straight through. Then they're on about the cement hadn't dried properly, the foundations were faulty. Bull...."

"...Look, Mr. Manion." the man interrupted. "If that wall weren't built properly, it wouldn't be safe. A kid leaning on it would be enough to push it over. And then what? Eh? We know better than to allow that to happen. It was as firm and sound as bloody Nelson's Column, that was. No doubt about it."

"We told them all that at the meeting, last week. Anyway, we'll have to see. But I think there's more to this than someone's letting on," Mark said. And then he added; "So does the Police Chief. He's made that very clear. Anyhow, keep up the good work. We'll have it damn well right this time."

"They'll not drive a tank though it when we've finished, Mr. Manion. You can be sure about that."

"Well, I'll be back in a day or two. If I need to test it, I'll bring a tank with me." Both men laughed, and Mark returned to his car.

He drove up the hill to the village and found the Huntsman, where he was able to buy a sandwich and some beer. Then, having already noticed the little house with the 'police office' incorporated, he made his way there. Constable John Harvey was sitting behind the little desk in Eric Brewer's office when Mark entered. Harvey looked uncomfortable, because he didn't want to be there, out in the sticks, in that dingy, pokey little place. Also, he didn't much like usurping Eric Brewer, whom he regarded as a decent chap, and this was his patch. Still, orders were orders, but he hoped that this case would soon be solved and he could hand back to Eric and return to 'civilisation' once again. Manion introduced himself: "Mark Manion, Technical Officer, County Surveyor's Department."

"I suppose you'll want to be sure they make a good job of the wall, this time," Harvey said.

"It was a bloody good job, last time, mate."

"So you say."

"I do say. It must've been a much bigger strike than they're making out," Manion told him.

"Well, we've just had the preliminary report on the vehicle. Brakes appear to have been in good order and everything else was fine, too"

"How can they say that? It was a mangled wreck."

"They can tell. They'll make allowances for the impact."

"Allowances? Bloody hell!"

"They can work it out. Don't ask me how. Ratios and things. Anyway, the point is that the tractor was in good working order before the crash."

"So they're saying," Mark pointed out.

"Well? They're the experts, Mr. Manion."

"Could they tell if, say, a tyre had burst, or something? There'd be no tyres left after a drop like that. Thirty bloody feet to the river, you know."

"Well I can only tell you what the report says. The tractor wasn't faulty," said Harvey.

"I don't believe that," Mark said. "Anyway, thanks for the information." Then he changed course.

"Oh, by the way, at the meeting, last week, there was a police woman. W.P.C. 'Dawson', was it?"

"Yes. Sara Dawson. She usually helps when there are women or families involved. You know the sort of thing."

"Actually, I think she knows my sister. I could do with a word with her. She won't know that our kid's getting married."

"Well, if you're down here tomorrow, you might bump into her. The lad's mother, you know, the lad that was drowned, she's coming over from Yorkshire. Sara will need to be here. Talk to her for a bit – even ferry her down to the accident site, I expect," Harvey told him.

"Oh, right. Thanks. I'll get down. Need to keep an eye on progress with the re-build."

"Of course," said Harvey. "But I wouldn't bother mentioning your sister. She'll see through that one, right away."

"It's worth a try, though, don't you think?"

"Well, I suppose it's better than 'Do you come here often?' "

* * * * *

On the following morning, a police car stood on the forecourt of the small railway station at Furness Bridge. The train from Manchester was seen to arrive and moments later W.P.C Sara Dawson escorted a thin, wizened looking woman from the station building. She carried a small overnight bag. Both women got into the rear seats of the car and the 'chauffeur' set off for Clough Top. The lady concerned was Fiona Wallace, as she had been known for the last twelve or more years, since Patrick Tudge had gone off with another bit of 'mutton dressed up as lamb' whom he thought he fancied. And just to prove that 'what was good for the goose was also as good for the gander', she had married Charlie Wallace - and regretted every day until he died last year. Patrick Tudge, who had returned to his home in the Irish Republic, taking his 'mutton' with him, had also passed away.

When the car reached Fell Lane End, Sara suggested that the driver stop for a few moments. Men were still there, re-building the wall, with the area cordoned off with tape and cones, and there was one 'official' type man making inspections and writing onto a clip board. The men glanced up as the car stopped. Sara said, "This is where it happened, Mrs. Wallace. The tractor went straight through the wall."

"Oh, aye," was Mrs. Wallace's curt reply.

"We thought perhaps you'd like to come back here, later. To lay some flowers or something."

"Naw. I don't want ta da that. Naw."

"Well, would you like to get out? Have a closer look, now?"

"Naw. I've sin all I want."

"All right, then. If you're sure. Drive on, Bill." And the car went on up the hill and into the village, and pulled up outside the Huntsman Inn.

Mrs. Wallace was greeted and registered – which merely meant that she was required to sign a 'Guest Book' – and shown to a small single bedroom at the front, overlooking the street. Sara waited downstairs, having arranged to have lunch served to the two of them in the equally small and squalid dining room. Conversation at lunch was difficult, with Sara having to initiate any talk at all. She did learn that William was never wanted, and when he turned out to be 'daft', as

Mrs. Wallace put it, neither she, nor his father, wanted anything more to do with him. "Better if tha'd strankled 'im at birth. I've allus sed saw," was her only comment.

"But he was a child, your son, Mrs. Wallace. Surely..." Sara said. She was horrified, incredulous.

"Nay, 'e's bin nowt ter me. Never 'as."

They finished the meal in silence. Sara felt very sad, as well as angry, but she had to subdue her feelings. Afterwards, Mrs. Wallace said she'd like to rest for a while, lie down in her room. Sara said that she quite understood and would call back later, and then take her to see Mrs, Marsh. This was agreed and the ladies parted. Sara wanted to cry, but she also wanted to shout at Mrs. Wallace, 'He was your son, he needed your care – yours more than anyone's – and you refused it. You rejected him because he wasn't 'normal', as they say'. Her own car had been left on the piece of open ground at the back of the inn – not quite a car park, but good enough. She went to the car and sat in the driving seat. She didn't move, but she was fighting back the tears. A few moments passed, and then there was a tap on the car window. A man was standing there, and she recognised him as the 'official' who had been down at Fell Lane End that morning. She wound down the car window and said quite sternly, "Yes? What do you want?"

"Hello," said the man. "I just noticed you there."

"Well?"

"You'll remember me. I was at the meeting in Wilmslow last week."

"Oh yes…"

"Mark Manion, Technical Officer, County Surveyor's Department. I sat across the table, opposite…."

"Yes," said Sara, beginning to regain her composure. "I knew I'd seen you somewhere."

"Well, once seen, never forgotten, as they say. Especially girls – well, nice girls anyway. You know what I mean?" He gave a confident wink. "You seemed quite upset. If you want cheering up, you know, I'm your man."

"No, I'm all right, honestly. Thank you". She turned away, trying not to encourage him.

"I'm sorry. Am I interrupting…?"

"No, no, not really. I was just gathering my thoughts, you know."

"Trying to solve the mystery?" He took a packet of cigarettes from his pocket. "Want one?"

"No thanks, I don't, well, not often."

"You did last week – at the meeting. Remember?"

"Yes. Under duress."

"Had to conform?"

"Something like that. Superintendent Tozer can be quite intimidating."

"Blimey! Anyway, a fag does help. Calms the nerves, you know. Sure?"

"Sure, thank you."

"Ok then." Mark then realised that she was winding the window up again. "Oh, are we any nearer to knowing how that bl -. that tractor got into the river?"

"Not yet, Mr. Manion," said Sara. But no doubt we will. Much more clever heads than mine are working on it, believe me."

"Maybe more clever heads, miss, but never prettier ones."

"I will have to go, now, Mr. Manion. There's lots to do today, yet So will you excuse me, please?"

"Yes. Sure. But please keep me informed of progress. That wall had been constructed well. It would have stood a lot of pressure, you know. Not just a glancing blow from a slow moving vehicle."

"I can't comment, I'm afraid. These technical matters are quite beyond me." Then she closed the car window, started the engine and drove away.

However, she only drove as far, as Eric Brewer's 'police house', barely fifty yards away. She went into the little office where John Harvey was still sitting behind the desk. He could see that she was upset. "Hello," he said. Enjoy your lunch?"

"Not really," Sara replied.

"At the expense of the Constabulary? I would have thought...."

"Damn the Constabulary."

"Oh, dear. What on Earth...?"

"Some stupid people, John. They deserve a spell inside. And I'd gladly turn the key, myself."

"Why? What's the matter? What's it all...?"

"That woman. Mrs.Wallace, the lad's mother. She doesn't want to know. Her own flesh and blood and she doesn't want to know."

"I thought she'd be grieving."

"Grieving? The only grieving in her mind is the fact that she'd had to come over here at all. All the way from Halifax. William wasn't wanted in the first place, just a stupid mistake, she said. And then when he showed signs of being a bit 'different', the father got out fast and she more or less threw William out. An innocent, vulnerable, poorly little boy and she got rid of him. I tell you, John, I feel sick. I really feel sick."

"Try not to get too distressed, Sara, there's a girl."

"It's not right, though, is it, John? He needed her love and her care more than most. And she couldn't care less."

"People can be like that. But I know just how you feel."

"She's not a bit bothered that he might have suffered in the accident and then had an awful drowning in the river. Just think what he might have gone through? Flailing about in that torrent, unable to do anything to save himself?   And I get the impression that she's saying to herself, 'Thank goodness.   He won't cause me any more trouble.   At last I'm free of him.   Free of any responsibility'."

"You don't know she's thinking that."

"But I get that feeling, John.   She's glad to be rid of him, all right."

"Oh well, there you go."

"I mean, that Mrs. Marsh, the woman he was lodging with, she had more concern, even grief, than this one.   Mrs. Marsh was very upset when Eric Brewer and I broke the news to her.   And she said then that the mother wouldn't care.   She was right."

"I thought you were arranging a meeting between them?"

"Yes, later on.   And that encounter should be very interesting.   At the moment, Mrs. Marsh is at a church meeting and 'Madame' is having a lie down.   I'm going back in a while."

"Right.   Oh, there's been a telephone call for you.   Someone in the County Surveyor's Office.   'Alan

Hardisty'? I said you'd phone back. Here's the number."

"I don't know anyone - oh, yes, I do remember now. He was a young man taking the minutes at the meeting in Wilmslow, last week. Probably wants to check something. I'll ring him. Tomorrow, perhaps." Then she left the office and returned to her car.

Later in the afternoon, she went back to the Huntsman and found Mrs. Wallace. As Betty Marsh's cottage was only a few doors along the street, the two of them walked to their meeting. Betty opened her front door. "Ya'd better come in," she said. Once inside, Mrs. Wallace asked: "Where's 'is room, then?"

"I'll show yer." They went up the stairs to the small back room. Mrs. Wallace looked around. She opened the wardrobe and examined the coats inside, feeling in the pockets.

"Nowt in theer," she said.

"There was just this envelope. The police found your address inside, an' there's some other papers, personal ones. That's all he 'ad. That an' th' Bible," Betty told her.

"No money, then?"

"William never 'ad no money. The little 'e earned, 'e spent. An 'e only gave me a pound or two rent. When 'e could."

"More 'n 'e ever giv' me. That's fer sure."

"Is there anything else here that you wish to take away, Mrs. Wallace?" asked Sara. "The Bible, perhaps?"

"Nay, I don't want that. Why would I want that?"

"I don't know. A memory?" Mrs. Wallace grimaced – she wanted to laugh, but she couldn't.

"I've enough memories of 'im fer a lifetime, luv. I don't want n' more." She turned to Betty, "Might as well burn the lot. Ya don't knaw where it might've bin."

"What about the envelope? There's 'is birth certificate."

"Aye. 'Spose I'd better tak' that. Don't know what fer, thaw. Might burn that an' all, meself, before long."

"That will be your prerog...your choice, Mrs. Wallace. Shall we go now? Leave Mrs. Marsh in peace?" They moved to the door and as Mrs. Wallace went out, Sara turned, took Betty's hand and squeezed it. Both had tears in their eyes. "I'll see you," she whispered. Then she walked with Mrs. Wallace back to the inn. The lady went inside, but Sara returned to her car, signed off duty, and went home.

* * * * *

At 9.30 the following morning the same chauffeur-driven police car drew up outside the Huntsman and Mrs. Wallace emerged from the inn, carrying her overnight bag. The driver opened a rear door and Mrs. Wallace handed the bag to him, and again took a seat in the back. Sara was on the other side of her.

"Good morning," she forced herself to say.

The driver said, "Mrs. Wallace. I have to tell you that the Coroner has ordered an inquest into your son's death. Headquarters have been notified this morning. You probably won't have to come, but you are at liberty to do so, if you wish. The details will be sent to you in due course."

"Aye, well I mayn't bother. It's a long way ter coom, fer that."

"And what about the funeral? There's arrangements...."

"Same agen. It's a long way. Eh, it won't cost owt, will it?"

"No. That will be taken care of, I expect."

"It better be. I've no brass ter waste on funerals."

"That's understood, Mrs. Wallace. In the circumstances...."

"Ya'd better get on," Mrs. Wallace said. "I don't want ter miss train."

"There's plenty of time," Sara said, as the car gathered speed on the hill down from the village. Soon they had passed Fell Lane End, and within a few minutes they had arrived at the station at Furness Bridge The driver, with the bag in his hand, opened the door and Mrs. Wallace got out. She took the bag and walked into the station. She would have a wait of about twenty minutes. Sara got out of the back and took the front passenger seat next to the driver. He knew that she was fuming. "Back to base?" he asked.

"As fast as you can, Bill," said Sara. "I hope I never ever set eyes on that woman again."

"She was over-awed, nervous. Didn't know what to do, or say."

"Good morning, please, thank you, I'm grateful for your kindness. That would have been a good start." The car was speeding back to Clough Top now.

"Courtesy doesn't come easy to some folk, Sara," the driver said.

"That word just isn't in her vocabulary, Bill. Neither are tender loving care, kindness, and many other human attributes. You know that she virtually threw that poor lad out because she didn't want the responsibility. She's a monster." Sara was weeping again.

"I shouldn't let it get to you, though. She's not worth it."

"You know, when I took her to his lodgings, yesterday, all she was concerned about was whether he'd left money around. She'd've taken a last few pence if it had been there. And she couldn't even be civil to the lady he'd been lodging with. I tell you, she's a monster, Bill. And that about the funeral!"

"I must admit I didn't believe what I was hearing. Her own son!"

"Good riddance to her, that's all I can say."

It still wasn't ten o'clock, and they were back in Clough Top, outside the 'police office'. "Come on," the driver said. "Time for a brew. Coffee or tea?"

* * * * *

Even Betty Marsh was flabbergasted when Sara called on her later in the morning and told her what had been said. The two ladies fell into each other's arms and cried together. Finally, Betty broke away. She said "Ya knaw, Miss Dawson, we have a little fund at church for situations like this. There's not a lot, but there should be enough. We'll give that lad a funeral fit for anyone. I'll talk t' th' Vicar."

oooooOooooo

CHAPTER TEN

The funeral of William Tudge was held at the Parish Church on the Wednesday of the following week. It was not an elaborate affair, but a good number of folk from the village – at least everyone who was able – came to the short service taken by the Vicar. Edith and Jim Gregson, and Jenny, walked behind the coffin with Betty Marsh. Joe and Martha Hodge were there; so too were Annie Halstead and her husband, Brian, P.C. Eric Brewer, came as a villager, rather than a representative of the Constabulary, with that role being assigned to Sara Dawson, and Alice, who closed her shop for twenty minutes or so, just the duration of the service, after which she hurried back and opened up once again. Bella Warrington sat alone in the back pew. There were two hymns, some prayers, including one for William's family, and the Vicar delivered a short, but kind and well composed eulogy, before William was laid to rest in a grave in the churchyard. Afterwards, sandwiches, tea and coffee were provided free of charge at the Huntsman, for anyone who wanted them, and some folk did, just for the opportunity of seeing inside the pub, which normally they never would. Sara went in, really to accompany Betty Marsh, who needed to be there, and she had to admit that these lunchtime refreshments were rather better than the usual packed lunch that she ate in the car. This was her second free meal at the pub in a week, even though her first lunch in the dubious company of William's mother had drawbacks.

A few days earlier, the Coroner had opened and adjourned an inquest into William's death, before releasing the body for burial. The inquest would resume as soon as the police had finalised enquiries.

At length, the funeral gathering dispersed, Betty Marsh went back to her cottage, only a few doors away, and Sara made her way through the inn, to a door that led to the 'car park' at the rear. She was about to go out, when she heard a man's voice. "Hello again. My favourite police person." It was Mark Manion. Sara turned and smiled.

"Oh, hello," she said. "Were you at the funeral?"

"No. I didn't get up here in time. Been inspecting the wall. You know, the re-building work."

"Not finished it yet, then?" Sara remarked. She thought also that Manion had never intended to be at the funeral anyway.

"Yes, just. That's why I was here. Making sure, you know. Should stand up to many more bangs and bumps, now. A really good job."

"So nasty accidents are unlikely in future?" Sara asked, teasingly.

"That was more than an accident, last time, darling. We're convinced of that. We'd swear by it. In court if necessary."

"You might have to, yet. The Coroner will want to be satisfied."

"He'll have to be. Anyway, how about making an inspection yourself? We can go down now if you like, and I'll show you. Your own personal examination. Come on."

Out of a genuine curiosity, Sara agreed, although she had not the slightest intention that he should take any other motive from her willingness to accompany him. They walked together the two hundred yards down the hill to Fell Lane End. She enjoyed the fresh air and Mark was pleased with himself. He thought he might be making progress. "Do you live here - in Clough Top?" he asked, as they walked.

"No," she replied. "We're over in Rainley. In the next valley. Nearer to Macclesfield, of course. We like it there."

Manion knew well where Rainley was, but that didn't matter. "We?" he ventured to ask.

"My mum and dad and I. In fact I was born there. Went to the village school. And then Macclesfield High."

"And now the police force? Like it?"

"Yes, well part of it is a bit like social services, really, and I enjoy that. I'm studying for my sergeants' exam which covers all areas of police work, and I need to pass that before I can specialise in any particular area. I'm not too happy with that but, if it means promotion, it's ok."

"Good bit of reasoning, that, I should say. So you're not a proper copper?"

"Oh yes I am. Or I will be one day. What about you, then? You live in Chester?" Deliberately, she had chosen to become the inquisitor.

"Near enough. I'm in lodgings," he told her. They reached the bottom of the hill and walked over to the newly repaired wall. Mark explained how much of the original stone had been recovered from the waters – less swollen now, which made the job easier – and how the wall had been reconstructed with strengthening and lots of cement. Now it all looked very sturdy, dry, safe and able to withstand a great deal of pressure. "A bull-dozer would have a struggle with that," he said.

Sara looked around her, and then walked over to the grassy croft where Jim had left the tractor and trailer. She saw the deep tyre grooves in the turf and the slight incline from the parking spot to the edge of the tarmac of the road. She realised that it was almost impossible for anyone to move the tractor and trailer from that spot, with the ground softened by rain, without mechanical aid. But Jim Gregson had the ignition keys. So how…? Manion came to her.

"Come and look at this, darling," he said, and began to walk a short way up Fell Lane. He pointed out that there were gouge marks on the grassy banks here and there, marks on the trunks of two trees on the roadside, and scrapes on the stone walls. All the marks were about the same height from the ground, at indefinite intervals, and could be traced up the hill for some distance. Eventually they seemed to disappear, but they were there, obvious and clear. "We only noticed them yesterday," he said. "What do you think?"

"I think this should be reported to my superiors," said Sara. "How high are they from the ground do you think? A couple of feet?"

"Nineteen inches," Manion told her, "Every one the same. We've measured most of them."

By this time they had reached the end of the path that led across in front of Bella Warrington's and the adjoining bungalows and, via the 'backs', to the centre of Spring Street. Both of them knew the 'short cut', and took it without comment. They passed the three bungalows and were in the open, on the edge of the Common, the distance was only about fifty yards.

Manion placed a hand on Sara's arm. For a moment, she let it stay there and then, very gently but very deliberately, she pulled her arm away. Neither said a word.

Within minutes they were back at the Huntsman. "I'll see if P.C. Harvey's in his office. I'll tell him about those marks."

"Yes, right," said Manion.

"Where's your car?"

"At the back, same as yours. But I'm hoping the pub might still be open. I fancy a drink."

"I don't think you'll be lucky," Sara said, "But you can try."

Manion wanted to ask if he could see her again, but he thought better of it. 'I'll devise a way', he mused. He just said "Right, 'bye, then."

"Goodbye, Mr. Manion," she replied. Then they went their separate ways.

* * * * *

"Yes, I've seen a report about that," said John Harvey, when Sara told him about the marks on the side of Fell Lane. "Seems some silly bugger tried to drive a

194

Council lorry up there, and had to reverse down again.
The lorry was too wide, and the road too narrow. It
happens, you know, Sara."

"But why would he want to do that, John?

"Thought he was taking a short cut, I suppose.
You must agree it's quicker than going all round via
Furness Bridge. "

"Well, Mark Manion, the Technical Officer,
didn't seem to know about the lorry."

"No, well, it's not something you boast about.
The driver would want to keep it as quiet as possible,
especially from the Council officers.   Eric Brewer
reported it here."

"Oh, right.   Apparently no significance? I'll let
Mr. Manion know."

"You'll be seeing him, then?"

"Quite probably. He just seems to turn up."

"Yes."

"I'm not encouraging him, John, if that's what
you mean."

"I don't mean anything, Sara. Except that – well
he's made a few enquiries."

"About me? What have you said?"

"Nothing. Just that you're a good girl with your mind on your job."

"Thanks, John. Actually I think he's a bit of a twit. And I don't like his eyes. They scare me."

"A squint? He can't help that, you know."

"No, but I still don't like them." She shuddered.

"He told me that he thought you knew his sister."

"He never mentioned that to me."

"No. I don't think he's even got a sister."

"Oh, I see. Right. Well don't worry. He might try, but he'll not get anywhere. I'll soon see him off."

Sara spent a few more minutes in the office and freshened up in the small toilet that was there. Then she went back to the car park. There was no sign of Manion, or his car, and the inn was closed for the afternoon. She opened her car and sat in the driver's seat for a while. It was her first opportunity to think. Mark Manion had made her acquaintance and had made a pass at her almost right away. She regarded that as insignificant at the time, and she knew she was considered attractive by some people, men especially. One or two women had told her, just as a compliment, that she was good-looking, although she never tried to be anything other than quite natural and pleasant with people – women or men – and hoped no more than that her appearance and her friendly personality would be accepted only for what they were. After all, kindness and friendliness were necessary attributes in her work. But now this man, for reasons of his own, had continued making advances, inviting her company on the walk down to Fell Lane End, which she undertook purely for her own genuine interest, and then he had held her arm, which surprised her, and was something she certainly did not want. She had, of course, been out with boys and had one or two 'casual' affairs, none of which lasted very long. But Mark wasn't a boy, he was a man. He would want far more than she was willing to give at the moment. She was studying for career exams, trying to succeed in a very demanding occupation, and the last thing she needed was a 'romantic' attachment of the sort that he would have in mind. But even more important was the fact that she did not particularly like him. He was older that she was – by at least five years, she thought – and she was unhappy about his manner; he was 'pushy' and 'showy', probably considered himself 'God's gift to girls'. 'I don't think so', she thought.   She knew she had done the right thing in her firm rejection of his touch.   Whether or not she was wearing her police uniform, he had no right to touch her and she would not let him touch her again.   And as for calling her 'darling'!   'No,' she thought 'I'm going to stop this in its tracks.'

* * * * *

The inquest into the death of William Tudge was resumed in Macclesfield Town Hall during the following week.   The police could not offer any clear explanation of the events leading up to the drowning in the river, but it was obviously connected to the crash at Fell Lane End involving the tractor and trailer.   A theory was advanced whereby some unknown person had attempted to remove the vehicles from the croft on which they were safely parked, and that William, in trying to prevent this, had thwarted their intentions, but found himself sitting on the tractor as it moved, uncontrollably, across the road, crashed through the wall, and dropped into the swirling waters.   Whilst the Coroner would not settle for this, he felt that something on these lines had taken place   Betty Marsh, in spite of her apprehension, was called to testify to William's good character, and she did this as well as she could.   Jim Gregson was asked about the boy's employment, and he was able to say that, although William was only a casual worker, he did everything well, was conscientious, willing, helpful, honest, trustworthy and quite reliable, once he had been set to a task and told exactly what to do.   Eric Brewer testified that William had never been in any trouble with the police.   William's mother did not attend the inquest.

A question also arose regarding the accusation made by Karen Dinnet.   The fact that this was pure fantasy by an immature schoolgirl was not important, but rather, whether, if William had heard of the accusation, it might have caused him to take his own life.   W.P.C. Sara Dawson said that she had made enquiries but was unable to determine precisely how far the accusation had spread, although she was inclined to the view that William did not know what the girl had said and that there was some doubt as to whether, in any case, he would have been aware of the serious implications that would have ensued.

The Coroner decided to put this question aside Obviously, the boy had gone into the water at the same time as the vehicles, and it would have been a very unnecessary and complicated, if not impossible, way to commit suicide – he could much more easily have jumped over the wall from the road.

The final verdict was 'misadventure', but the Coroner said that he remained unhappy on at least two matters. Whilst accepting that the vehicles had been parked regularly on what was known locally as 'the croft' without previous incident, and that such practices were common in rural, farming areas, he was anxious that this should not be regarded as normal, and extra care should be taken in future when any farm vehicles were left unattended in public places. The use of securely locked garages or compounds was preferable at all times. He was also critical of the Highways Authority. This wall had only recently been re-built, and despite the certifications of the technical officers, it might not have settled or dried out sufficiently for it to be completely safe. The heavy rains of preceding days might have softened the mortar even more, and in these circumstances an adequate safety barrier would have been required. This might not have stopped the vehicle, however slowly it was travelling, but it was perhaps fortunate that no-one had leaned on the wall, perhaps to observe the waters in full flow, and thereby dislodged the insecure masonry, and fallen to their deaths as well The proceedings closed.

W.P.C. Sara Dawson descended the wide staircase into the main entrance hall of the building, and as she did so, a hand tapped her arm. She turned to see Mark Manion standing there. "Oh, hello," she said, and smiled, showing her lovely row of white teeth.

"What did you think of that, then?" he asked.

"Fair enough, I suppose. Nothing else was possible in the circumstances."

"I think it was a bloody cheek," Manion said. "That wall was as safe as houses, darling, heavy rain or not. We're not idiots, you know."

"Probably the Coroner was just being pedantic. Covering every aspect. I shouldn't worry about it," Sara said.

"Our boss'll worry about it, though. Take it as a personal criticism. Life in the office won't be worth living for days."

"Oh well, he'll get over it. In any case, you know, it was only a comment. Something to consider for the future."

"We'll certainly do that, my love. You can bet we will. And by the way, what came of finding those marks and scrapes on the side of Fell Lane? You said you'd report it?"

"Yes, I did," Sara said. "And you're not going to like this. It seems that one of your drivers tried to take a wide lorry up there and got stuck. Had to reverse down again."

"Who told you that? First I've heard of it. Mind you, our lot wouldn't want to report that, I suppose. There's some right idiots, I can tell you. But I'll soon find out who the idiot driver was, and then there'll be hell to pay. Anyway, I'm off for a pint. Fancy one? Or something else if you don't like beer?"

"Well no, not really. I've got rather a lot to..."

"Come on," he said, trying to take her arm, "I bet you're dying for something. I'd like to buy you…" But at that moment Sara noticed Alan Hardisty coming down the stairs and crossing towards the exit. She pulled away from Manion.

"Oh, there's Mr. Hardisty. I must catch him. I owe him an apology. Thanks for the invite, but sorry. I must go." She hurried away, through the main doors and caught up with Hardisty just outside. "Mr. Hardisty," she called. He turned and smiled.

"Hello. I saw you giving evidence. You did well," he said.

"Oh, yes. Thanks. Anyway, Mr. Hardisty, I want to apologise. I didn't return your phone call, last week. I'm terribly sorry!"

"No, don't worry about it. It was a tiny question that I really shouldn't have bothered you about. I sorted it out anyway."

"Well I….I'm still sorry."

"No, don't be. But look, I was just hoping to find a little café somewhere, just for a sandwich and a cup of tea. Do you know anywhere?"

"I think I do," Sara said. "There's one just along the main street. I'm going that way. I'll show you." Mark Manion came out of the Town Hall doors, just in time to see Sara Dawson and Alan Hardisty disappearing around the first bend in the road.

* * * * *

After the inquest, life at Clough Top began to return to some normality. Most folk agreed with the Coroner's verdict, although no one really could fathom what had happened. A reporter from the local newspaper came around trying to glean information, and wrote a fair and accurate account of the inquest, as well as another article about the village and the curious events of the recent weeks. Similar stories appeared in other papers but, because Bella Warrington never wrote under her own name, it was impossible to tell if any of the reports were hers. In the late summer, she contributed a short piece to her 'Country Woman" series:

'Periods of dry, warm weather, and weeks when it has been wet and cold, have kept the flora in good shape this year. The green turf on the hillside might have turned brown if we had had long, hot spells – so loved by

the sun bathers – but they have been tempered by the rains and cool winds, when sandals, shorts and colourful tops were replaced by wellies, warm trousers or skirts, and thick macintoshes. Most of our bushes are still in flower, few leaves have descended yet from the trees, and my neighbour cut his small but immaculate lawn every morning last week. They forecast that autumn will be cold and wet, but there's no sign of bad weather yet, and no one here is grumbling.'

But the forecast was quite wrong In the middle of October, there was a glorious, though very short, Indian Summer. For a few days the heat was quite intense. Everyone resorted once again to shorts and open shirts or blouses; some men went around stripped to the waist, and some younger women were happy in bikinis On one of the days, Bella Warrington left her bungalow and walked across the 'backs' to Spring Street. She wore a long loose-fitting dress without sleeves and sandals without stockings. She walked quite slowly; the heat was uncomfortable and she was perspiring. She went into Alice's shop, made two or three purchases, and then said "Oh, Alice, love, my father has been taken seriously ill in

Manchester, so I'm going there for a while. Just to be with my mum."

"I'm sorry to hear that, Miss Warrington," said Alice. "But I'm sure your mother will need you at a time like this. How serious is it, do you think?

"He's quite old, Alice. It could be the end." There were tears in Bella's eyes.

"Eh, it might not be, love. These old 'uns have a habit of rallying sometimes, you know. If he's getting the right care."

"Oh, yes. He's in a private clinic. But…"

"I know how you must feel though. It must be very worrying."

"It is, Alice. Anyway, I want to cancel my newspapers for a while, please. No more after tomorrow."

"Of course, Miss Warrington. I'll see to that."

"Oh, let me settle up with you to date then."

"Certainly." Alice found her ledger, and reckoned up what Bella owed.

Bella paid her, but as she did so, she seemed to slump forward onto the counter. Alice was alarmed.

"Oh, Miss Warrington, love. What's the matter? Are you all right?" Bella tried to stand, but couldn't. At one side of the shop there always stood a small chair. Alice rushed around the counter and took Bella's arm. "Come on, love," she said. "Sit here for a bit. Can I get you some water?"

"Yes, thank you, Alice. I'm so dry. It must be the heat." Alice went into a back room of the shop and returned a moment later with a glass of water.

"There," she said. "Have a good drink. This heat is enough to knock anyone sideways." But as she sat down, Bella had let her dress tighten around her, and Alice noticed the large bump in the region of her stomach. She knew exactly the cause of the incident. Bella sat for a few minutes, sipping the water and regaining her composure. Another customer came in and Alice served the person in her usual business-like manner. Then Bella rose, said that she was feeling much better and needed the fresh air that the walk home would give her. "Well, you be careful, Miss Warrington. Take it easy, now won't you."

"Yes, I will, Alice. Thank you. I hope to see you around Christmas."

"Very good, Miss Warrington. See you then." Bella walked from the shop and Alice watched her until she turned off Spring Street and into the footpath that went across the 'backs.' 'Well,' Alice thought. 'the hot weather isn't entirely responsible for that incident.'

ooooOooooo

CHAPTER ELEVEN

In those days, compared to later times, Christmas was never celebrated well at Clough Top. It is true that most of the inhabitants decorated some of the interior rooms of their cottages and houses, some put up trees and enjoyed decorating them as well, and one or two of the doorways displayed small wreaths of holly, Some neighbours and friends exchanged cards and presents, and on the day itself the Huntsman extended opening hours and the bar was continually full of folk, some making too much of an excuse to get drunk! The children were catered for, with a party on Christmas Eve in the Church Hall, when Father Christmas arrived to distribute small gifts: Arthur Benson, Gregson's fellow farmer, usually obliged and played the part. But as soon as darkness fell, the village was silent, dark, huddled against the cold wind that blew now from the higher fells beyond Moorside Farm. Nevertheless, those who liked Christmas enjoyed it, and those who didn't, took it all in good humour and simply sighed with relief when it was all over. New Year was little different, except that on the stroke of midnight on the day, two or three houses received callers -'First footers' as they would be termed in Scotland - and there were shouts of greeting and signs of merriment that lasted a while. By half past midnight, all was quiet, the Huntsman had closed its doors, lights in the windows were going out and the darkness and silence returned.

It was the third week in January before Bella Warrington returned to her bungalow. Alice, diplomatic as ever, had casually informed the one or two people who might have either wondered or enquired that Miss Warrington had gone to be with her mother in Manchester for a while, because her father was seriously ill. Alice had also scanned the 'Deaths' columns of the newspapers, although she never found any announcement relating to a 'Mr. Warrington'. She noted that 'Country Girl' continued to appear once a week in the same national daily, except for a fortnight at Christmas and New Year, times when perhaps she never appeared in any year. At least two of the articles, however, featured nature in urban parks, a definite contrast to the usual 'country' themes.

On one day that week, right out of the blue, Bella came into the shop. She looked well, had lost weight – as well as the obvious bump – and she wore a neat trouser suit that made her look good. Alice was quite stunned at the contrast with her previous visit, that day in the Indian Summer.

"My, hello, Miss Warrington. How are you?"

"I'm well, Alice," Bella told her. "Quite a change from – last year."

"Indeed it is, love. You look marvellous."

"I've been away longer than I expected, but it's been necessary."

"Your father? How is he?"

"Not too bad at the moment, Alice. He's rallied a bit in the last week or so, and it's made things easier for Mother. Which is why I've been able to come back for a while. I need to get some work done. And I'm having a telephone put in tomorrow. Then she can phone me, and I can return straight away. It's only an hour to Manchester in the car, you know."

"That's better then, love," said Alice. "Now, do you want to resume your newspapers?"

"Oh, yes please, Alice. Do I owe you anything?"

"No. If you remember, you paid up-to-date the last time you were in."

"Oh, that hot, fateful day. I remember now. It seems ages ago."

"That short hot spell. We've had it a lot colder since."

"Yes, we have. And Christmas as well. What was that like here?"

"Nothing unusual. Same as always. But I think everyone enjoyed themselves."

"That's good," said Bella. "Now, Alice, I don't think this is going to surprise you too much. I'm a mother. I've had a baby!"

"No, love, it doesn't surprise me. When you were in, last time, I knew it wasn't just the heat. And I saw...I knew you were expecting."

"I thought you would realise."

"But don't worry, Miss Warrington. I don't go in for tittle-tattle.. No-one knows anything."

"I expect they soon will, though. Then the gossiping will begin."

"And the child? When and what?"

"A little girl, ten days before Christmas. I've called her 'Jane'."

"That's lovely, my dear. Congratulations. Where is she now?"

"On the back seat of my car, just outside. Come and have a look."

"Oh, I will. Thank you." Alice came from behind the shop counter, just as she had done on that previous occasion. Bella walked towards the door, and then turned to her.

"By the way. It's all true about my father. He is terminally ill, but has surprised us all that he's putting up a fight. I planned to have the baby in Manchester, and the illness just coincided. Nothing was fabricated."

"I would never have suspected anything of the sort, love, honestly. And anyway, at least your father has been able to see his grandchild. It's his first, I assume? I mean, you've no brothers or sisters?"

"It is his first, Alice. I'm an only child." They went out to the car. There was a chill wind blowing, but the baby was lying in a 'carrycot', swathed in blankets and wearing a knitted bonnet. She looked very cosy and warm. Alice peeped in and made girgly sounds with her mouth.

"Hello," she said. "Hello, little Jane. Have you missed your mummy? Well, she's here now. There." Alice looked back at Bella. "She's beautiful, Miss Warrington. She really is."

"Thank you, Alice." Bella said, as she got into the driver's seat. "I'm sure you'll see more of her in the future."

"I'm sure I shall. And don't worry, Miss Warrington, I shall say nothing until the right time comes."

"I know, Alice. Thank you." Then Bella drove the car away, down the hill to Fell Lane End and up the steep hill to her bungalow.

* * * * *

No sooner had Bella's telephone been installed than she had an urgent call from her mother. Her father had been rushed back to hospital and her mother needed her. It was already eight o'clock in the evening, but Bella packed her suitcase immediately, gathered together all the things necessary for the baby, loaded everything into the car, closed and locked the bungalow, and headed off for Manchester   Patches of dense fog hindered her progress and it was nearly eleven by the time she reached her parents' house in the city, but the baby slept through it all.

Bella found her mother in a state. The condition of her father had worsened, but on top of it all, she realised that her daughter had travelled with her baby, in difficult conditions at night – risking life and limb, all because she had summoned her. Should she not have waited until the morning?   Conditions might have improved, making the journey easier and safer.

"Don't worry about that now, Mother. We're here, safely. That's all that matters." Bella tried to re assure her, although not very successfully.

"But I just didn't think, Bella. Oh, oh dear!"

There was nothing Bella, or anybody else at the hospital, could do for Bella's father. It was just a matter of time. But now Bella had arrived, the baby was put safely into a cot, permanently kept in the room that Bella herself would use, and the two women sat down by the lounge fire, each with a hot drink. It was midnight.

They sat up well into the night, discussing the situation, Bella trying to comfort her mother, who was, even then, beginning to grieve. At almost one-o'clock, the baby was heard crying and Bella, who was breast-feeding, knew what was required. She went to attend to it and, on her return, found her mother fast asleep in her chair. She covered her with a rug, dimmed the lights, and soon she herself fell asleep.

It was still dark when, early in the morning, they were wakened by the telephone. Bella answered it and was advised by the hospital to come as quickly as possible. They made drinks, had whatever food they could easily manage – bread, biscuits, cake – while they were hurriedly preparing themselves and Bella fed the baby. Then they set off in Bella's car, still in the half light, negotiating early morning work traffic and travelling the three miles to the hospital. They were shown straight into the private room which was occupied by Bella's father. He was unconscious. His wife took his hand. Bella touched his arm. She then turned to a nurse, who beckoned her away. Still with the baby in her arms, she followed the nurse. "We've done all we can now, my dear," the nurse said. "I'm afraid it's just a matter of time." Bella wept. "Also, can we help with the child? It's preferable that it's kept outside the ward."

"Yes. I should have known that. I'm sorry," said Bella.

"That's all right," said the nurse. "Don't worry about that. I'll try to arrange something better for you. You can't be expected to stay out here with the child for very long."

"I don't mind, really," said Bella. But the nurse hurried away. And Bella walked up and down the short corridor, rocking little Jane in her arms. Later, someone brought a small easy chair for Bella, and she sat down outside the door of the ward. Everything was silent. There was no movement for twenty or more minutes. Then the baby woke, girgled and began to cry. She needed more feed, and Bella, unbuttoning the blouse into which she had changed earlier, obliged once more. This private intimacy with her darling little one was the most precious and marvellous experience she had ever known.

But then she heard the ringing of a bell, and a doctor, followed by two nurses who came along the corridor swiftly and went into the ward. Bella knew then that the end had come.

Moments later, her mother came out, crying uncontrollably. "It's over, Bella," she said. "Your father is dead." A nurse was on hand, and she took the baby aside, while mother and daughter fell into each other's arms and cried. Finally, they were taken into a little separate room and given tea. Bella's mother received a sedative. Once they were sufficiently composed, mother, daughter and the baby left the hospital. Bella drove them back to her mother's home.

Two days later, back at Clough Top, Alice was able to read the short notice in the national daily: "WALTER WARRINGTON. BELOVED HUSBAND OF MILDRED, FATHER OF BELLA, AND GRANDPA OF JANE, PASSED AWAY IN MANCHESTER ON WEDNESDAY, AGED 81. ENQUIRIES...." 'No.' she thought, 'This proves it wasn't a lie, Miss Warrington.'

The days following her father's death were very busy ones for Bella. Her mother went to pieces completely and her own doctor gave her medication and recommended that she stay in bed. Bella contacted undertakers, who were very kind, understanding and helpful, but she still had to receive friends who called, deal with the local rector, who would be taking the service at the parish church, contact two relatives, who lived in the South of England and thought it was impossible to get to Manchester in time for the funeral, and inform other appropriate people of the arrangements. Her father had many connections: his former office, his club, the local charities that he supported, not only with generous cash donations, but often with time and expertise as well. He even had contacts with the City Council, and at least two of the councillors, if not the Mayor himself, hoped to be present at the funeral. And on top of it all, Bella still needed to look after the baby.

By the time of the funeral, Bella was completely exhausted, but she continued manfully, reading a short lesson in the funeral service, and afterwards returning with her mother to the house, where refreshments were served to all who wished to come.

For just two hours in that day, a kind neighbour, who couldn't get to the church, volunteered to take the baby, and Bella gratefully left her for that short time.

When it was all over, Bella's mother's condition did not improve; in fact her grief worsened. Her doctor prescribed more medication and more bed rest and Bella was obliged to stay with her much longer than she had anticipated. Every conversation that her mother had, no matter what its original purpose, always got around to her husband, what a good, wonderful man he was, and how she felt she could not continue living without him. The only other feature of any conversation was Bella's baby. Bella's mother told everyone, over and over again, that a year ago, Bella had married quietly at the church in the village where she was now living, but her husband was very involved with his own affairs and thus unable to accompany her on her frequent journeys, although few people were fooled when Bella's supposed husband did not turn up for the funeral of his father-in-law. Bella suspected, in fact she knew, that the shock of the truth, that she was not married, and the baby was illegitimate, was another factor in her mother's illness. Nevertheless, after some days there was an improvement; Bella's mother managed to get out of bed, go downstairs and eat a small, but nourishing meal. Afterwards, Bella took the opportunity she had been waiting for. "Look, Mother," she said, "I'm going to have to go home very soon. I need to do some of my own work. Why not come with us? The change will do you good."

"Oh no, dear. I don't think I could manage..."

"Of course you could manage it. It's only an hour in the car."

"But there's no room for me at Clough Top."

"There is, Mother. You can have my room, and I've got a camp bed that will go easily into the office. I can use that, and Jane's cot will fit in there as well.

"Well, I don't know. I really need to be close to Doctor Blakeney."

"My doctor will see you, if that's necessary. I've told you, it's a lady and she's very nice." The discussion continued in this manner for some time, but eventually Bella's mother ran out of reasons to oppose the plan, and reluctantly she accepted her daughter's proposal. So, on the following day, the three left

Manchester, all arrangements having been made for leaving the house in the care of a neighbour, and with the doctor and other necessary people fully informed. In an hour, they had arrived safely at the bungalow in Clough Top.

With her mother in residence, and able to keep an eye on baby Jane for at least some parts of the day, Bella was able to resume work with gusto and was soon making headway. Also, she was able to pop across to Spring Street. On the second day, she went into Alice's shop.

"Why, hello, Miss Warrington, love. Back at last then?"

"Yes, back to my work, Alice. It's been sadly neglected and I need to earn some money."

"And where's the little one?"

"She's at home. My mother's come to stay with us for a while. She's badly in need of a change." Bella told her.

"Oh yes. I saw the announcement in the paper – your father I mean. I'm sorry, love."

"Well, that's how it is, Alice. But mother's taken it very badly. She's still quite poorly. I'm just hoping that being here for a while will help."

"Grief can be a terrible thing," said Alice. "But let's hope – perhaps looking after the baby will help as well. Take her mind off – you know."

"You could be right, Alice. She's not really come to terms with my– with the birth yet, either – but I'm sure she will. It might be a blessing in disguise."

"'Course it will, love. Now, what can I get for you?"

* * * * *

Just a few days later there was the first warm day of the year. Bella's mother had much improved; she didn't mention her husband's death, but played with the baby, read a newspaper, and even peeped into the office to see what Bella was writing. So Bella decided that the time had come to 'run the gauntlet'. She would take them both into Spring Street, even go into Alice's shop, and announce to the inhabitants of Clough Top that she was a mother. She knew full well what the result would be, but hoped for at least some understanding, some acceptance; for she was not the first, nor would she be the last, 'fallen' woman in the world.

They went across the 'backs', into Spring Street, and into Alice's shop. Bella introduced her mother, and soon Alice was talking 'baby talk' to little Jane. "She's beautiful," she said. "Both of you must be very proud." After making a few purchases – even Bella's mother needed certain things – they finally left and walked off, chatting naturally to each other, down the hill towards Fell Lane End.

Within five minutes, Annie Halstead, flustered and almost bursting with curiosity rushed into the shop. "Alice," she almost shouted. "I've just seen that woman from the Fell Lane bungalow, you know, Miss Warrington,"

"Oh yes," said Alice.

"Well, my eyes must be deceiving me. But I'm sure she was pushing a pram. Another, more elderly lady was with her."

"That would be her mother, Annie. She's come to stay with Miss Warrington for a while. Miss Warrington's father died about three weeks ago."

"Yes, but, but," she was having trouble with the words, "but…the baby?"

"Miss Warrington's," said Alice. "A little girl. I've just seen her. She's beautiful."

"Hers! You mean she's got herself …. had a child?"

"That would seem to be so," said Alice

"But, but she's still Miss Warrington? She's not married?"

"I don't know anything about that, Annie."

"But you knew she'd had a baby? Really, Alice, how could you not tell m... somebody?"

"It's not my business to tell anybody," said Alice, "I don't think it's anybody's business, really."

"I suppose she confided in you from the beginning and you enjoyed keeping it secret."

"There's no secret. You've seen it for yourself, Annie."

"Now, yes, but only accidentally. This might have gone on for months, and we didn't know. Anyway, who's the father? That's what we must find out, right away."

"You must ask Miss Warrington herself. I don't know."

"But someone must know. I suppose it's some 'highfaluting' young man she's been having a secret affair with. Isn't that disgusting?" By this time, Annie was becoming incandescent with rage. "Mind you, I've always thought she was devious, you know. Up to something.. And now this just proves it." But her anger was more to do with not being aware of Bella's situation, rather than any moral judgments – they would come later.

At that moment, Betty Marsh entered the shop. Annie accosted her right away. "My dear Betty," she said. "You'll never believe what I've just witnessed."

"Tell me, then," requested Betty.

"That woman, you know, lives in the first bungalow up Fell Lane."

"Bella Warrington, yer mean?"

"Yes. MISS Bella Warrington, Betty."

"Aye?"

"She's had a child."

"She 'asn't!" exclaimed Betty. "Ow d'yer knaw that, Annie?"

"I've just seen her. Pushing the pram, as large as life   Quite brazen about it, too".

"Might not be 'er's thaw. 'Ow d'yer knaw it's 'ers?"

"It's hers all right. It seems that Alice has known about it for a while. Not told anyone, though."

"Well," said Betty. "That's a shock, I must say. Did no one knaw she were pregnant? Did yer knaw that an' all, Alice?"

"Only a few days ago, for sure," Alice lied, "She showed the child to me, a lovely little girl. You'll adore her."

"Adore her? A bastard? cried Annie.

"Oh, come on, Annie, we don't know that do we? We don't know the circumstances.

"She's not married! A bastard. They're enough circumstances, Alice."

"Yer think she might've bin attacked or summat, Alice?" asked Betty.

"All I'm saying is that it could be something like that.   We just don't know, do we?   And the most charitable thing is to wait until we do."

"No, I'm not having that," said Annie. "She's been seeing somebody behind our backs. And this is the result. It's immoral and it's disgraceful."

"I wonder if th' Vicar knows about it," asked Betty Marsh.

"I bet he doesn't," said Annie. "The likes of her wouldn't confide in him. Anyway, he'll be up here in the morning. I'll be doing the flowers. I'll let him know, then. Mind you, she never comes to church. That could have a lot to do with it." Both the ladies made small purchases, paid Alice and left the shop.

* * * * *.

A darts match had been arranged at the Huntsman on the following evening, Among the members of the opposing teams were Steve Dinnet, Eric Brewer, Bob Benson - one of the sons of Jim Gregson's fellow farmer - Ken Laws, one of the joiners, a man named Bert, who had come up from Furness Bridge, and Jim Gregson himself. The air in the small bar was thick with the smoke of cigarettes; pint glasses of beer were being consumed in considerable numbers; there was much loud chatter and raucous music played over a loud speaker was trying to compete. A considerable number of women sat or stood around, some watching the match and cheering or shouting encouragement to one side or the other   In one small corner sat Annie Halstead, Mavis Dinnet, Steve's 'missus', and several other women, but neither Betty Marsh nor Edith Gregson was among them.

"I've allus thawt she were a bit stuck up, yer knaw. Aye, I allus thawt that," said Mavis Dinnet.

"Aye well, this'll mebbe bring 'er down a beet. 'Avin a babbie an' no proper father," another woman said.

"Theer all alike when eet comes ta that sort a thing thaw," said Mavis. "Coppulatin'.   It's just that some can afford ta bring um up proper, but others 'ave ta struggle. I bet likes of 'er won't struggle much."

"It'll depend on who it is, though," said Annie.

"We don't knaw that, thaw, d'we?   I mean eet could be anyone.   Someone 'ere now, fer all we knaw," said Mavis.   They all looked around, Mavis giggled. "Well, I knaw oo eet won't be. It won't be my Steve."

"Yer don't knaw that, thaw, d'yer, Mave. You can't be certin."

"Nay. 'E knaws better 'n that. 'E knaws if 'e did owt like that, I'd murder 'im wi' me own 'ands. An' I would too."

There was a break in the darts match. The players and others went to refill their glasses, some headed for the toilets. Eric Brewer came to lean on a ledge near to where the ladies were sitting.

"We're just talkin' about yon woman up Fell Lane. You knaw she's 'ad a baby, Eric?" asked Mavis.

"Aye. Quite a surprise."

"She's not married, you know," said Annie.

"No, I didn't think she were," said Brewer. "But it's not a criminal offence these days. Two hundred years ago she'd 've been publicly whipped. Mind you, the feller probably would've got off, scot-free."

"Well, 'oo is the bloke, then? Ya knaw, the father?" asked another woman.

"I think it's a man she's been seeing outside the village," said Annie.

"Could be," said Brewer. "But that's not what I've 'eard."

"What's that, then Eric? What've yer 'eard?"

"Well. Think back. How old's the kid, now?"

"About three months. Born just before Christmas, so I'm told," said Annie.

"Yes, well then, go back nine months before. Well, just about a year ago. What was going on here then?"

"Well, that was the time of the acc....Oh no! No, it couldn't be him," said Annie.

"William!" exclaimed Mavis Dinnet, laughing.

"The 'Leprechaun'. That's what I used to call him," said Brewer.

"But 'e wouldn't know much abart that sort o' thing. 'E might 've bin a bit daft, but 'e allus kept clear of girls. 'E were scared of 'em," said Mavis.

"Girls, yes. But a grown woman who perhaps encouraged him? It's possible, you know."

"And when he thought he'd done wrong, he drowned himself," Annie considered.

"There were summat goin' round last year about 'im getting' a girl; int' trouble. It never came t'nowt, but 'no smoke wi'out fire' eh?" said the other woman.

"Wan't it your girl as said 'e'd done summat, Mavis? I seem ta remember…"

"Nay, that were nowt," said Mavis Dinnet, quickly.

"Aye, but she might've 'eard summat, an' tried ta be clever. These young 'uns can be like that, ya knaw."

"Anyway," Brewer butted in. "I'm only telling you what I've heard. Probably a bit doubtful, but possible."

"Quite possible," said Annie. "Well, who'd've thought that? William eh, and 'er? Well well."

The darts match continued, more beer was consumed and the bar became noisier and noisier. But the ladies found it difficult to refrain from talking about what had been going on in secret, and in their village.

ooooooOoooooo

CHAPTER TWELVE

It was three days later. Bella and her mother had just finished lunch, her mother had gone into the sitting room and was attempting a crossword - usually she was very good with crosswords - and Bella, with baby Jane in a 'carrycot', had settled in the little office. There was a knock on the front door and Bella went to open it. She rather expected the visitor, the Vicar of Furness Bridge – Clough Top was still part of the Parish.

The Reverend Christopher Nuttall had been Vicar for four years, and was not expected to remain there for more than another two or three. He was a tall, thin man, aged about forty, and wore a black pin-striped suit and his dog collar. Today, he also wore a thin raincoat and a trilby hat. As Bella appeared at the door, he raised his hat and bowed slightly. "Miss Warrington?" he enquired.

"Good afternoon. Yes, I'm Bella Warrington."

"Christopher Nuttall, Vicar of Furness Bridge."

"Yes, I know," said Bella, holding out her hand, which he shook.

"Good afternoon," he said.   I trust I'm not imposing upon you, but I'd like to discuss something with you, please"

"Why, of course," answered Bella. "Do come in."

"Thank you." He entered and removed his hat.

"My mother is staying with me at the moment and she's in the sitting room. But I'm sure she won't mind if we..."

"No, no, please don't let me disrupt anything. I've heard that your father died recently and so it will be very upsetting...."

"Mother won't mind. She'll probably be ready to lie down in her room."   They went into the sitting room. "Mother, here's the Reverend Nuttall come to see us. He's our Vicar."   Mother became somewhat flustered now. She put her pen down, shuffled the crossword paper from her knee and looked up.

"Oh," she said. "Good afternoon, Mr. Nuttall."

"Good afternoon, Mrs. Warrington. No, don't get up." He offered his hand. She shook it.

"I've heard about your recent bereavement, madam. I'm very sorry. Very sorry indeed. Please accept my condolences."

"Thank you," Bella's mother said meekly, and tears came into her eyes. "Yes, my husband was... such a good man. So thoughtful... and kind. I shall miss him... very much." This she said between sobs.

"Yes, I'm sure you will. But you mustn't distress yourself." He looked at Bella. "Perhaps I should...." But mother carried on without any hesitation:

"He had connections in the church, our local church, Saint Bartholomew's, in Manchester, I mean. He was on the Parochial Church Council for many years, and served as sidesman, and warden at various times. Such a good man."

"Then you have reason to be very proud," said the Vicar. "And now I am sure that you will take comfort in the knowledge that your loved one is at peace and in the place reserved for him by our Lord in Heaven," he added.

"Yes, of course, Mr. Nuttall," said Bella's mother, still sobbing. "He was such a good, devout man. I'm sure that..." But here Bella cut the conversation short.

"Mother, I think Mr. Nuttall wishes to discuss something with me. I wonder if you'd mind...? Your lie-down, perhaps?"

"No, dear, "she said, recovering some of her composure, "I shall go into the garden. I can lie down later."

"That's a lovely idea It's such a beautiful day. You might take Jane with you."

"Yes, dear. If that's what you wish. She'll be all right with me."

"Just take the carrycot as it is. Can you manage? Or shall I...?

"I'll manage perfectly, dear." She turned to the Vicar. "Jane is our...my daughter's....em."

"Thank you, Mother." Then she added as her mother went out, "The air in the garden will do you both the world of good." Bella then turned to the Vicar.

"Do please sit down, Mr. Nuttall. Can I get you some tea?"

"Oh no, thank you, Miss Warrington. I've already made four calls on parishioners today, and at each there was tea. Any more, and I shall suffer severe bladder problems." He sat down and so did Bella.   There was a silence for a few moments and then he coughed nervously and began: "Miss Warrington, I don't wish to intrude on your privacy, but it's come to my notice, and here it is even more obvious, that you have recently given birth. That is correct, isn't it?"

"That is quite correct, Mr. Nuttall. I have a baby daughter.   She's eleven weeks old, now.   You might wish to see her later."

"That would be lovely, thank you.   But for the moment I would like to ask you about baptism or christening?   Have you made any arrangements for that? At Saint Bartholomew's, in Manchester, perhaps?"

"No, I haven't," said Bella.   "And it is not my intention to do so."

"I   see.   This   is   rather   perplexing,   Miss Warrington.   I would have thought that....?"

"My view is that a ceremony such as that would encumber the child with allegiances at a much too early stage in life.   If in say, ten or more years, she decided herself to embrace a faith, any faith, I would be delighted, and I would stand by her, support her, encourage her in every way I could.   But it would have to be her own free choice, a choice that she can make with knowledge and understanding.   Such a commitment...."

"Forgive me, Miss Warrington, but christening is formal naming, it need not be a commitment."

"But by implication..."

"There is no implication."

"Oh, I think there is, Vicar.   And for many parents there is no problem.   But as I understand the matter, at a christening pledges are given to bring the child up in the Christian faith."

"It is the only true faith, Miss Warrington. Obviously, your own father was very certain of that."

"Yes.   And I know you are certain of that too. I have no wish to dispute it.   But if I had my daughter christened, I would want to abide by the promises that I would have to make, and I cannot do that."

"At least I'm grateful for your honesty, Miss Warrington."

"And I'm truly grateful for your concerns, Vicar. I know they are well meaning and sincere.   I am just as sincere.   Jane will not be christened."

"Very well," he said.   "If that is your wish. Although I might return to the subject again later on.   But now there is just another matter that I must raise."

"Yes, please do."

He shifted himself nervously in the chair. Then he asked, "Who is the child's father?"

"I expected you to enquire about that," said Bella. "But I do not choose to tell you."

"On the birth certificate?"

"There's no name.   The circumstances are such that…...."

"You see, I wonder whether he has exerted any influence in this matter?   On your reluctance to have the child christened?"

"Oh no," she said

"But you've discussed the matter with him?"

"I've discussed it with nobody.   The decision is entirely mine."

"Miss Warrington, rumour is going around the village here…."

"Rumour and gossip! Tittle-tattle. Really Vicar!"

"A certain person has been suggested as the father, and it might be in your best interests to at least clarify, one way or the other. And I sincerely hope that you can categorically state that the particular person is not involved."

"I will not do that, whoever it is," stated Bella quite forcibly. "No-one has any right to question me on such a personal and intimate subject as this is. I will say nothing more."

"I think you might wish to, when you know the person's identity. You will remember the tragic accident that occurred here just twelve months ago. The young man

"William Tudge? Yes, I remember it well."

"Then you can confirm that he isn't the father?"

"No, Vicar, I can't do that. I'm sorry."

"Does that mean that it could be, but you don't know?"

"Really, Vicar. That implication is scandalous."

"Well, there's no alternative conclusion."

"It means that I am not prepared to confirm or deny anything. If I say it isn't one person, you might or might not believe me, and if you do believe me, your suspicions will fall on someone else. That isn't very fair. The matter is private, and it will remain so."

"Miss Warrington. A few days before the accident, the terrible event, the young man attended one of my Bible classes, one of a series. Afterwards, on this particular day, he stayed behind and indicated to me as well as he was able to, that he was worried about something. I pressed him on the matter, and he said that it was connected with a lady. He was very confused. His knowledge of, might I say, the biological facts of life were very limited. I tried to counsel him as well as I could. Now it is a constant worry to me that my efforts were inadequate, and in vain."

"I don't think you need worry too much about that, Vicar. After all, young men will be young men, you know."

"But he was so immature, inadequate. Can you not just put my mind at rest on this one point?"

"No, I'm afraid I can't. Whatever I say might not be believed. And so I shall say nothing."

"Miss Warrington, please!"

"I'm sorry, no!"

"That is very unfair."

"I am sure that there are quite a few ladies in Clough Top, some church members, some not, who will wish to speculate as to the father of my child. But I expect it will all die down in a few weeks. Whether or not that turns out to be so, I intend to keep silent on the matter. The gossip can have full sway."

"It is not gossip, Miss Warrington. It is sincere concern, especially in this one case, where the person involved cannot defend himself. Will you not clarify that one case?"

"No I will not, Vicar. I'm sorry." Realizing that Bella was adamant, the clergyman tried another approach.

"Miss Warrington. From what your mother said just now, it seems clear that your father was a regular churchgoer, and a Christian. I am to understand that you did not whole heartedly share his faith? His commitment?"

"That is probably correct, Vicar, although I loved and admired my father very much. I understood his faith and his commitment, and I admired that, too."

"Then I am sure that he would wish you to help us. Surely, as a tribute to his memory?"   Here, Bella detected a kind of blackmail.

"I think we should leave my father out of the matter," she said.

"Did he know of the child?" the Vicar asked.

"Yes.   In the few days before he died, I took her to his bedside."

"And he approved?"

"He was overjoyed to have a grandchild. If he had lived, I think he would have worshipped her."

"Even in the circum...." He was afraid of going too far.

"By that time, he was very poorly. He never referred to my circumstances."

"And your mother?"

"Mother thinks that there is a man somewhere who, even now, will make an honest woman of me. I regret that she will be disappointed."

"That's very sad," the Vicar said.

"But now, Vicar, you said you'd like to see my little one. Come on, let's go into the garden."

"I'd be delighted," he said, and they went out to the rear of the bungalow. Bella's mother was asleep in a deckchair, placed on a small area of grass that they always called the 'lawn', although the name suggested something much more grand and was hardly accurate

The carrycot in which the baby was lying stood on a small wooden box beside the older lady. Two blue eyes looked out from under a blanket as Jane was gazing silently and contentedly at the sky above Bella folded some of the blanket back, so that more of the child became visible. Hoping not to wake her mother, she whispered gently, "There, now here's a gentleman to see you." The Vicar looked into the cot and smiled. Bella's mother awakened.

"Oh, oh dear," she said. "Is everything all right?"

"Yes, Mother, everything's fine. Reverend Nuttall has just come out to look at baby Jane."

"A lovely child, Mrs. Warrington," said the Vicar.

"She's beautiful, isn't she, Mr. Nuttall? Now you must tell me, has the date been fixed?"

"The date, Mother?"

"For the christening."

"No, Mother, there isn't going to be a christening."

"Of course there is, dear. Really, sir! Just because of the circumstances of the birth, you have no reason, or no right, to refuse to christen her. This is quite outrageous. Was this your decision?"

"No, Mrs. Warrington."

"Then whose was it? The Parochial Church Council or the Bishop himself?"

"It was neither, madam. It was your daughter's own decision."

"Bella's?" She looked with incredulity at her daughter.

"That's right, Mother. I don't want Jane to be christened."

"But of course she must be christened. I wish it, and if your father was still alive, I'm certain that he would have insisted upon it." She began to weep. "He would be horrified to think that his own granddaughter was not to receive that sacrament. What are you thinking about, Bella?"

"I'm thinking about my daughter, Mother. I want her to have freedom of choice."

"You cannot let this happen, reverend sir. Really you can't."

"I think, ladies, that this is a matter for reflection," said the Vicar. "You might wish to discuss it between you. But please be aware, Miss Warrington, that your decision need not be final. The Church will always be ready, and willing, to give your child a christening at any time in the future. Now, I must leave you, as I have other calls to make and I've a service of Evensong to conduct at Furness Bridge before dinner. So, if you'll excuse me...?"

"Of course, Vicar. I'll see you to the door," said Bella

As they moved back towards the bungalow, the Vicar called, "Goodbye, Mrs. Warrrington. I'm sure I shall see you again." Bella saw him away from the front porch, and stood for a few moments, contemplating the situation. She prepared herself for an explosion from her mother. Then she returned to the garden.

But the explosion did not come. Instead Bella's mother sat silently, while Bella picked up the carrycot and said, "Come on, little one, it's time for your feed, and I expect you'll want a change as well," and she carried the cot into the house and into the office. She began to attend to the baby, removing a nappy, cleaning, and substituting a fresh one. Soon she heard footsteps outside; the bedroom door opened and then closed again with quite a bang. She unfastened her blouse, and supplied the needs of her infant. "There," she said, "Is that better? Is that what you want? Is it? Granny isn't very pleased though, is she? Well, never mind. She'll soon get over it. Yes, she will." She completed her task, put the baby back into the carrycot and settled her down to sleep. Then she resumed her work.

Sometime later, she went out to the kitchen and began to prepare the evening meal, and then she knocked on the bedroom door. "Mother. Mother, are you all right?" There was no reply. "Mother, come on. What's the matter?"

"I'm ill," a faint little voice said.

"Can I come in, then?"

"If you like." Bella went into the bedroom. Her mother was lying motionless on the bed. "I want to go home tomorrow," she said.

"Right, fine," said Bella. "The car is ready." There was silence for a few moments, before her mother said, "I don't understand you, Bella."

"You don't understand why I won't have Jane christened?"

"Your father would be horrified. It would be his greatest wish."

"I want Jane to make her own choices. I think Daddy would have agreed with that."

"I know he always gave in to you. He didn't always agree, you know, but he always gave in. Just like the occasion when you went away with that bookseller man. He was horrified by that."

"He never said so."

"I presume you slept with the man." This was, of course, something about which she had always wanted confirmation, but had never dared to ask. Now she took the chance. "What if you had become pregnant then? Think of the disgrace, Bella. I know your father was worried sick. And as headstrong as you always are, you wouldn't marry the man after all, in the end."

"I hardly think Daddy would have approved of that. Oliver is a Catholic. I didn't know until later. He told me on the way home from Cambridge"

"A bit late, wasn't it?"

"Not really. Oliver didn't know my feelings about that sort of thing."

"Bella, you should never have.....! Anyway, we're getting away from the main point."

"You were getting away from it, Mother. Now let me make it quite clear. I do not want to have my daughter christened. That is a choice for her to make when she is old enough to do so. I will not make it for her."

"Oh. So when your father and I had you christened, we did wrong. You've resented it ever since you were old enough to understand. Is that it?"

"I never said that," replied Bella. "You did what you thought was the right thing at the time. It was your choice for me, and I've never held it against you, and I never will. But now I'm in that situation, I want my daughter to have the freedom of choice."

"But you are her parent and her guardian. You must make whatever choices for her, if they are for her own good and in her best interests, and this clearly is. Bella, please!"

"No, Mother."

"And her father? I don't know who he is – you won't even tell me that. Has he had a say in the matter? Has he influenced this ridiculous decision?"

"I've told you, Mother. All responsibility has been ceded to me. No one else influences anything. I make all decisions alone."

"That is wrong, anyway. Someone's getting away without facing any responsibilities," But Bella could see that this continued argument was taking a toll on the older lady. She tried to calm the situation, and said that the meal would soon be ready. "I don't want a meal. I don't feel like eating anything."

"Don't be silly. Of course you must eat. But don't hurry. Take your time. I'll call you when it's on the table." Then Bella went back to the kitchen.

Yet in spite of being called three times, her mother did not come out for her meal. Bella ate alone, and then put some of the food and a cup of hot coffee on a tray and took it into the bedroom. Her mother was still lying motionless on the bed. "I've brought you your meal, Mother. You can eat it when you're ready. But at least try to drink the coffee before it goes cold." Then without further argument she left the room and returned to clear her table, wash the dishes and tend to the baby. Finally, when all seemed quiet and the baby was asleep, she settled down to resume her work. Sometime later she heard the bedroom door open, but her mother only went into the bathroom and then returned to the bedroom again.

At last, Bella went to lock the doors of the bungalow, before settling down for the night. She found her mother's tray with the plate, a dish and cup, all empty, on the floor outside the bedroom door. She picked it up and chuckled to herself. Mother ill? She wasn't falling for that one.

Baby Jane disturbed the calm of that night, and three times Bella had to get out of bed to deal with her. On one occasion, she only wanted a comforting touch, a little caress, before sleeping again, but on the two later occasions a feed was necessary, and Bella was ready with her breast, and on the last time, a change and a dry nappy was required. As a result, breakfast the next morning was later than usual. When it was made, Bella took the tray into her mother once again. The old lady woke from her sleep and looked at the bedside clock. "Oh," she exclaimed. "We are late this morning."

"I've been up with Jane in the night. I've overslept a bit."

"Is Jane all right?" At least, Mother was alarmed about her grandchild.

"Of course. She just wanted a little attention. Here's your breakfast."

"I'm still not hungry."

"You ate everything last night."

"It made me sick. I had to go to the bathroom…"

"You weren't sick, Mother. Don't try that with me."

"So, you don't believe me now. I feel very ill."

"Well, stay in bed. No going home, and I'll call the doctor."

"That's right, be sarcastic."

"I'm not being sarcastic! But if you say you're ill, then you need a doctor. I've told you that my doctor is a lady. She's very nice and very good."

"I don't need your doctor."

"Then what...?"

"I just need you to see sense."

"Oh, don't go back to that. I've made my decision and I'm going to stick to it. Jane will not be christened. Accept it, Mother. It isn't the end of the world!"

"It is, for me. She is my granddaughter, you know."

"Well, I'm sorry, Mother, but that's my final word. Now, do you want me to take you home, today? You've no need to go, and I'd rather you didn't. But it's your choice. Just say."

But her mother decided to stay. In fact, she stayed another week. Finally, she said that there were things at home that required her attention, and so they set off in the car, with the baby safely on the back seat. By then, Bella noticed, her mother had improved. In fact, she seemed in better health than ever. She did try, once again, to change Bella's mind about the christening but, realising that the effort was useless, gave up completely. She hugged the child, and kissed Bella before they left and returned to the bungalow at Clough Top – just the two of them.

ooooooOooooo

CHAPTER THIRTEEN

Bella's intuition, that the birth of her baby would be little more than a 'nine-day wonder' in Clough Top, proved to be correct. By the time she returned to the bungalow, the village had settled back to its routine once again and life continued as it had always done. A brand new, shining tractor with an equally new trailer was often seen parked on the 'croft' – Jim Gregson had good insurance – and the new wall above the riverbank was strong, and people leaned over it to peer into the waters below, without the slightest fear of any disastrous consequences. One or two of the ladies, notably Annie Halstead, still speculated as to the father of Bella's child, and Betty Marsh adamantly maintained that it could not possibly be William Tudge. Others were not so sure.

But the months passed by. Bella was often seen pushing the little pram up or down the hill from her bungalow to Fell Lane End, and from there to Spring Street, or across the 'backs' by the direct route to or from Spring Street. She was a regular customer at Alice's shop, and usually Alice had time to come from the counter and look at little Jane. "My, she's growing already, for sure she is. Cutting a tooth? Yes, I can see it.... Bit painful now, but it will pass.....You'll be taking her to the dentist before you know it, Miss Warrington."

After a year or so, the little girl could be seen trotting along beside Bella, holding her hand or breaking loose to run into a little pool of water, or to pick a wayside flower, scruff her feet in piles of fallen leaves in autumn, or slip and slide in the ice and snow in winter.

Jane, herself, began to have memories. She remembered going in the car with her mummy, to see some doctors at the little house in Furness Bridge, actually the nearest health clinic, and she had to pull up her top and let them listen to her tummy with a funny tube thing. Then a man looked into her mouth and touched her teeth.

She also remembered going with her mummy to a funeral at the church in Spring Street. They just waited outside and saw some people in black or dark clothes come out of the church and the men were carrying a large wooden box called a 'coffin'. Everyone was sad, and poor Mr. Gregson came out with his daughter, Jenny, and they were crying very much. Then they all got into some very big cars and went away. Edith Gregson had died of cancer, very suddenly. Later, they walked across part of the Common, and onto the lane that went to Moorside Farm. At the farm, Mr. Gregson seemed very unhappy, but he was pleased to see them, and while her mummy stayed in the house and talked to Mr. Gregson for a few minutes, Jenny took her down to see the pigs, and some rabbits in a cage. There were two cats in the yard as well, and Ricky, the dog, tied to a little post. Brack had died two years previously. Before they left, Mr. Gregson smiled at them and thanked them for coming. Jane thought that was funny, because she liked going there and seeing the animals and Jenny was very friendly to her, so they should say 'thank you' to him. When they returned to the bungalow, Jane said how much she had liked that, how kind Jenny was, and that she hoped that Mummy would take her there again, another day.

School was the next thing. She started at the Church Infants', off Spring Street, and she liked it very much. There was so much to learn. But one day she went home and her mummy was very angry. It was all because she asked the question, "Mummy, what is a bastard?" Bella told her never ever to say that word again. It was a naughty word, and only naughty people said it. But Bella was really heartbroken, and as soon as the child had gone into the garden to play for a while, she wept bitterly. She also determined to discuss the matter with the head teacher, which she did on the very next day.

Mrs. Formain, the head teacher, tried to apologise for the occurrence, but pointed out that children use words they don't understand, without any malice or prejudice, and that it was just unfortunate that Jane heard it and picked it up. She realised the difficulties that had been created for Bella, but hoped that she would let it pass. Secretly, however, the thought was in her mind that the situation was entirely of Bella's own making, and she ought to be prepared for whatever brick-bats might come her way, and not be so sensitive.

On another occasion, Jane asked Bella why, unlike other children, she hadn't got a daddy? Bella told her that her daddy had gone away for a long, long time, but he loved her just the same. This seemed to satisfy the child for that moment, but Bella knew that it puzzled Jane, and just hoped that the question would not arise again until Jane was old enough to understand more effectively.

Not long afterwards, Jane remembered, there was something else at the church. It was a wedding, and everyone was very happy this time, and dressed in lovely clothes, pretty frocks and very big hats with feathers or flowers. She saw the bride, Karen Dinnet, come out of the church with her husband, and everyone threw pettly things over them, and laughed and shouted funny things. Then they all drove away in big cars covered with ribbons and flowers and bows. Karen married a boy from Clough Top, and although some suspected that it was none too soon, she didn't in fact have her first child until almost two years later.

Then there was another funeral, but this time it was a long way from the village, at a big church in Manchester. Granny had died, and mummy was very upset – well so was Jane really, but she didn't like being sad and so she tried to keep happy instead. Mummy read something out of a big book – the Bible – in the church, and there were lots of hymns and prayers and things. And then they went to a big hotel and had a party, with nice things to eat and drink – in fact that was the best part – and they stayed for a night in Granny's old house, before coming home on the next day.

When Jane was about eight, Bella arranged another farm visit, but this time to Mr. Benson's, at the other end of the village from Mr. Gregson's. Mr. Benson kept ponies, and Bella thought that Jane would enjoy a little ride. Jane was very nervous at first, but Hilary, another very nice lady who looked after the horses and ponies for Mr. Benson, showed her one called 'Mat', and very carefully sat the child on his back and held her tight as the animal took a few gentle steps. Jane began to relax and enjoy the ride then and thought that she would learn to ride a pony, like some of the other girls in the village, when she was a bit older. Hilary said that she could come again and have some lessons.

It was almost two years later when Jane had the biggest thrill of all. Jenny Gregson was getting married, and she asked Jane if she would like to be a bridesmaid. There was an older girl called Wendy Mason who was going to be one as well. Jane could hardly sleep for what seemed like lots of nights while the excitement grew. In fact, Bella knew that she was having a good eight hours sleep every night, and the periods of excitement were of no more than ten minutes between her getting into her bed and falling fast asleep.

The day came when her mummy took Jane to Macclesfield, and they went to a shop where she was measured and fitted for the dress that she would wear. They were shown the material, a lovely yellow satin to match the one for Wendy and fit in with the one that Jenny would wear. A few days later they had to go to the Parish Church for a rehearsal, and to find out exactly what they each had to do on the big day. Jane, intelligent as ever, thought that this was rather funny, doing everything as if it was real then; the only difference being that they would be wearing the wedding clothes instead of the jeans and tops they had on that night. She met Thomas, the boy that Jenny was going to marry, and thought he was very handsome and lovely to talk to. He even came to her and talked to her, calling her 'Jane', as if he had known her for a long time. She also thought that the Vicar was very nice, but of course it was Reverend Crossley, Reverend Nuttall, having left six years ago now, was a

Rural Dean somewhere in Wales. They had to return to the shop in Macclesfield for a final fitting and when she saw her dress for the first time, she thought it was the loveliest thing she had ever seen, and could hardly believe that she would wear it and that it would be hers to keep forever.

It is true to say that Jane did not sleep very much on the night before the wedding. She was so excited and thought only of putting on the dress and wearing it for all to see – some of her school friends would be very envious and next week she could tell them all about the whole thing. Actually, she was asleep when her mummy came into her bedroom – the room that used to be Bella's office – and said that it was time to get up. The 'office' had now been dispersed between Bella's bedroom and the sitting room. Jane had a bath, and some breakfast, before dressing, and Bella helped her with getting the dress exactly right. Then Mrs. Walpole, the lady now living in the bungalow next to theirs, came in to see her and said how lovely she looked. At half past ten, a car arrived on Fell Lane and Bella watched her as she walked out to it, got in, and, as it went away down the hill, she waved almost as a royal princess would, though not quite as regally, for Jane was just an ordinary little girl, very thrilled and happy and still ready to share that happiness with the whole world.

They went to Moorside Farm, where she met Wendy Mason, who looked 'almost' as lovely as she did. Soon, Jenny came down from her room wearing a really gorgeous white dress, with its long flared skirt, the bodice allowing a generous view of her beautiful neck and the shapeliness of her bust. She wore a lovely hat as well, with a veil, and carried a colourful bouquet of spring flowers. When she came into the room she went to greet both Wendy and Jane immediately, kissing both of them on the cheek, but then declaring how stupid she was, because both girls would need to remove traces of lipstick, and Jenny would have to re-apply the colouring to her own lips in order to look perfect.

Both Jane and Wendy were taken to the church in the large motor car and they had to wait until Jenny and Mr. Gregson arrived. Then they walked behind Jenny and Mr Gregson down the aisle of the church. Everyone in the church pews turned and looked at them as they passed by, eager to see Jenny's appearance, but also Wendy's and her own. People smiled and nodded their heads as they went along, but soon they reached the place where the Vicar was standing, facing everyone. Thomas was there with another young man, whom Jane did not know, but she knew he was the best man. As they walked along, Jane could see her mummy standing at the end of a row, looking very smart in a dress which she had just bought, a light coat, and a very pretty hat. She also looked very proud.

The Vicar conducted the service. They sang a hymn, had a reading from the Bible and said prayers. The Vicar asked both Jenny and Thomas some questions and they said 'I do' and other things at the right time. Thomas put a ring on Jenny's finger, and they kissed each other. They went into a side 'vestry', where they signed registers and certificates, before coming back into the church. The organ was playing full blast as they walked back down to the church door, Jenny and Thomas together and Wendy and Jane behind. The best man and other people came along as well. It was a dry but cloudy day, and they stood at the church entrance for what seemed like ages while lots of photographs were taken.

The wedding reception was held at the Huntsman and although Jenny and Thomas were taken there in the wedding car, everyone else had to walk the distance of only a hundred yards from the church. The best man, whose name was Phillip, came to Wendy and Jane and invited them to walk with him, each girl linking one of his arms. This was the first time in her life that Jane had ever been so close to a boy, but she liked the experience very much.

Long tables were placed in the large upstairs room at the inn, with one across the ends of the others. Jenny and Thomas sat in the centre of this 'top' table, and Jane and Wendy and Phillip sat next to them. Mr. Gregson and Thomas's mother and father also sat there with one or two other people whom Jane did not know. A nice lady called Sara sat next to Mr. Gregson. Waiters and waitresses served them with lots of lovely food, although Jane could not eat everything, and even thought she was going to be sick. She had orange juice to drink, except when there were speeches and she was given a little glass of champagne, which she didn't really like and only sipped.

Throughout the meal, Jane could see her mummy sitting near the end of one of the tables, keeping a watchful eye on her, but still looking very pleased, happy and proud.

At the end of the meal, Phillip stood up and made a funny speech. Then he proposed a toast 'to the bridesmaids'. Everyone stood up and drank and then clapped, and she felt very important. Both she and Wendy were given gifts – hers was a lovely bottle of perfume – and many people told them how pretty they both looked.

The meal and the speeches were followed by dancing – after the tables and chairs had been cleared and a record player installed for the music. Immediately, Phillip asked Wendy to dance with him, and she did so. Jane, on the other hand, could not dance, but her mummy came to her, took her onto the floor and showed her what to do. At this stage it was just sort of 'Rock 'n Roll' and all Jane had to do was to move her body to the rhythm of the music and copy her mummy, but later there was a

Barn Dance and the Veleta, which she had difficulty with at first, but she soon picked up some basic steps and enjoyed the fun.

One or two other nice people came to talk to her. One was Mr. Eric Brewer, whom she soon discovered had once been a policeman in the village. Now he had become a Chief Inspector of a force near Birmingham and lived on the south side of that city. However, he did not want to miss the marriage, because Jim Gregson and he had always been very good friends and he was very fond of 'young Jenny'.

The lady called 'Sara' also came to talk to her. She said that she had been a police lady, once upon a time, and often had to look after people in Clough Top. She remembered the time of the 'accident', when a young man was drowned, and how she was able to assist Mr. Gregson. Jenny was still a schoolgirl at that time, and both she and her mother were very frightened until it became clear that Mr. Gregson was safe. She also cared for Mrs. Marsh, who looked after William, the boy who died. Mrs. Marsh was now being cared for in a home in Macclesfield. Sara said that she, too, was so pleased to be at the wedding, and to accompany Mr. Gregson, who, she thought, still missed his wife, very much.

In the middle of the evening, Jenny and her new husband disappeared for a while. When they re-appeared, they had changed from their wedding clothes and were now wearing clothes for a journey. No-one knew where they were going for the honeymoon, although Jane heard someone say "Well, they won't get far tonight, the last train from Furness Bridge will be off in twenty minutes." But a taxi arrived outside the inn door, luggage was loaded, and with shouts of 'Goodbye', remarks, some appropriate and some not, hugs and kisses to everyone, the couple finally got into the car, and were whisked down the hill towards Furness Bridge.

Bella then decided that it was high time she took her daughter home to bed. She was looking very tired and becoming irritable, But as they began to say their thanks and farewells, the best man, Phillip, came across. He took Jane's hand, thanked her for being "Such a lovely bridesmaid" and kissed her on the cheek. She smiled, blushed, and, as he moved away, tried to kiss him back, but she missed and he did not notice. Bella did notice, but she just said, "Come on, darling, time for bed; you look very tired."   Other farewells were said as they crossed to the door, but soon Bella's car was speeding down to Fell Lane End and then up to the bungalow.

Jane was very unhappy now, because she had to take off her lovely dress. She had enjoyed wearing it so much. She began to cry, but Bella helped her, and told her that she would be able to wear it again, quite often. Soon she was in her pyjamas, her face washed and her teeth cleaned and lying in her warm, comfortable little bed. For a few minutes she thought about the day, the wedding, the lovely time at the Huntsman, and the very interesting people she had met, including those who really wanted to meet her.   She thought about Jenny and Thomas, married now, and wondered what that would be like, and she thought about putting her arm into Phillip's arm, even though Wendy was doing the same on the other arm, and then the kiss he gave her, and how she had been too slow to properly kiss him back. Then she fell asleep, and did not wake again for eight hours. It was the next morning.

ooooooOooooo

CHAPTER FOURTEEN

After Sara Dawson had left Macclesfield Town Hall following the inquest on William Tudge, she had walked with Alan Hardisty to a little café in Mill Street, a main thoroughfare leading from the market place. Years later, by means of bypasses and diversions, the narrow street would be given over to pedestrians only, but at the time, it saw a flow of traffic in both directions, with jams and hold-ups of vehicles a regular occurrence. The couple went into the café; Alan ordered a hot snack of some kind, with a pot of tea, and invited Sara to join him. "I really shouldn't," she said, but the food looked good and she was hungry. "I'll perhaps have a sandwich, and a cup of tea. Thank you." Alan was delighted, he ordered for her, and they sat together at a little table.

When they had settled and began eating, they both chose the same moment to begin a conversation. "This seems a pleasant town," was Alan's opening, as Sara said,

"This isn't one of my regular….oh, sorry," she chuckled.

"No, it's all right. It saves me finding an alternative to the cliché, 'Do you come here often?' "

"I don't actually," Sara said. I bring sandwiches for lunch with a flask of coffee or a bottle of water. I have them in the car. It saves time."

"Well, this is better than a car park. It's warmer, you see, and more comfortable I should imagine."

"Often I'm out in the countryside and there are some nice views. I have my favourite spots. And the car is quite warm – cosy in fact."

"And a bit of peace and quiet, eh?"

"For a short time. I don't get long, though."

"Where do you go? Whereabouts, normally?"

"Oh, the forest or the reservoir. There's a small unofficial lay-by on the Old Road. I try to get there if I can. Not always possible, though. Mind you, sometimes I finish up quite near home, so I can pop in and chat to my mum and eat at the same time. That's better in the winter, anyway. A warm fire and all that."

At that moment, Alan, who was facing the window, saw Mark Manion pass along the pavement. Although he looked in the café and surely noticed them, he walked on quickly. At that moment, Alan felt a glow of satisfaction, even though he would have preferred not to have been seen, and he was not really in the business of scoring points off his colleague. When Sara had finished her sandwich and tea, she glanced at her watch. "Well, it's high time I was on my way," she said. "I've a busy schedule."

"Oh, must you?" Alan asked, hoping he could delay her.

"Yes, I really must. And I insist on paying for my food." She placed a few coins, equal to the cost she had calculated, on the table.

"Honestly, there's no need...."

"Yes there is. Now, I'll let you finish your lunch in peace." She held out her hand. "Goodbye, Mr. Hardisty. You must excuse me."

Alan took her hand and wanted to kiss it. But he thought better of it, and politely shook it. He stood up as she moved away, then resumed his meal, delighted at the encounter, at what she had told him and certain that, somehow, he would see her again.

In the days that followed, Sara worked enthusiastically, engrossed in her duties. She visited Betty Marsh a couple of times, comforting her in the same manner as if Betty had been a mother grieving at the loss of her only son. Sara also went to Moorside Farm, where she ensured that everything was well with the Gregsons and enjoyed chatting with Edith, who, Sara had noticed, was becoming increasingly unwell. On one occasion, she passed the Huntsman, just as Mark Manion came round from the back, having left his car on the land there. "Hello," he said, "I'm going for a pie and a pint. Care to join me?"

"Oh, no thanks," Sara said. "I've got my lunch in the car."

"Bit cold for that, today, isn't it? There'll be a warm fire in the bar. Hot food as well. Come on."

"No," she said. "I need to get on. I haven't time. I'm sorry, Mr. Manion." He reached out towards her arm, but she pulled away. "Mr. Manion, please. I haven't got time, today."

"But you must have time for lunch. You're allowed that, you know."

"I've told you, it's in the car. It's what I prefer."

"You prefer not to have lunch with me? That's it, isn't it?"

"Of course not. Don't be so silly."

"Well what, then? You had lunch with poor little Hardisty, the other day."

"I never...Oh, after the inquest, in Macclesfield. Mr. Hardisty was just looking for somewhere to eat. I knew that café and took him there. That's all."

"Well, you still had lunch."

"A sandwich. I just felt like having one. Anyhow, he had no reason to tell you."

"He didn't, love. But I passed the window and I saw you. Now come on , have a bite with me. It's only fair."

"Don't you understand, Mr. Manion? I'm busy. I can't afford to waste my time in any pub at the moment. Thank you for the offer, but I'm afraid I must decline."

"Well can I see you again? When you're less busy?"

"I really don't know. I can't promise anything at the moment."

"Please. I must see…"

"That's silly, Mr. Manion, really. You mustn't pester me like this."

"But don't you realize how attractive you are? You're a smashing girl!"

"How can you say such a thing? You hardly know me."

"I've seen you enough. The eye of the beholder, you know."

"Look, I really must go, Mr. Manion. I've a lot of work to get though today. Now, excuse me, please."

She began to move away, and he thought again that he would hold her arm. But caution restrained him. Then he said: "Ok, then. But I will see you again, and I know it will be soon. Goodbye, just for now." After they parted, Manion went into the Huntsman and Sara hurried to her car after saying "Goodbye".

The audacity of the man began to alarm her. She knew she didn't even like him; he was loud, brassy, pushy. If she wanted a companion, a boy friend, which at that time she didn't, he would be the last person she would think of. The very thought of being with him appalled her. But she didn't want to be rude to him – that wasn't in her nature, even though, in her job, she often had to be firm. And as for finding her attractive, she was sure that she was neither the first nor the last woman that he would say that to. She would have to be firm and, if necessary, use the authority that her uniform gave her. She was determined to be rid of him, and rid of him she would be.

But it wasn't as easy as that. Two days passed, and after she finished work on the second day, Sara drove to her home in Rainley, parked her car as usual and began to walk the few yards to the gate of her parents' house. Then she heard a footstep behind her and Manion's voice "Hello," he said. She turned to see him standing there. "You told me you lived in the village. I've been hoping to catch you."

"You've been hanging around?"

"Not exactly. There's a job on the main road I've had to keep an eye on. Otherwise these navvies get away with murder."

"But they'll have finished and gone home hours ago!"

Manion looked at his watch. "No, about half an hour, that's all. They're working late to get the job done. Overtime, of course. Not that they deserve it. Lazy buggers."

"That's not my kind of language, Mr. Manion. If you don't mind..."

"Oh come off it, darling. I'll bet you've heard worse than that in your business. Cops aren't saints, you know. I've heard the way they talk – even the criminals aren't in the same league. Anyway, look, I really wanted to apologize for the other day. I shouldn't have delayed you."

"You were delaying me, Mr. Manion, and I don't want you to do it again."

"But if I need to talk to you..."

"There's no need for you to talk to me. I'd rather you didn't."

"That's not very polite, not very nice."

"It's the truth, though. I have to speak my mind."

"I only wanted to apologize."

"There was no need. It doesn't matter."

"Why don't you want me to talk to you?"

"What's the point?"

"I want us to be friends. Why can't we be friends?"

"I hardly think we're on the same wavelength, Mr. Manion. I have a career to pursue, studies to contend with, and a demanding job to do."

"I'm not asking you to..."

"You're asking me to go out with you. Of course you are. I'm sorry, sir" - she used the word deliberately -. "I'm not interested, and I'm never likely to be."

"Sir!" he laughed. "What on Earth?"   At that moment, a man appeared at the front door of Sara's house. He was a middle-aged, well-dressed senior executive, and he looked strong, fit and healthy.

"Sara, are you all right, my dear?"

"Yes, Dad, I'm fine. I'm just on my way."

"Well, we're just going to start dinner. Don't be too long."

"I must go," Sara said to Manion. "Now please leave me alone. I don't wish to have a friendship with you.   Just go away and don't waste any more of my precious time."   She moved away. "Coming, Dad," she called, went into the house, and closed the door behind her.

Days passed, during which Sara continued her work, her studies, and enjoyed free time when she went out for walks, met up with friends and did the other things in her normal routine. On the following Saturday she was on duty, and she did various tasks: some paperwork in the office and some visits, including to one family where the father was due to appear in court on a very serious charge on the following Monday morning. By lunch time, she was able to drive out onto the Old Road that climbed steadily out of the town and into the open fell country. She went to the area of verge she knew. It was sufficiently stable to have become an unofficial lay-by, and there she parked up and reached into the back seat of her car for her lunch box and coffee flask. It was very quiet and so peaceful, with the silence disturbed only by birdsong, the bleating of sheep on a nearby hillside and the very occasional motor vehicle that passed by. She finished her lunch and then leaned back for just a few minutes of rest. She closed her eyes and had soon dozed off

She was wakened by someone knocking on the car window. At first she didn't recognize the young man who stood there. He was wearing an open-necked check shirt, a light jacket, old flannel trousers and a cap. He also carried a small rucksack. Being aroused from her sleep so abruptly, she was annoyed, irritable and in somewhat of a daze. But she subdued those feelings, because someone needed her assistance and that was her duty. After a moment, she wound her car window down. "Hello," she said. "What can I do for you, sir?" The man removed his cap.

"Miss Dawson," he said. "You remember me, Alan, Alan Hardisty?"

"Oh hello, Mr. Hardisty. I'm so sorry. I think I must've been dozing and I didn't recognize you."

"That's all right," he said. "I saw the car and thought it might be you." Of course, Sara realised right away that she had told him, that day in the café, how she often parked up on the Old Road to have her lunch. She could not help wondering whether he had come looking for her, or at least had chosen to come that way on the off chance that he would encounter her. But she put aside these thoughts for the time being.

"It's a nice day for walking," she observed. "Where are you heading for?"

"Macclesfield. I've come over from Furness Bridge via Clough Top and along the ridge. There's a train back from Macclesfield about four."

"Well, you're in good time. You should get to the station in half an hour from here."

"Yes, there's no need for me to hurry." As he stood there, he removed the rucksack and opened it to find a flask. He took a drink.

"You enjoy walking on the hills, then?" Sara asked him.

"Yes. I do a lot of it at home, in the Lakes, you know. Mind you, it's real hiking up there. The hills are much higher and steeper. Some real mountains, in fact. Scafell Pike, Great Gable, Helvellyn, Skiddaw. I've been on them all."

"You've seen some good views, then?"

"Yes, but we don't do it for the views, Miss Dawson. It's the walking and the climbing: the serious physical effort.. And it can be tricky in bad weather. I was on Great Gable in a hailstorm once. Not very nice, but very invigorating. And quite a challenge, as well. You've got to have a challenge in life, you know."

"Yes, I'm sure that's right, Mr. Hardisty."

"Oh, call me Alan, please."

"Well, if you wish."

"And you are 'Sara'?" Sara nodded somewhat reluctantly. Then he went on, "I think Christian names are much more preferable to surnames, don't you? I mean 'Mr.' this, and 'Miss' that, is so unfriendly. It's like going back to the days of Jane Austen."

"Formality is sometimes necessary, Alan. It's very important, especially in a job like mine."

"Yes, of course. I understand that. But imagine going out with someone and still calling him 'Mr'? You wouldn't do that, would you? Not in this day and age anyway, Sara."

"No, of course not." Then she shuffled in her seat, turned and began putting her own flask and lunch box into a compartment in the car. "Well, I must be on my way," she said. "I've still got plenty to do. In fact, I'm going over to Clough Top   And you mustn't linger too long,. You don't want to miss your train."

He would have gladly missed the last train that day if he could have prolonged this conversation with her, He knew then that he loved her, but he was very unsure about how he should handle the situation, although he told himself that he was being sufficiently wise not to put any pressure on her.   For a start, he had no idea of the differences in their respective lives.   She would have established routines, friendships, relationships which he knew nothing about and she might not wish to abandon any of them just for him.   He was sure of his feelings for her, but whether, or if ever, they were reciprocated was something he could not know.   He knew, nonetheless that the time would come when he would declare his feelings and he only hoped that she would respond and come to love him, too. For that moment, at least, he just stood back, allowed her to tidy her car, start the engine and shout "Goodbye, then," as she closed the window and drove away, on up the hill towards the ridge and over it to Clough Top. Replacing his rucksack, and with the joy of knowing that he had at least spoken with her again, he headed off in the direction of Macclesfield Hibel Road railway station.

A few days passed without further incident until Sara arrived home late in the afternoon of a particular day. As she emerged from her car and stooped to reach her bags from the back seat, she heard a footstep close behind her and then Manion's voice. "Hi," he said. "What good timing. I thought I might find you here." Sara straightened herself, locked her car door and turned to face him.

"What do you want, Mr. Manion?" she asked with as much ferocity as she could manage.

"A word with you, please. That's all," Manion said.

"Well make it quick, I'm in a hurry."

"In a hurry, eh? You're always in a hurry. That's not a very nice way to greet a boy friend. What's the matter with you?"

"Since when have you been a boy friend? You're certainly not mine."

"Well, have you got one? Who is he? Not little Hardisty, for God's sake?" Sara noticed, and not for the first time, either, his deliberate attempts to belittle Alan as much as possible and at every opportunity.

"Don't be so impudent. It's nothing to do with you," she said.

"It has everything to do with me, darling," he responded "When you're my girl, I won't let you out of my sight." Sara laughed.

"And you really think I'm going to be your girl? That's the last thing...."

"Oh, just wait a while. You'll see. Anyway, I'm going to watch the motor racing at Oulton Park next Saturday. Thought you might like to come."

"Next Saturday? I'm on duty. But in any case...."

"You're always on duty. Obviously the police force are working you too hard, my love. When do you get some time off?"

"I was going to say that I have no desire to go to see motor racing at Oulton Park with you or anyone else, thank you very much. Now, will you please..." She had started to walk away, but he blocked her path.

"I asked you when you had some time off?" he persisted.

"That's my business, Mr. Manion. Now please let me pass." He reached out to hold her arm, but she evaded him "And don't you dare try to touch me. Do you hear?"

"Answer my question, then."

"Why? It's none of your business."

"I'd like to take you out somewhere. Anywhere."

"And I don't want you to take me out anywhere, anytime. Can't you understand?"

"No. I know quite a few girls who would give anything to go out with me. You don't know how lucky you might be, my love"

"I'm not your love. So why not ask one of the others? And just leave me alone."

"None of the others matter. It's you I want. Sara. You see, I'm using your first name now. And you must call me Mark."

"I have no intention of....I asked you to leave me alone. I must go. I've got better things to do. Now please...." He could see that she was determined. She was also flustered and upset. He decided to leave her for that time, let her calm down. But at least he had told her of his feelings, made it clear that he wanted her. That was a step forward. He stood back and let her pass.

"Thank you," she said. And she hurried away to her parents' house, and disappeared through the front door.

On the following nights, she took evasive action. She managed to get away from work early, so that she could park and go to the house long before he could be there. Alternatively, she stayed late – there was always plenty of paper work to do – so that he might tire of waiting, give up and go home, that is assuming that he had tried to catch her at all. One day, she parked near a friend's house at the other end of the village, walked home and then returned to retrieve the car in the company of her father as he took the dog for its evening walk. But she never set eyes on Mark Manion.

* * * * *

Sara didn't know that Alan Hardisty was interested in acting. He had been a member of an amateur dramatic society in the village, near Windermere, where he had grown up, and he had played a few small parts. Now he was eyeing up a dramatic society in Chester with a view to joining them. Sara's office phone rang one morning and she heard the voice say "Hello, this is Alan. Alan Hardisty."

"Oh, hello," she said.

"Look, em, are you interested in seeing plays? At the theatre?"

"Well, I could be. Why?"

"My local society is doing a good one next week. 'Ring Round the Moon' by Jean Anouilh. He's the latest French dramatist. Very good, and I think the play would appeal to you. Do you think you'd like to come, er, with me? I've got a spare ticket for next Wednesday."

"That sounds very nice," Sara said, and she accepted the invitation, although she wouldn't be able to use her police vehicle and would have to go to Chester by train. There was also a late train back to Manchester that night, but because it would arrive too late to connect with anything to Macclesfield, her dad would have to meet her there with his own car, which he readily agreed to do.

She had a lovely evening. Alan met her at Chester Station and took her to a small restaurant for a meal. Realizing that he had never seen her in 'civvies' before, he admired her lovely red wine coloured dress with a full skirt, the V of the neck showing just sufficient of her chest and shapely neck to be quite alluring. She had a light raincoat over the outfit and a silky scarf, and she carried a handbag. Alan wore a casual jacket and trousers, and a tie. They walked to the 'theatre', which was actually a village hall. There was a stage with serviceable curtains, and rows of individual chairs on a flat floor. Alan and Sara sat together, several rows back from the front, and soon the lights in the hall were switched off – manually. The curtains drew back and they were transported to an extravagantly furnished French chateau, with a conservatory-like verandah, filled with potted palms and bushes and plants. There was a butler, a collection of the most outlandish and eccentric main characters Sara had ever encountered, and most intriguingly of all, identical twins, both obviously played by the same actor. Of course, the two characters never appeared on the stage together at any time during the play.

Sara thought the poetic dialogue was wonderful, although there were one or two 'sticky' moments when the actors forgot their lines and had to be 'prompted'. Two characters dancing the tango together in the second act were rather stiff and became entangled in each other's clothing, which caused laughter from the audience, but it didn't stop them playing on manfully, and all was well. There was long applause at the end, and three curtain calls.

Too soon, however, Sara and Alan had to rush away, because they had little time to spare before her train left the Chester station. They made it in time and, before boarding the train Sara paid Alan for her seat at the theatre, as well as her share of the cost of the meal. He didn't want the money, but equally he didn't want to upset her. As she boarded the train, she turned and thanked him for a lovely evening. He wanted to kiss her, but he refrained. He went back to his lodgings, thrilled that he had been privileged to have taken her out and certain that this was just the start of a long and beautiful relationship. Mr. Dawson met his daughter at Manchester Central Station and was soon driving her home in his large, powerful car.   Then she was in bed, thinking about the play, the acting – especially the hideous 'tango' scene – and the man who played the twin characters in the one performance.   But she thought little of Alan Hardisty, and she was soon asleep.

* * * * *

Now that several days had gone by without incident, Sara had resumed her habit of parking near to her home, although she still took alternative routes from work and varied her times as much as she could.   Two days after her theatre visit, as she emerged from her car, she heard a step behind her and the familiar voice. "Hello.   Not seen you, lately."   It was Manion.   "Been avoiding me, have you?"

"I might've been," replied Sara.

"Well, that's a nice way to treat a bloke. Especially one who thinks the world of you."

"I'm sorry to disappoint you.   I don't reciprocate your thoughts."

"Not yet, perhaps, but….. Anyway, I didn't know you liked seeing plays…at the theatre."

This really came as a bombshell. How did he know? Alan must have been talking, boasting even. She felt shattered, betrayed. She could hear Alan's voice – 'I took her out you know. Went to see a play. She came all the way to Chester by train and caught the last one back.' Perhaps he said more, invented things even. 'We had a cuddle and kissed afterwards – and I'll be seeing her again soon.' But Sara managed to keep calm.

"What I do is none of your business," she managed to say.

"Not now, perhaps. But one day soon."

"One day never."

"So you prefer Alan Hardisty? Can't think why. He's a bit of a twerp, you know."

"I enjoy plays," she said. "That one was extremely good."

"Plenty of steamy passion was there? I bet he got the girl in the end, didn't he?"

"It wasn't that kind of a..... Look, Mr. Manion, I'm not going to stand here talking rubbish like that with you. Now will you please leave me alone, otherwise I shall call my father."

"I didn't think Alan liked that kind of thing either. Bit of a dark horse he's turning out to be. Still, you never can tell." He reached his hand towards her.

"Leave me alone, will you?"

"All right, all right. Keep your knickers on!"

"Dad! Dad!" she called. "You're filthy, Mr. Manion. Just get away from me." Then she was able to push past him and run towards the house. Manion rushed to his car and drove away as fast as he could.

A week-end intervened, but in the middle of the following Monday morning the telephone rang on Alan Hardisty's desk in the County Surveyor's Department. "Alan Hardisty," he announced into the receiver.

"It's me. Sara."

"Oh, Hello. Monday morning's looking better already."

"It won't when I've finished, Alan."

"Why? What's the matter?" He detected the threatening tone in her voice.

"Did you enjoy telling your mates about our theatre visit?

"Telling who? About what?"

"Your office mates. Our going to see the play?"

"Sara, honestly, I don't know what you're talking about. I wanted that evening to be secret. I haven't said anything to anyone. And I wouldn't mention it to anyone here. They're blooming women mad."

"What about Mark Manion?"

"I certainly wouldn't mention anything to....He's not been seeing you, has he?"

"He's been trying to. And he knows about our outing."

"Well, not from me, he doesn't. Believe me, Sara, love, I wouldn't talk about you to anyone, and especially not to that bloke. How does he get to see you?"

"He tries to meet me as I arrive home from work. I've been managing to avoid him, but I wasn't careful enough on Friday afternoon. He knew all about our evening."

"All I can think is that he must have known someone there, and they've informed him. But please believe me, my dear, nothing's come from me."

Over the week-end, Sara calmed down a little, and she decided to give Alan the benefit of the doubt. She had begun to like him, although the thought of anything more than a casual friendship with him had never entered her head. But at least he might somehow put a stop to Manion's attentions, and that, in itself, would be a good thing, even though she despised herself for the very thought of using Alan just to get rid of Manion. Alan implored her to trust him, to believe him, and to leave everything to him. He would find out what was going on and 'sort Manion out' once and for all. Sara doubted his capacity to do that, because she was quite sure that Manion was unlikely to heed any warnings from Alan, but at least he could try. So she agreed to his request and promised to tell him immediately if Manion approached her again. He said he would phone her back very soon

In spite of Sara's doubts, Alan did have the guts to tackle Mark Manion. First of all, he wanted to know how Mark knew about the visit to the play. Manion had heard about it from a member of the drawing office staff, who was also a member of the dramatic society and had spotted them. The description of the girl fitted Sara, and, of course, it didn't take Manion long to get confirmation from Sara that she had been at the performance.

Alan told him what Sara had said about pestering her and insisted that it had to stop immediately. Manion asked what right Alan had to make such a demand, and Alan claimed, he realised quite falsely, that she was his girl friend now.

"That's nothing," Manion said. "You're not engaged to her, are you?"

"Not yet. Give us time."

"Anyway, I wouldn't care if you were. I'd still be after her."

"Leave her alone for God's sake. You know she doesn't want you around."

"She's just playing hard to get. I've at least sussed that out. But give me half a chance and I'd bed her in no time." Alan cringed at the thought of this big, ugly uncouth lout having the slightest contact with Sara.

"Leave her alone, Mark, do you hear? And don't forget that she's a police officer. She could get you done for stalking, or harassment, both even." Manion laughed. "She could. Mark. And don't think she won't." They continued to argue for a while and then Manion finally decided to leave it and walked away. Of course, he hadn't given up, but he needed to think about the situation and perhaps adopt a different strategy.

Two days passed before Alan was able to reach Sara by phone – she had not been in her office for more than a few moments and he hadn't left any message. When he did contact her, he told her about the other staff member who had spotted them at the play and informed Manion. Sara accepted this as the truth and apologized to Alan for accusing him of bragging. He then asked if he could see her again and she agreed to meet him in the following week, this time in Manchester. The day before they were due to meet, Manion, who had been discreetly tracking her, contrived to bump into her on a street in Macclesfield. "Oh, hello," he said, a broad grin on his face. "We meet again, I knew we would."

"I didn't know you were psychic, Mr.Manion."

"I'm many things, darling. You'd be surprised."

"Probably I wouldn't," Sara said. "Anyway, I must hurry on. Please excuse me."

"You didn't tell me little Hardisty was your regular boy friend. You could do a lot better than that, you know. Of course, if I'd known that..." And to her eternal credit, Sara decided at that moment to play along with the deception.

"Alan?" she said. "Oh yes. He's super. And such a gentleman"

Sara met Alan again in Manchester as they had arranged, and it was early enough for them to go to the 'first house' at the pictures. They enjoyed the film and Sara insisted on sharing the cost. After the film, they returned to the railway station, where they would each catch separate trains. Alan's was due out first, but as they stood with a few minutes to spare, they talked about the film, and she was impressed by his comprehension of the plot, many of the details of which she had overlooked. Finally, with only a minute or two to spare, she said, "Oh, I met Mr. Manion the other day."

"God! He's not been...."

"No, listen. According to him, Alan, you are my steady boy friend." Alan's heart sank. Manion had ruined everything for him.

"Sara, honestly, I had to pretend, to hopefully put an end to his chasing you. But honestly, I never meant..."

"Look, don't miss your train. Just go for it." He moved away because the train's doors were slamming. "Alan!" she called, and he looked back at her. "I don't mind," she shouted. He boarded the train, and lowered the window. She was right there. He managed to lean out and touch her. She squeezed his hand. The train drew away.

Alan saw no-one else in the train carriage, even though it was full of people. He noticed no-one boarding or leaving the train at the numerous stops on the journey, and only very vaguely did he remember showing his ticket to an inspector as he came around. For the whole of that journey, he thought only of Sara and could not fully comprehend what she had said. 'I don't mind'. Had she meant that she didn't object to the pretence that she was his girl, or did she mean that she wanted the reality itself? She wanted to be his girl, his sweetheart, his lover and perhaps, one day, his wife? If the train had not began to move at that moment, he knew he would have returned to the platform, stayed with her, held her.

Even a pretend romance should be sealed with a kiss! But as it was, he must wait, agonize. There was, of course, a positive side to all of this. She was not angry, she wasn't going to abandon him but, rather, she would be around to continue the friendship; he would see her again, and again, and again. Alan reached his home station, left the train and ran all the way to his lodgings. Of one thing he was certain: he was in love with Sara and perhaps, just perhaps, she was in love with him as well.

For her part, Sara found her own train, boarded it and managed to find a seat next to a middle-aged lady in an otherwise crowded carriage. What had she just said? 'I don't mind'. What had she meant? Alan would be confused; she herself was confused too. Was she being fair in letting him think what now she knew he would be thinking? Or was she content to continue a deception in order to at least rid herself of that contemptible Manion? Now she had almost committed herself to a friendship with a man about whom she knew very little and it could develop, very rapidly, into the sort of friendship she knew she didn't want at this stage in her life.

There was a moment when the train came to a halt not at any station, but out on the tracks, nowhere in particular. Several minutes passed and Sara was still thinking of Alan. Suddenly, the lady sitting next to her said: "Typical! We'll not be 'ome before daybreak it this rate."

"Oh?" said Sara. "I don't expect it will be that long. Just a short interruption. Something to do with the points, I should think."

"Bloody points! It's time they got 'em seen to, then. I cum inta town three times a week, an' this allus 'appens. Summat's wrong, but I don't know owt about points." Then there was silence again, except for other people chattering, laughing, coughing. Corridor doors opened and closed again, people shuffled. At the far end of the carriage, a man who obviously had been drinking began to sing. A voice said,

"Oh God, don't let him start. Ernie, be quiet, lad."

Although the delay seemed like a good half hour, it was in fact only a few minutes before the train moved off again. Eventually, Sara arrived at Macclesfield

Station, walked to her car in the Police compound, and drove home.

There was a message for her to phone Alan Hardisty when she went into her office the next day. She did so and was ready with her answer to the question that she was sure he would ask. "Yes, Alan. If you'd like to continue our friendship, 'go out' with me, as they say, I don't mind."

"So what I pretended to Manion might be true?"

"You must understand, Alan, that I have a demanding job to do, and I have career exams to study for. We won't be seeing each other every night, or even every week."

"Yes, of course I understand that. I promise, I'll not interfere with your work, or anything. Please trust me. But if we're 'going out', like you say...."

"Don't say any more now. We'll meet soon and talk then."

"When shall we meet? Sara, I must have something...."

They met in Manchester again in the following week. Then, with a half day due to her, Sara went to

Chester, where she met Alan and they had a meal and walked around the city. While they were on the city walls, Alan put his hand into hers for the first time. She let it stay there. But she had to catch an early train back and soon they were on the platform. They had both enjoyed the day, and this time it was she who was boarding the train. As she did so, instinctively, she turned to face him. And just as instinctively, he put an arm out to her, pulled her towards him and kissed her. Soon the train left the platform, and she was waving from the window until neither could see the other any longer.

ooooo0ooooo

CHAPTER FIFTEEN

Two weeks after the inquest at Macclesfield, John Harvey went over from Clough Top for a discussion with Chief Superintendent Tozer. The Chief was well aware of Harvey's dissatisfaction with being placed in the village, which he regarded as dirty, squalid and a bit of a 'hell-hole'. 'Whoever in their right minds would choose to live here?' he often asked himself, although, being a town dweller all his life, he had never managed to appreciate the beauties of the countryside, nor the unique qualities possessed by many of its characters. He admitted to Tozer that his investigation was getting nowhere. It seemed that no one knew anything, or if they did, they weren't giving anything away, not at least to him. "I honestly think it would be better if Eric Brewer came back, sir. He knows these people, and is more likely to hear something, a whisper, a snippet dropped carelessly, than I ever would.

"Have you talked to the farmer, Gregson?"

"Many times. But it's always the same. I've tried, sir, really I have, but there's nothing. He left the vehicle properly parked at the bottom of the hill, on the piece of ground they call 'the croft', and had the ignition keys in his pocket. He's as baffled by the affair as we are, sir."

"John, he's a bloody liar. You know that, don't you? I'm damn sure the Coroner did."

"But I can't get to him. He just repeats the same thing. Vehicle parked and the keys in his pocket. The spares were hanging on a nail in the farmhouse kitchen. And he was away all day, mending walls on the moors."

"It still doesn't add up, though. That lad, who was a bloody loony anyway, couldn't have shifted that tractor an inch. It must've been near axle deep in the mud. The ground was sodden. And the County Surveyor is convinced that the wall would've stood up to much more than the force it would've received from a tractor travelling a few yards at bugger all speed. I agree with him."

"But Gregson is adamant."

"Yes, I know. Still, you might be right about Eric Brewer. And there's another job in Crewe that I want you for. I'll re-instate Brewer and you can come over. But I want Sara Dawson regularly in Clough Top, as well. You never know what she might pick up from the women folk. One of these days, someone will talk."

So within hours, Eric Brewer was back in the little office in Clough Top. Both he and John Harvey were pleased. Alec Tozer could be all right when he wanted to be. But no one at Clough Top said a word in the months that went by.

On one of her regular morning visits to Brewer's office, Sara asked once again if there was 'anything new?'

"Not a sausage," said Brewer. "Silent as the grave. You?"

"No. Most people think it *was* suicide, now William must have managed it somehow."

"I can't see how, love. It would have taken six men, possibly more. The Leprechaun didn't have one mate, let alone six."

"Unless it was a gang from somewhere, and they pushed it while he tried to stop them. That theory was suggested at the inquest," said Sara.

"I don't buy that for a moment." Brewer told her.

"Nor do I, really, but…"

"By the way," Brewer interjected. "I believe you know a chap called Manion. County Surveyor's office."

"What about him?"

"He was around here yesterday, asking after you. I didn't know you were getting serious with a feller."

"I suppose he told you that."

"I got the impression that he fancied you and the feeling was mutual."

"Huh!" exclaimed Sara. "That's what he'd like you to believe. He's been causing problems for me for weeks. I can't bear the man, but he won't leave me alone."

"So he's been pestering you?"

"Yes."

"In what way, love? How?"

"He's been waiting for me when I get home from work. Waiting near where I park the car. Or he turns up, somewhere else I happen to be."

"What does he want?"

"I would have thought that was pretty obvious."

"No, well, I mean, does he ask you out or something like that?"

"Oh, can we have a drink? Go out for lunch? He even wanted to take me to watch motor racing at Oulton Park."

"You've always turned him down?"

"I can't stand the man.   He's so conceited, so full of himself,   Even implied that I should consider myself lucky to have his attentions."

"I see.   Right, leave it to me, Sara.   I'll have a word.   I'll put the fear of God, or at least the Constabulary, in him in no time."

"All right, thanks Eric.   Oh, but try not to swear at him.   He thinks the police are worse than the criminals in that respect.   It would be nice to prove him wrong."

"Right," said Brewer.   "I'll talk like a choirboy.   I used to be one, you know."

Sara decided to take the opportunity to confide in Brewer.   She told him about Alan Hardisty, how she was seeing him and growing to love him.   "I just don't seem to be able to help it, Eric.   I don't know why."

"Don't even ask yourself why, love.   Just follow your instincts, obey your heart and enjoy.   I'm delighted." That was all he said on the matter.

* * * * *

It took Eric Brewer a couple of days to discover that Mark Manion had been assigned to a project only a few miles from Clough Top, where the County Council were constructing a new road bridge across a small river. Brewer drove over there one morning and observed Manion measuring, testing, weighing-up stresses, and giving instructions to his workmen. There was no doubt that he knew what he was about, After a while, Brewer got out of his car and strolled down to the site. He was wearing his police uniform. A workman saw him and indicated to Manion, who broke off from his tasks. "Oh hello," he said. "I didn't know this was still your patch."

"It isn't my usual one, but it's near enough."

"Yes, I suppose it is. Anyway what's new? No, don't tell me. You've solved the Clough Top drowning mystery. And that won't be before time, either."

"I wish we had, mate," Brewer said. "That really would make my day."

"Well, it's taking you long enough. One thing you can be sure of though. There was nothing wrong with that structure, that wall. It was as safe as houses. So don't try blaming that."

"We're not blaming anything yet, Mr. Manion. It's just a mystery. But there's another thing I do want to mention."

"Oh, aye?" said Manion. "You've got a message for me from Sara. You know, that girl of mine?"

"Well, not exactly. But there've been quite a few break-ins, recently, over Rainley way. Someone's reported seeing a bloke hanging round there. Fits your description. Just thought you ought to know. Our chaps might be giving you a call."

"But I had a job over there a few weeks back. Road repairs. I needed to be around the place. Bloody hell!"

"Well, I just thought you should know, that's all. Oh, and another thing. One of our lads is a very fit, welterweight boxer Won every match so far, and usually with knock outs. He's got something going with our Sara. So watch it, my friend. If he hears you calling her 'your girl' you'll finish up in Emergency Ward Ten. This is just a friendly warning. Watch it. Ok?"

"Right. I'll bear it in mind. Thanks."

"You'd better, Mr. Manion. Otherwise…..!" Brewer never knew how much of this Manion actually believed, or whether he suspected that Sara was behind it all, but nevertheless. Manion was visibly shaken and deflated at being spoken to in an aggressive manner by a police officer in front of his workmen. He sloped away towards his own car, got in, slammed the door, and stayed there for almost an hour. Eric Brewer had already phoned Alan Hardisty and told him not to believe anything Manion might say to him about a welterweight boxer. In fact, Manion said nothing, carried on with his work, and was, within days, eying up a pretty little typist in the general office.

* * * * *

Alan Hardisty came regularly now to Sunday lunch at Sara's parents' home, and then the four of them would walk on the hills, Sara holding Alan's hand the whole time. At Christmas that year, the same year that Bella gave birth to Jane and Bella's father died, Sara went up to join Alan's family at a very well appointed cottage in the village of Winster, near Windermere. Although Boxing Day was frosty, cold and crisp, Alan and Sara wrapped in warm clothing climbed Gummer's Howe, a hill at just over 2000 feet and therefore classed as a mountain, near the southern end of the Lake. They climbed steadily and then scrambled the final twenty or so feet of rock to the cairn at the summit. Standing together, above a layer of cloud, they could see for many miles: Morecambe Bay to the south; the Coniston and Langdale fells to the west; Loughrigg to the north; and round to the Eastern fells –the Northern Pennines - bordering Yorkshire. There was a chill in the air and Alan noticed Sara shiver a little. He put his arm around her. She was warmer. Then, at last, he asked, "Sara, will you marry me?"

She stood motionless for a few moments on the top of that Lakeland fell. Thoughts, emotions, fears, delights all seemed to cram her brain in those first few seconds after the sound of Alan's voice faded. She had come to love this man. Yes, strangely, unaccountably it was love that she felt for him and being without him now would be unthinkable. But she knew that she had allowed the friendship to continue and to flourish in spite of her commitment to a demanding career and her utter determination to gain promotion and get to the top – to be the first woman chief constable. And now this! Was she going to jeopardise all that for something she had never seriously considered? Minutes passed as she stood there, feeling the warmth and protection of his arms around her. She felt a damp tear trickle onto her cheek At last she was able to speak. "Darling," she said. "Can you give me some time? Please. I want to think. I need to...."

"Of course. I didn't expect a reply right away. I just want you to know that marrying you would make me the happiest of men. I love you very much. I want you so much. Please, don't keep me in suspense for very long. I don't think I could bear that,"

"No, I won't do that," was the promise in her reply.

Alan had noticed that the mist below them was getting thicker and it was time for them to return to the safety of lower ground. He pointed this out to Sara and, holding each other so tightly, they descended to the surfaced fell road, along which they would walk back to the village of Winster.

The couple returned to Manchester by the early train the next morning and there they parted, Sara for Macclesfield and Alan for Chester. She thanked him for a lovely Christmas, said she would contact him very soon, and they embraced. On the journey back, Alan thought only of her and remembered the same journey, only months ago, when she had left him in suspense then too. Sara also remembered her journey on that evening, when she wondered why she had suddenly, almost impulsively, told Alan that she 'didn't mind'. Didn't mind what? And she remembered the old lady complaining of the delays and the drunk who started to sing.

Sara finally decided to accept Alan's proposal and invited him to her parents' home on New Year's Eve, but she told him that she wanted to continue her career, her studies and fulfil her ambitions. He agreed to that, after all, financially it would be beneficial to them both.

The wedding was planned for the following October and, in the meantime, Sara gained promotion to a more senior position in the Manchester Constabulary. The coupled managed to put a deposit on a little property in Knutsford, the Cheshire town that was convenient for both of them to commute quite easily. And so they were wed. There followed days and nights of complete bliss. Alan, so kind and considerate, so loving and caring; Sara so understanding, helpful and passionate.   They both worked hard, and enjoyed week-ends with the chores, the shopping, and work in the house and garden.   Christmas, spring, Easter came and went.   It was in the late summer that Sara realised a change within herself and she was sure that she was pregnant.   It was soon confirmed, and when she told Alan he was ecstatic.

Their first child, Andrew, was born the following Easter.   Sara had resigned her post with the Manchester Constabulary on the understanding that, with her qualifications and experience, she could return to a similar post and advance her career, once the age of the child made it possible for her to do so   She enjoyed her time at home and cared for the baby with great joy and complete devotion..   She did the usual things, went to clinics; saw to immunisation and all the other necessities of young motherhood.   Yet she was restless.   She still yearned for her work, which she had always found fascinating.   Thus it was with some mixed emotions that she greeted the news that she was expecting again in the following year.   In due time, her daughter, Lucy came along.   Dutifully and joyfully, she gave the same care, attention and love to her new charge, and then took a genuine motherly delight in watching both her children grow.

One of the most striking topographical features of the town of Knutsford is its Heath, a wide expanse of open grassland, bounded by main arterial roads and the rear of a residential estate. Except at its corner nearest to the town centre, no buildings have been constructed on its boundaries. The Heath covers about thirty acres, and has been used for many public events, including horse racing, and May Day celebrations. As a child, the novelist, Elizabeth Gaskell, lived with her aunt in a house overlooking this grassy expanse. Although Sara and Alan did not live next to the Heath, their house was within easy walking distance, and Sara took the children there almost daily. They would scamper around, play in the grass or just enjoy the open air.

Sara had been coming to the Heath for months. Then one day, while she was crossing there alone, she saw an unmistakable figure. A gentleman, bolt upright, striding out along the path that had been worn by the feet of many thousands as they crossed to or from the town centre. The gentleman was carrying a dog lead, as well as using a walking stick. His dog was busy sniffing and foraging in the grass. Sara was in no doubt that he was Chief Superintendent Alec Tozer. He wore a green suit, collar and tie, and his trouser leg bottoms were tucked into his socks in the style of a golfer. He reached Sara, and was about to pass by, oblivious of any recognition. But she was having none of that. "Good afternoon, Mr Tozer," she said. He stopped and looked at her quizzically.

"I'm sorry, madam, I don't think I…"

"Sara Hardisty. I was W.P.C. Sara Dawson, Cheshire Constabulary."

"Oh … yes," he said, obviously recognising her now "Raffles, come here, boy. Heel." The dog obeyed instantly. "How do you do."

"My husband and I live in Knutsford and I find this a very pleasant place to walk."

"Yes," Tozer replied.

"Usually, I bring the children, but Alan is home today, so they're with him. I'm having a little break."

"You've left the force then?"

"Only temporarily, I hope.   When the children start going to school, I'm planning to return.   That's if they'll have me, of course."

"I've packed it in, you know."

"I didn't know that, sir," Sara said truthfully.

"You were in on that drowning case weren't you? You remember, the affair at that dingy little place, Clough Top, was it?

"Yes, I was.   The poor boy who drowned.   I remember it well.   I couldn't ever understand his mother. I think she was relieved by his death.   He was unwanted from the start, you know."

"That's the case that did for me.   We never solved it, and I always said that if there was a case I couldn't clear up, I'd retire."

"But surely, Mr. Tozer," – Sara deliberately dispensed with the 'sir' – the case hasn't closed.   I mean, we might find the answer one of these days."

"Someone might, some day.   But it won't be me, madam.   I'm out of it, now."

"Enjoying life in retirement, I hope."

"Well, I suppose. Mrs. Tozer and I went abroad last summer. Italy."

"Oh, I'll bet that was lovely. Lucky you. Did you have good weather?"

"Too hot for me, really. But she enjoyed it. Worst of it was, though, we had to put the dog in kennels for a fortnight. We won't do that again, will we boy?" The dog sniffed the ground near its owner's shoes. "He didn't like it. Moped the whole time, and lost pounds in weight. No, we won't do it again. That's the end of 'going away' for us. We'll stay at home from now on." Sara thought it was absurd that the requirements of an animal, no matter how much loved and appreciated, could take precedence over the choice of a holiday. But it seemed to have done so.

"Well, Mr. Tozer, it can be very restful at home, in a familiar environment. Do you live here, in Knutsford?" she asked.

"No We're a few miles down the road. Handy enough for a nice walk on the Heath, now and again, isn't it, boy?" The dog looked up, sniffed, snorted and began to move away. "Well, he wants to move on. Time we did.

It's been nice meeting you again, madam. Goodbye and good luck." He followed the dog away from her.

"Goodbye, Mr. Tozer," she called after him, and then she, too, went on her way.

The drowning of William Tudge and the investigation that followed was discussed now and again by Sara and Alan during their marriage. After all, if the incident had never occurred, it is very unlikely that they would have met at all, but, as Sara well knew, the same could be said about her encounters with Mark Manion. Neither Sara nor Alan could ever come to a conclusion regarding the affair, but whereas Alan took the view that the lad was trying, in some way, to prevent the theft of the vehicles from the croft, Sara was not so sure and thought that however much she liked and admired Jim Gregson, he knew a lot more about the events of that day, than ever he was prepared to tell.

The pretty young typist in the general office soon became weary of the attentions of Mark Manion, at the very same time that he obtained another post in the highways department of a local authority in Southern England. There he managed to attract a girl whom he married, and they had a large family   But Sara never set eyes on him again.

oooooOooooo

CHAPTER SIXTEEN.

'Just a few days ago I was sitting in the garden of my daughter's home in deepest Surrey. The lawns were immaculate, the herbaceous borders, stocked with the choicest of plants, now a rainbow of colour, blues of delphiniums –Elatum; reds of geraniums – Sanguineum; yellows of marigolds – Calendula officianalis; and whites of a variety of rose, mingled with red ones as well as bushes of fuchsia – parviflora; their delicate, bell-like heads hanging downwards from the stems adding further colour. In the centre, wallflowers and antirrhinums were bedded out and beginning to burst into bloom, and at the far end of the lawn were various flowering bushes, two semi-mature Japanese maples – Acer; which seemed to just shimmer in the sunlight, while beyond them, larger bushes and trees provided a backdrop. The scents from some of the blooms wafted on the air; there was the tinkle of water from the miniature fountain Jane had installed, and the noise of birdsong was everywhere – in the early evening, we heard the Nightingale. Yet these were the only sounds, and often there was complete silence. Who

would believe that we were barely twenty-five miles from London's Marble Arch?'

So wrote 'Country Girl' in her contribution for a week, over thirty-five years after her first article appeared.

Just a few days later, Jane Lomax was tending the same garden in the early afternoon, when the house telephone rang. She had the portable extension with her. "Hello, Jane Lomax."

"Oh, Mrs. Lomax," a voice said at the other end. "This 'ere's Mavis Fish. I live next door to Miss Warrington, in Clough Top."

"That's my mother," said Jane.

"I thought she were, 'cos she's got your number written 'ere in 'er book."

"Yes. Well, what's the matter, Mrs. Fish?"

"She's taken a nasty turn, this mornin', dear. I think she's very poorly. She's in bed now and we've sent for th' doctor, of course, but 'e's taking 'is time. I think ya'd better come up if ya can, and soon, if possible."

"Oh, right," said Jane. "I can set off later this afternoon, and I, or we, will be there this evening."

"Good, Mrs. Lomax. I think ya'd better do that, luv. I really do."

"Yes. Thank you, Mrs. Fish. Look after her, please. And see if you can hurry that doctor."

"Right, will do. Meantime, I'd 'urry yerself if ya can, but take care an' all. See ya later."

"Yes, see you tonight. Thanks again. 'Bye."

Jane replaced the receiver and hurried into the house. She needed to think now. Simon was in Rome and would be there for two more days. She would phone his P.A. and ask her to get a message to him. Both the girls were at school, but would be home in an hour, and she would have to take them with her, whether they, or the school, liked it or not. She would pack cases for them and install them in the car. She would have a pot of tea and some snack ready to be eaten the moment the girls came home. Then they could be on the road by five o'clock and in Clough Top by half past nine, traffic permitting.

But it was after ten by the time the car climbed the steep hill on Fell Lane and stopped near the end of the track to the bungalow. The girls were tired, aching, and petulant. Jane knew this, and was sorry for them. But there had not been any alternative. She had to bring them.

Mavis Fish, a woman somewhat older than Jane, stood on the verandah to Bella's bungalow. Stanley, her husband, stood behind her. Mavis was a large woman, with dark hair, now straggled, framing her face. She wore a very plain dress and a small apron.. Stanley was tall, quite thin, and going bald; he wore a t-shirt. He was very dependable and kind, and over the three years that the couple had lived next door to Bella, he and Mavis had helped her in small but practical ways on many occasions.

The stress of the five-hour journey and the anxiety of her mother's health were reflected vividly in Jane's face, but she smiled and shook hands with Mavis and Stanley. The girls were still squabbling over something in the car as Jane looked about her. "How is she?" she asked.

"They've taken 'er to th' 'ospital in Macclesfield, dear. Doctor came about an hour after I phoned ya, and 'e sent for an amb'lance, right away. I went with 'er, and they've done all they can for th' moment. She was unconscious, and she's in a single room. I told them ya were on th' way up and they said ya could phone when ya got 'ere, if ya like.. But ya must be 'ungry and tired, especially the girls. What can we do for ya? Stan'll put the kettle on, for a start." And Stanley went into the kitchen and did so. The girls came in, still arguing over some small problem, but Jane quickly put a stop to it.

"Here we are with your grandma very, very poorly, and all you can do is squabble. Stop it at once."

"But Mum…;" Emma tried to protest

"Stop it, Emma. Now! Do you hear?" Of course, Jane realised how tired they were, but it made no difference. Both girls sulked away, but fell silent.

"Oh, I've another message for ya, Jane, I may call ya Jane, mayn't I?" Mavis put in.

"Of course, and can I call you Mavis?"

"Aye. An' 'e's Stanley."

Jane noted the reference to 'he', rather than 'my husband', but she knew that nothing disrespectful was intended. She just said, "And the girls are Sally and Emma. Sally's the older one."

"Right. Now yer 'usband rung up from Rome. 'E said as ya'd given 'im my name an' e'd found our number through 'directory' or summat. Any road, 'e said 'owever late it were, ya've to ring 'im back tonight, whenever ya arrive. 'E'll leave 'is mobile phone switched on all the time, he said."

"I'll do that right away then. Thanks, Mavis."

While the tea was being prepared and served, Jane phoned the hospital, but all she could glean was that her mother was sleeping; there was no change in her condition – she was 'stable', and that they could visit any time on the following morning. She then rang Simon and brought him up-to-date with the situation. He said, "Listen, darling, I've got a meeting early in the morning here and then I'm finished. So I'm booked on a mid-day flight direct to Manchester and they're hiring a car for me at the Airport. I'll drive over to Macclesfield Hospital and should be there by half-past four. Shall we meet there?"

"Yes, of course, love."

"Then we can assess the whole situation. Ok?"

"Right, yes, my darling. See you then."

"Jane, you sound tired. Try to get some sleep – and that goes for the girls as well."

"Yes, we'll organise something, love. Don't worry. See you tomorrow."

"Bye then. Love you."

"Yes. Me too. Bye." And Jane replaced the receiver.

Mavis and Stanley organised a meal for them and offered sleeping accommodation for the two girls. This was accepted gratefully, and Jane was able to sleep in her mother's bed.

Sleeping in a strange house, away from home, even though their mother was only next door, seemed to excite Sally and Emma, and they forgot their squabble. They were given the room at the back of the bungalow, in the equivalent position to Bella's office. There were twin beds, and the close vicinity to the bathroom was another advantage. Both would have baths in the morning, but now, at the late hour, they just tumbled into their beds and very soon were fast asleep.

At her mother's bungalow, Jane needed first to collect her thoughts: her mother was dangerously ill in hospital, and if the worst did happen, she, Jane, would have many things to do. Of course, she knew now that Simon would arrive tomorrow and he would give her one hundred per cent support. How much she needed that! Something, however, made her go into Bella's office. She wanted to see if anything vital had been left undone, or left on view, particularly confidential items that should have been put away. However, everything was tidy – at least as tidy as Bella's office ever was - and there was nothing awaiting attention. But being there, she realised that once this was her own little bedroom and that it was here that she played, did homework and studied for exams. And it was here that she first put on that beautiful little bridesmaid's dress that made her feel so lovely, and so important. She remembered the wedding – Jenny Gregson's wedding – the boy, Phillip, whose arm she linked, and who later kissed her, although she failed to properly kiss him back. She also remembered the agony of having to take the dress off again. She did wear it on other occasions, although, as she grew, it became too small. She wondered what happened to it, did she take it when she left home? Or could it still be here somewhere? She couldn't remember. Perhaps she would find it again, somewhere.

But now tiredness got the better of her. She locked the bungalow, had a wash and undressed, got into the bed, put the side lamp off and was soon asleep. Nevertheless, it was not a long, restful, refreshing sleep. She woke several times, thinking mainly about her mother and wondering what she would find when they went to the hospital in the morning. She worried about the girls, uprooted from the routine of school work at a moment's notice – albeit for only a short time, for they could return next week – and being whisked away up here, arriving late at night, tired, fretful and quarrelsome. How grateful she was for the kindness of Mavis and Stanley Fish, and their devotion to her mother over the few years they had lived next door. She thought, too, of Simon, away from her in Rome, but now able to come back tomorrow. Then he would take charge, tell them what to do, advise, help, comfort. Oh, how she wished he was there with her, now. But she must be patient just a little while longer. She slept, woke suddenly, dozed again, then dreamed something awful, but couldn't remember what it was. She cried, trembled, thought of getting up and doing something – anything! But she didn't. She knew that rest, even if it was not sleep, was better for her, bolstering her for the trauma that she might have to endure.

When dawn came, she rose and went out onto the verandah, with a mug of hot tea in her hand. The air was still and smelt fresh with morning dew. The sun came up, lighting first the roof tops of the cottages at Fell Lane End, where once the Hodges had lived. Birds began to chirp and fly over the small field on the other side of the track that led in front of the Fish's bungalow and then across 'the backs' to Spring Street, and she even saw a rabbit – or probably it was a hare, dart from a small bank near the roadside wall All was calm and at peace. At least it was outside - inside, in Jane's heart, there was only turmoil, fretfulness and anguish.

At twelve fifteen on that day, Bella Warrington passed away. Jane, Sally and Emma were at her hospital bedside. Although she had not opened her eyes, they were assured that she knew of their presence - hearing is the final faculty to die – and Jane was certain that, at one moment, Bella had applied pressure to her own hand as she held hers. The medical staff left them for a while, as they cried, hugged each other, kissed Bella's face, kissed each other, and cried some more. Finally, two nurses returned and gently helped them out into the corridor, where Mavis and Stanley were seated. They rose and, knowing the end had come, took each into their arms, embraced them, wept, cried, sobbed and sobbed again. The nurses took them into a small, private room, where a pot of tea was provided. Eventually it was agreed that Mavis and Stanley would take the girls back to Clough Top and Jane would wait at the hospital for Simon to arrive. She had, however, already sent him a short text message, hoping he would pick it up on his mobile phone – 'MOTHER DIED 12. 15 P.M. WITHOUT PAIN OR DISTRESS. WE HAVE TO BEAR IT NOW. WAITING FOR YOU AS PLANNED. TRY TO HURRY, BUT KEEP SAFE. LOVE YOU, ALWAYS, J."

* * * * *

When they arrived back at Clough Top, Mavis and Stanley provided a snack for Sally and Emma, although they were not very hungry. Afterwards, it was suggested that the girls should go out for a walk in the warm sunshine and country air. The pair went out, walking together down the steep hill to Fell Lane End. The croft no longer bore the deep ruts and tractor tyre marks of Jim Gregson's day, but was level; its grass was short and dotted with daisies, dandelions and other wild flowers in the seasons.

Sally and Emma went over to the stone wall above the ravine and the flowing waters of the river. They watched as birds fluttered between the banks and to and from the bushes and trees. Now there was nothing to hint at the tragedy that occurred over forty years previously, the same year, in fact, that their own mother was born. Neither girl knew anything of those events. They sauntered up the steep hill to the village itself. There was a good new surface on the road and Spring Street had pavements as well. Many of the old cottages had been renovated, repaired or extended. The Huntsman looked inviting with newly painted signs, pretty window boxes and a large glassed extension at the side and rear providing excellent restaurant facilities. The Parish Church had been cleaned and was even floodlit at night. In fact, everywhere was as clean and tidy as any village street could be. A small group of boys stood near the inn and eyed the girls with interest, but Sally and Emma just smiled, giggled a little, and went on up the street. They reached the point where the road was wider, making it possible for buses and other larger vehicles to turn round. Beyond that, the road narrowed considerably as it continued, past the entrance to

Moorside Farm, and on to the higher fell country. Deciding not to venture further, the girls turned back, braved the posse of boys once again, found the entrance to the footpath across the 'backs', that Stanley had already told them about, and returned to the bungalow that way.

* * * * *

In the grounds of Macclesfield General Hospital, Jane sat on a seat, waiting eagerly for Simon to appear. The spot overlooked a small lake which was partly surrounded by trees and shrubbery, producing a pleasant atmosphere of peace and calm. The contrast with the bleak and austere settings of hospitals in many places and in previous generations could not have been greater. Simon came in on a back road that led straight to an alternative car park, while she was watching the hospital road from the main entrance at the front. As a result she did not see his approach, but he had spotted her, and had noticed how tired and forlorn she looked. As he got closer, he called to her. "Darling!" She turned and saw him coming towards her: tall, slender and with an unruly mop of fairish hair falling over blue eyes and a fresh looking – still almost boyish - face. He tried to smile.

Jane ran to him and was immediately engulfed in his large, gangly arms. He held her tightly.

"Oh, Darling," she said. "This is a nightmare. Mother died at about mid-day." Then she just cried bitterly in his arms. He tried to comfort her and his embrace went a little way to doing so. But she was exhausted, both physically and mentally, and he could see that she was in no fit state to drive her car. He arranged for his hire car to be left and paid for at local agents in Macclesfield, so that he could drive them back to Clough Top in Jane's car.

The day was Friday, and it was impossible to make any definite arrangements, such as those for a funeral, until the death had been registered on the following Monday. Jane could then expect to be a very busy person, and she would need to stay in the area. Simon and the girls, however, had to return home for a few days at least, and so it was agreed that they would fly to London on the Sunday. On the Saturday, Jane was able to rest, regain her composure, and prepare for the week ahead. Simon looked after them all very well. She did not enjoy saying 'goodbye' to them at Manchester Airport, but as she drove her car back again to Clough Top, she felt more confident and knew that she would be able to cope with everything that would confront her in the week ahead.

Bella's funeral was arranged for the following Friday, at Macclesfield Parish Church and would be followed by cremation, which Bella had stipulated in a will that Simon had found in her desk drawer. The death was announced in the national press and an obituary appeared in her own paper. Thousands of readers wrote in with letters of grief, expressing sadness that 'Country Girl', at least written by Bella Warrington, would appear no more. As many as could manage it would be at the funeral service. Jane contacted as many of Bella's friends as she could trace - a large number were farmers or landowners in the area, and journalists and writers with whom she had worked and held her in high regard and esteem. Family members were few, but Jane did find a cousin, related on Bella's mother's side, who lived in Dorset, but he was somewhat disinterested, and just sent a card expressing 'Sadness at your loss.' The undertakers were very helpful and nothing was too much trouble for them. The Rural Dean was appointed to conduct the service, and he interviewed Jane twice to ascertain, and check, details of

Bella's life to be included in his eulogy.   But she was unable to help at all with the identity of her own father.

On the Thursday evening, Simon arrived again with the two girls, using his own large, luxurious car that covered the journey in just over three hours.   It was wonderful to see them again, and after hugs and kisses with each of them, and a long, sensual embrace with Simon, Jane served them all with a delightful dinner.   Simon was relieved to see that Jane's usual composure had returned; she was coping now and looked much better.   He felt that, although tomorrow would be an ordeal for her, not least because she had asked to read a favourite poem in the service, she would blossom again, laugh and find interest and joy in daily living once more.   The two girls were accommodated with Mavis and Stanley Fish again, and Jane and Simon remained at the bungalow.

Very early on the following morning, the hearse carrying the coffin arrived on Fell Lane, near the end of the bungalow track.   With the vehicle halted there, Jane recalled being picked up at the very same spot when she was a bridesmaid at Jenny Gregson's wedding all those years ago. Her excitement then, and her utter despair now, made such a contrast. The line from Blake about 'Joy and Woe' being 'woven fine' came to her. 'How utterly true that is', she thought. 'Then I stood here in joy, now I stand here in woe'. At the given time, they began the journey back across the fell and into Macclesfield town. The mourner's car, with Jane, Simon, Sally and Emma, was followed by Stanley and Mavis in their car, and another vehicle with a couple from the village, whom Jane only knew by sight. She thought, 'How kind of them to come.'

At ten-thirty precisely, the cortege entered the Market Square and stopped at the church gate, where everyone waited for the coffin to be taken from the hearse. It bore one floral wreath from the family. The spot was within only a few yards of that where, many years before, Mark Manion had stood to see Sara Dawson and Alan Hardisty go off in search of a café. The Rural Dean greeted the mourners at the door of the church and they followed the coffin, borne by four sturdy undertakers' assistants into the large, wide, but surprisingly bright and modern interior. "I am the Resurrection, and the Life, saith the Lord: He that believeth on Me, though he die, yet shall he live: and whosoever liveth and believeth on Me shall never die." "I know that my Redeemer liveth." "Blessed are they that mourn: for they shall be comforted."

When the congregation stood up the funeral procession moved down the centre aisle, and Jane was taken by surprise and completely overwhelmed by the number of people present. Holding Simon's arm very tightly, she followed the Dean, and behind them came Sally and Emma. A church officer carrying a dark wooden stave made up the rear. The coffin was placed reverentially before the altar, and the family were ushered into the 'reserved' front pew. The service began: A hymn, prayers, Jane's reading, and a short, but kindly tribute by the Dean. Bella's hostility to the Church was well known, although when Jane decided for herself that she wanted to be baptised and then confirmed, Bella gave her complete and unfailing support. So, too, when Sally and Emma were born, they were christened, Simon saw to that, and again Bella attended the ceremonies. The Dean, therefore, concentrated on Bella's ability to convey in words many of the wonders of nature, an ability that God had given to her, and its result in a kind of ministry to thousands of readers nationwide, even though Bella herself would never have recognised it as such. The service ended with another hymn, and the Dean led them again behind the coffin, to the steps of the church. There, Jane shook hands with what seemed like hundreds of folk, inviting many to join them all at a local hostelry, to which the family would return after the final committal. Only the family went on to the crematorium, where this took place. Then it was all over.

The function that followed, which in bygone times would have been called a 'funeral tea', was held at a large public house, near to a prominent road junction in the town. Many people did attend, and two or three hours passed in condolences, reminiscences and memories. Jane was told many things, some of great interest, though others not. One person, though, stood out for Jane. It was Oliver Grant.: now in his seventies with a grey beard and hardly any other hair on his head, but slim, and still quite robust. He told Jane how he had fallen in love with Bella, and that his love for her had remained to this day. He did not tell her of their intimacy, although Jane began to wonder, and imagined if, in fact, this could be her own father. He said that he had been married, though his wife died a few years ago, and that they had had two sons, now grown up and married with families of their own. Although he had given up his bookshop, he retained his interest in books in his retirement by being a part-time dealer. He gave her his card.

One other person renewed his acquaintance with her that day. It was Eric Brewer, the retired Chief Police Inspector, who lived near Malvern now, but came up especially to pay his respects to Bella. He told Jane that he was still in contact with Jim Gregson, who once had Moorside Farm, but had for many years lived with his daughter and son-in-law, at their public house in Bristol. None of them could come up for the funeral – Jim was, in fact, quite lame and infirm, and losing his eyesight, – but they all sent condolences. Jane remembered them well. She recalled her visit to the farm, Jenny's kindness and, even more vividly, being a bridesmaid when Jenny married. And when Eric Brewer said his farewells that day, he took Jane's hand very tightly and he kissed it. Jane's hand was often kissed at many 'official' functions, but this time she felt that there was something special. She just wondered.

Mavis and Stanley Fish were stalwarts again that day. Always there in the background, helping, supporting, comforting. It was their pleasure too, to accommodate the two girls for one more night Both of them had, in fact, come to look upon Sally and Emma almost as 'family' and Stanley especially felt a sort of bond with them, to the extent of calling them 'our little girls'.

On the following day, the family left Clough Top and returned to London. Mavis and Stanley agreed to look after the bungalow, forward mail, and keep in touch until the family could return to 'sort things out' in just a few weeks' time.

oooooOooooo

CHAPTER SEVENTEEN.

Bella Warrington was astute when it came to her finances, and, with sound advice, she had been able to leave the whole of her estate to Jane and Simon, Sally and Emma. Her money was in trust for the children, and the bungalow at Clough Top with its contents was inherited by Jane. After much discussion, Jane and Simon decided to keep the property as a second home – a kind of country retreat – where they could spend weekends or longer holidays, away from the hectic lives that they all led in London.

But it was several months before any of them managed to return there. Both Sally and Emma had college exams to study for and sit, Simon had two more trips abroad – Rome again, and then India – and Jane was busy seeing to their needs, helping where she could, and continually tending the garden as the summer progressed. Then there was the usual annual family holiday – a fortnight in Portugal in August - which Jane envisaged would be the last one together as a family, for she knew that both girls were wanting to go their separate ways in the next year.

Therefore, it was in the middle of September when Jane finally got away and drove for three or more hours before arriving at the bungalow in the middle of a Thursday afternoon. It was planned that she would have a whole day there, alone, before Simon would drive up with the girls on the Friday night: then they would spend the weekend together. Mavis and Stanley had prepared everything for her arrival; the house was warm, food was in the pantry as well as the fridge; and there were oceans of hot water. The couple welcomed her as though she was a long-lost relative – hugs and kisses from both, a pot of tea immediately, cakes, biscuits....

"It's lovely to see ya back, Jane, really it is."

"I'd have come up sooner, if it had been possible. But life at home is very hectic at the moment. Even now, I feel guilty. Sally's got a job interview next week. She needs me for moral support, if nothing else."

"Well, she'll be 'ere tomorrer, and ya'll be with 'er next week, luv. Coming up 'ere could be a nice break for 'er, as well as for yersel."

"Yes, you're quite right, Mavis.   And anyway, I must start going through mother's things   It's high time I did."

So when the pleasantries and the small chat were over, the couple left Jane in peace.   She began to take stock of what Bella had accumulated over the years.   In the bedroom, the wardrobes were full of dresses, coats, hats, and the drawers full of undies, handkerchiefs and many other pieces of fabric – things that only women hang on to in case they might be needed one day.

From the bedroom, Jane crossed to the sitting room. It contained a large book case.   She began to examine its contents.   There was a complete set of Dickens' novels, a set, complete so far as she could tell, of the novels of Sir Walter Scott, several sets and two one-volume complete works of Shakespeare, the poetry of Wordsworth, Shelley, Milton, Keats and Tennyson, as well as many lesser known poets, and a section that seemed to be devoted to female authors, Mrs.Gaskell, Jane Austen, the Brontes, Mrs. Banks and George Eliot.   Rebecca West, Virginia Woolf, Edith Sitwell and Nancy Mitford were among the more recent authors.   There were books by many others whose names Jane had never known before. All the books here were beautifully bound, tidily shelved and in excellent condition. She took one or two from the shelves, and noticed that several still had the shop label inside – 'Oliver Grant, Bookseller, Manchester'.

Finally, Jane went into Bella's office. This was the room she remembered as her own little bedroom, with its view of the back garden, the stone wall at the end, and then the rising ground of the Common and the low fells beyond. She recalled that she had once thought of those hills as 'mountains', though in fact none of them were more than five hundred feet in height. Inside, the room was completely changed: gone was her little bed; the chest of drawers in which she kept all her small clothes, as well as her toys; the wardrobe that contained all her dresses and coats, and hats, and many other things that a girl collects over her childhood years. Her little bookshelf was still fastened to the wall, but now the fairy stories and Enid Blyton, Elsie Oxenham and Angela Brazil had all disappeared and been replaced by directories, dictionaries and other reference books. And there was another, rather large bookcase containing books on nature, gardening and other rural pursuits.

Bella's desk was tidily arranged, as Simon had left it several months earlier, with telephone, computer, stationery trays and other similar items. The desk had five drawers, two of which were locked The unlocked drawers contained various kinds of papers – letters, drafts for articles, notes, pamphlets, and handbooks, which, Jane could see, would require sifting through, with decisions to be made regarding scrapping or keeping, although just what should be kept, and where, would require further thought - work that could not be done in the time she had available in that week-end. But then she saw that there were two locked drawers. Where were the keys? No doubt they would be somewhere in the bungalow. She made a cursory search of the office, but could not detect them. She went back into the bedroom and looked in bedside drawers and cupboards without success. Finally, she found Bella's handbag; inside it were what looked like desk drawer keys. She returned to the office and found that the keys fitted perfectly.

The first of the locked drawers contained a loose-leaf file in which there was a typed 'Journal', Bella's day-by-day record of her work and events in her life. The last page was dated four days before her death. –

'…….*Not feeling very well today. Still, I must press on – notes for 'Country Girl' next week, for a start. This morning it took me ages to walk over to Spring Street, and then up past Benson's old farm. But beyond, the countryside looked so lovely, summer foliage now well established, plenty of berries in the hedgerows and on the rocky banks, here and there –bilberries, soon ready for picking. Then I needed to return, this queer feeling was getting worse. Oh dear!*'

Jane felt tears coming to her eyes. But she turned a few pages and looked further back. This was a wonderful account of Bella's life, and it was labelled 'No. 34.' There would be thirty-three earlier ones, each one perhaps covering a year or more. She hoped that they had all been kept. She was determined that they must be found.

The second locked drawer contained a scrap book – newspaper cuttings from years gone by. Many of these were quite torn and 'dog-eared', but still perfectly readable.   And there was a separate folder with cuttings from over forty years ago. She browsed through and very quickly a headline startled her: **'MYSTERIOUS DROWNING AT CLOUGH TOP.'**   Then there was the account of the death of the young man, William Tudge. There were several other accounts, some no more than a few lines, but one had a photograph of a young man, poorly dressed, with untidy hair, quite bulging, penetrating eyes, and a small scar on the left side of his forehead. Jane thought he looked simple-minded.   Then there was an account of the inquest, held at Macclesfield, with a report of the accident with the tractor, and the uncertainty of how it had entered the river, given the place where it had been left, and the fact that the wall above the river had recently been re-enforced.   Mr. Gregson, who owned the tractor, gave evidence, as did Police Constable Eric Brewer, Chief Superintendent Tozer and Woman Police Constable Sara Dawson.   Then Jane remembered Mr. Gregson – his wife's funeral, and, of course, Jenny's wedding, at which, she had been a bridesmaid.   She remembered Eric Brewer, who talked to her then, and again, only four months ago, at Bella's funeral – now Chief Inspector, retired.   The name,

'Sara', also came to her, although she could not remember much about the lady. In Jane's mind, however, the whole affair took on a kind of significance which she had never known before. She began to ponder and read the cuttings over and over again. The very fact that Bella had kept this material, safely locked away here for so many years - the whole of Jane's own life, in fact - was something of importance, and it suggested - well, what exactly did it suggest? Could it be that this young man, William Tudge, had been someone special to Bella? Could they possibly have been lovers? Could he, William Tudge, even be her own father? The drowning, an accident? Suicide? To these questions, Jane wanted answers, and she decided, there and then, to find them.

Jane realised immediately that Bella's current Journal, No. 34, meant that there were the thirty-three previous ones somewhere. The current one began in the November of the previous year and the binder was by no means full, which indicated that the previous ones could cover at least forty years between them, perhaps the whole of Bella's time at Clough Top, and certainly the time of her own birth and the events surrounding the drowning of the young man, William. 'Where were they?' The question took on a great importance in her mind. Certainly they were not in the office, and Jane scoured the bungalow, which had several cupboards and store places, but they were not to be found.

It was getting late; Jane was tired, and hungry. She went into the kitchen, made herself a snack meal – soup, sandwiches, some cake and some yoghurt, with coffee, and settled down by the gas fire. She watched something on television for a while – yes, latterly, Bella had owned a good television set – but Jane soon switched that off. She was pondering the drowning, the circumstances surrounding it all were prominent in her mind.. Finding those previous journals was top priority – where could they be? But that would be something for tomorrow. She cleared everything, locked the house, and finally went to bed. She was soon asleep.

In mid-September, even though summer has officially ended, there are sometimes days when the sun shines from a clear blue sky from dawn to dusk; the air is still warm and one feels that perhaps summer has returned for a while. Friday was just such a day, although it did not herald an Indian summer like the one of over forty years ago when Bella went over to Alice's shop and Alice first noticed her condition. Jane woke, drew back the curtains, and saw the view, bathed in sunshine, across the pasture land, over the roofs of the cottages near Fell Lane End, and over to the higher ground on the other side of the river. She made breakfast and took it on a tray to the little table that Bella had always kept on the verandah. Still in her dressing gown, she sat there, breathing the fresh, warm air, and listening to the sound of birds as they flew here and there around the garden and over the field beyond. She also heard the 'baaa' of sheep not too far away, and then a dog barked somewhere down in the area where the cottages stood. This, as her mother had often said, was heavenly.

But as she sat, her thoughts quickly turned to the discoveries of the previous night: the scrapbook and the cuttings relating to the drowning of William – 'That poor boy,' she thought. Then the big question returned: 'Could he have been her father?' There was still something about it that didn't ring true. He seemed strange, almost simple, and hardly the sort of man to whom her mother could be attracted. Admittedly, her mother did have strange ideas, strange ways, but if this man was as he appeared, even her mother would surely have kept her distance. Nevertheless, for the first time in her life, Jane determined to un-earth the truth. To discover who her father really was. Of one thing she was almost completely certain – her father was not Oliver Grant. Yes, he had loved Bella; he had told Jane so and perhaps they had been lovers. But that must have been a long time before Bella had come to live at Clough Top, and she had lived there at least two or three years before Jane's own birth.

By the middle of the morning, Jane was ready to go out, and she was just about to do so when the phone rang in Bella's office. It was Simon. "Darling, I'm ready to leave as soon as the girls get home. They're going to try to make it early, so we should be up there by sevenish! I suggest that we all have dinner at a local hostelry - there's that one in the village. Can you book us a table?"

"Well, I'll do my best, my love, but if you're late...I mean, I don't know what time they stop serving," Jane remarked.

"Well, go and see. We can always cancel, if we have to."

"Yes, I know, but it's hardly fair, is it, Simon?"

"Oh, we'll make it up to them. Go tomorrow night, instead, and give them a bit extra. They won't mind."

"I'm on my way over there, now. I'll see what I can do, then."

"Yes. Good. Put on that charm of yours. You know it never fails."

"That's bribery."

"No. Just friendly persuasion. Oh, here's Emma home already. She's just come in. So as soon as Sally arrives, we'll be on our way."

"Well, take care. Don't speed. Do you hear, Simon?"

"Yes, I hear. Don't worry, darling. We'll all be there safely. You'll see. Anyway, 'bye for now. Love you."

Jane walked out to Fell Lane and descended the steep hill to Fell Lane End. At each side of the surfaced road, there was the uneven, grassy verge, dotted with small trees and shrubs, wild flowers still in bloom, and stony tufts or mounds, and beyond the verges were the dry-stone walls enclosing the field that the bungalow overlooked, and, on the other side, woodland which stretched away toward Furness Bridge. Although the woodland was private, she remembered playing there with other children in her schooldays. When she reached Fell Lane End, she noticed the croft, just as her daughters had seen it a few months earlier. She went over to the wall and peered into the ravine. The waters swirled far below, rushing down from the higher hills above the village to the lower lands of the valley below Furness Bridge. Ferns and small bushes sprouted from crevasses in the rocky sides and many places were covered with lichen. Birds chirped and hopped and flew across and around the dark, shaded area. Jane noted that the wall itself was very sturdy and strong; it seemed to have been moulded into the rocky banks and a great force would be required to dislodge any part of it. It was completely sound and secure.

In her head were the accounts of the accident that happened there all those years ago, when that young man was drowned. How it occurred was still a mystery, because unless the wall had been considerably less secure than it is now, it would have withstood a considerable force - much more than a strike from a slow-moving tractor.

Still, in those days, she thought, such security might not have been so stringent. She lingered there a little while. She was alone. One or two light vehicles passed, on the way to or from Spring Street, and something came down Fell Lane and then turned left, away from Clough Top, and continued down towards Furness Bridge. But there were moments when all was quiet, except for the birdsong and the waters gushing in the ravine far below. The thought came to Jane that this was the last spot on Earth seen by that boy, William, before his horrible and untimely death. Inevitably, then, the question returned, 'Was he her father?'

She walked up the hill to Spring Street. The General Store – Alice's old shop – had become a franchise of a chain of identical shops throughout the area. As she needed several items, she went in. A man of about the same age as herself greeted her. He wore the usual brown overall coat, with a pen and pencil clipped into the breast pocket and an open shirt and jeans and trainer shoes. "Mornin';" he greeted her.. "Nice day."

"Good morning," said Jane. "Yes, it's lovely."

"Bit unusual for September, though. Usually colder by now." There were many warm days in the month, as Jane could remember from childhood, but she didn't want to argue the point.

"We're fortunate, this year, then," was all she said, and she continued to look along the shelves.

The shop was now a mini self-service supermarket and she had collected a wire basket as she entered. She made her selection and took the basket to the counter. The man scanned the bar code of each item into the till, which totted up the total. "That's five pounds and thirty five pence, madam, please," announced the man and Jane paid him. Then she asked him

"Pardon my curiosity, but how long have you been here?"

"Here, in this shop, you mean?"

"Yes."

"Oh, getting on for five years, now. Hardly seems that long, though."

"I used to come in here as a child. The lady that was here then..... what was her name...?"

"Mrs. Chidlow, you mean? Alice Chidlow?"

"That's right, 'Alice'. She was lovely. She used to give me sweets."

"Aye, I can believe that. But that was her problem, you see. Too much generosity doesn't always pay, in business But then there was something even further back, I believe. She took sides in some village affair and it lost her quite a lot of trade. Folk went down to Furness Bridge instead, regardless of the inconvenience. Pity really. Because, as you say, she's a kind soul."

"Is she still around, then? In the village, I mean?"

"No. Her husband, died a few years back, and then she eventually decided to sell up. She went to live with her sister, I think. Somewhere in Wales."

"But she's still alive?"

"Well, I think so. I can find out…."

"No, no thank you. I just wondered, that's all. Don't worry about it, please. It's not important."

"You've lived here in Clough Top, then?"

"Yes, until I married and moved away with my husband. And that's over twenty years ago, now."

"You'll notice some changes."

"Quite a few. But some things are the same."

"Where did you live? If I may ask?"

"The first of the bungalows off the Fell Lane. My mother was Bella Warrington."

"Oh," he exclaimed. "Then you're just the person I need to see."

Really? How can I help?" The man hesitated a little, coughed nervously, and then said

"It's the papers, madam. There's an outstanding account."

"Is there? But of course, there must be." said Jane. "Really, I am sorry. I never realised and I do apologise. I'll pay you at once. How much is it?

The man went to a pile of papers behind the counter. He sorted through them, found the appropriate invoice and announced, "Thirteen pounds and twenty pence. We did send an invoice to the house."

"Then we must have overlooked it. I'm terribly sorry. We haven't been back since the funeral, you see." She paid him. "I only came back yesterday. Trying to sort a few things out."

"You've got a job on, then.. Best of luck."

"Thanks. I'm sure I'll need it. And your invoice is sure to be there somewhere. Shall I?...."

"Oh, just scrap it now," he said. "This is a receipt." And he handed Jane a slip of paper that came automatically from the till

"Right, thanks," she said. "Goodbye."

"'Bye, madam, and thank you."

Jane left the shop. She continued along Spring Street and reached the Huntsman Inn. How different it looked from when she went there as a child, and even from when she and a few senior school friends had their first real alcoholic drink there, over twenty years ago. Inside the front door, the hallway had been widened, carpeted, expensively decorated and made into a good reception area. A sign on the desk pointed to a bell push. PLEASE RING FOR ATTENTION. Jane rang the bell.

A tall, dark haired, 'leggy' young woman appeared after a few moments. She was immaculately dressed in a wine-coloured business suit – skirt and jacket – with a white blouse, to which her name badge was pinned, and a gold chain around her neck bearing a cross. She was made-up perfectly and displayed the latest 'hair do'. Jane expected an intelligent greeting. " 'Ello, luv, can I 'elp yer?" caused her some surprise. Jane explained her wish to book a table for dinner that evening, with the proviso that it depended on her family arriving in good time. "Oh, don't worry abart that, luv. We serve till nine, an' if yer can't make it, doesn't matter. We're never full on weekdays."

"Oh, that's all right, then," said Jane. "But we'll make it tonight if we possibly can. Otherwise it might be tomorrow night."

"Best 'buke' fer that, then. Saturdays are often very busy."

"I'll remember that. Thank you."

Before she left, Jane went through to the ladies' cloakrooms, where she observed that everything had been re-furbished; there were tiles, boxed-in washbasins with large, brass-handled taps, air blow hand dryers, a large vanity shelf and an equally large mirror on the wall, a box of floral paper handkerchiefs, and a vase of artificial, but nonetheless attractive, flowers It was a great contrast from the concrete floors, whitewashed walls, two hand basins bracketed to the wall, a towel hanging from a wooden roller, used by everyone and, as a result, always wet, a cracked mirror, and cubicles that didn't lock properly, chains you had to pull down, and one roll of toilet paper that seemed to be shared between users, as she remembered from all those years ago. 'My word,' she thought. 'Someone's spent some money here.'

Then she went to the rear part of the inn, where she found the large new conservatory area containing about ten separate tables, some of which were already occupied by people taking early lunch. The area extended around the side of the building and was light and airy, warm and refined. Jane hoped that dinner there would be possible that night. Then she left, crossed the road, and returned to the bungalow by way of the footpath across the 'backs'.

Simon and the girls arrived soon after seven o'clock. They were weary and felt dirty after so long on the road. Mavis Fish heard them on the track from the road and, after allowing a suitable time for family greetings, she went into their bungalow, just to re-enforce the arrangement for Sally and Emma to stay with her and Stanley. The girls went back with her, and each was able to wash, change clothes and put on fresh make-up, before the four of them set off for Spring Street and the Huntsman Inn. Simon and Jane managed to have a few moments together, but Simon wanted a wash and spruce-up before taking his beautiful three ladies out to dinner.

It was not until they were in bed that night that Jane was able to tell Simon about her discoveries. She told him of the scrap book with the cuttings relating to the drowning of William, the 'accident', if that was what it was, and the inquest. She told him of her suspicions that William might have been her father and, equally, her feelings that he might not be. "Did your mother never mention him?" asked Simon.

"Never in that way," replied Jane. "I seem to remember being told, or hearing about, the drowning.. But it's all quite vague."

"And you've seen your birth certificate?"

"Well, of course. You've seen it yourself, many times. It's been needed for the passports and things. You've never noticed?"

"Yes, it's blank. I remember. 'Father unknown' "

"Makes me feel like Orphan Annie. I wish I knew."

"Bit late for that, love.   If it was that lad, forty years! No chance, now."

"But was it him, Simon?   From the photograph in the cutting, he looks a bit mental – not, you know."

"Not a full shilling, as they say. So?"

"Mother would never – "

"There's never been any certainty about what your mother would do.   And that would explain the secrecy. She wouldn't want anyone to know – and especially not you."

"Aren't there ways of finding out, even now? DNA or something?"

"Yes, but you've got to have something from the person.   Some tissue, skin or saliva, blood or, I suppose, urine.   You've no chance of getting that   Was he cremated?"

"I don't know.   But there's a funeral report, I think."

"Mind you, even if it was a burial, I hardly think they'd even consider exhumation now.   Anyway, that would take weeks to organise."

"So? What's a few weeks, after forty years?"

"Darling, don't be silly. Such a thing would be damn near impossible."

"Even for you? With your connections?"

"Yes, especially for me. I don't know anyone…."

"Marion what's-her-name? In the Home Office?"

"Marion couldn't do anything. And even if I thought she could, I wouldn't ask her."

"Why not? Anyway, I'll find the scrap book again in the morning. If it was cremation, there's no point in arguing."

"Better get some sleep, then. That's what I need." He kissed her and turned onto his side. "Good night, darling."

"Good night," said Jane. Simon was soon asleep, but Jane lay awake, pondering the questions in her mind. She would get to the bottom of it all, and there was plenty of time to do it.

At breakfast the next morning, Jane produced the scrap book. The funeral report made it clear that William Tudge had been buried in the graveyard at the Parish Church. The family agreed that they would walk over, and, assuming that there was a headstone, they would find it. Actually, there was a headstone, and it was not difficult to find. The inscription was very brief: **"WILLIAM TUDGE, DROWNED AT CLOUGH TOP, AGED 19 YEARS"** followed by the date, and **"R.I.P."**

Simon could see that Jane was moved. She stood, silently staring at the headstone, and her eyes moistened a little. After a short while, he put is arm around her. "Come on," he said. "Let's see if they're serving coffee at the inn." Sally and Emma were standing close by, and they all strolled together to the Huntsman and, yes coffee was being served.

oooooOooooo

CHAPTER EIGHTEEN

Chief Inspector Eric Brewer had been retired for several years. He had a very good pension, and tried to enjoy life to the full. He had found a lovely country house with a good-sized garden, not very far from Malvern; from windows at one side, there was a good view of the pointed peaks rising from the flat lands that surrounded them. His passion was golf now, and he went regularly on golfing holidays. His wife, Mabel, could have been a golf widow, but she took part in many associated activities, ran a social club and accompanied him on all the holidays.

The Police Pension Fund forwarded a letter to him, from Jane Lomax.

'Dear Sir/Madam,

In connection with a personal family matter, I am trying to contact ex-Chief Inspector Eric Brewer, who, prior to retirement, was attached to a constabulary in the Birmingham/Midlands area. If you are able to contact Mr. Brewer on my behalf, I would be very grateful Alternatively, would you please inform me of his current address? Thank you.

Yours faithfully, Jane Lomax, nee Warrington –
Clough Top'.

A few days later, Eric Brewer phoned Jane. He remembered her, for they had met at her mother's funeral only a few months earlier. She told him how she had discovered the papers relating to the drowning of William Tudge, and that she would like to see him to discuss the matter. "Oh, that's a very long time ago, now, Mrs. Lomax. I remember it, of course. We never could get to the bottom of what happened, you know."

"It was only a few months before I was born. But it's become very important to me. I must know the truth."

"That's a problem though. No-one knows the truth. The lad went into the water, but how, has always been a mystery."

"I'm not talking so much about that, but I'd like to know the true identity of my father."

"Oh well. They always said … look, I think we'd better discuss this face to face. I'd invite you over, but, tomorrow, we're off to Portugal for a month. Can it wait till we get back?"

"Yes…well yes, of course," said Jane, hesitantly. "But in the meantime, is there anyone else I can see? There was a lady, a W.P.C.…."

"Sara? Sara Hardisty? Yes, I can give you her address. She's still on our Christmas Card list. Hang on." And he gave her Sara's address and phone number. Then he added, "And there's Jim Gregson, you know. Lives with his daughter and son-in-law in Bristol. They run a pub. Mind you, he spends half his time at a sea-side place in Devon. I can give you the Bristol address." He gave her the address, and then the conversation ended, but it would be resumed on his return from Portugal.

* * * * *

Soon after Sara Hardisty's encounter with Alec Tozer on the Heath at Knutsford, her eldest child, Andrew, started school. Knowing that she could put Lucy safely into a day nursery, one close to their home, she decided that she would be able to re-start her career. She put the idea to Alan, but he wouldn't hear of it.

"No, my dear" he said. "I want you to stay at home. Look after them properly, as a mother should."

"But Andrew's at school and Lucy will be all right. I know she will."

"How can you be so sure?"

"She's a bright child. She'll enjoy the nursery."

"She might not. Anyway, love, your place is at home. You should be…"

"My 'place'! My place is wherever I choose it to be."

"No, my dear," Alan said. "It's where I wish you to be."

"Oh, indeed!"

The arguments continued over several days. Sara reminded him that, even at the time of their marriage, they had agreed that her career would not be affected - interrupted, yes, if children came along - but it was never intended that she should abandon her aspirations completely, and for ever. Alan had agreed to this at the time. But he said that the situation had completely changed. She had two children, a husband and a home to look after, and that should be enough for any woman to cope with, never mind gadding off to a demanding job that might keep her away from home – from him, and more importantly, from the children – for days on end. She then pointed out that she would earn a very good wage and the extra money would be useful. Once again, Alan rebuffed her with the reminder that he had risen to be a senior administrator in the department and his salary was quite adequate   Finally it came to an ultimatum. Sara said, "Either I go back to work and continue my career with your complete agreement and blessing, Alan, or I leave you."

"Don't be silly, you can't leave me – us."

"Try me."

"Sara, please…."

"I said 'Try me', Alan. "   And that was the end of the matter.   On the following day she took the two children, only temporarily, Alan assumed, and returned to her parents' home. In the succeeding days, despite pleas from him, and her parents' desperate attempts to resolve the situation, she flatly refused any offer of reconciliation. To her, a promise once made should always be kept. It was sacred and the fact that Alan was ready to break it was inexcusable. She applied to Manchester Constabulary and within weeks had commenced a new job.

Alan's love for his wife never diminished and, for her sake as well as that of the children, he moved out of the Knutsford house, so that they could return, at least until things were sorted out, but they were not 'sorted out' for a long time. Andrew returned to his school and Lucy went to the nursery until the time arrived for her to move up as well. Sara allowed Alan access to them, and there even came a time when she thought he might accept her working again and there could be a happy outcome. But it was not to be.

Almost three years passed and then, one day, 'out of the blue', Alan arrived at the house. It was at a time when he knew that the children would be in bed. He came straight to the point "I want a divorce, Sara," he told her.

"Yes," was her steely reply.

"I can't go on living alone, you see. I just can't. I've met someone, someone special, and she's agreed to marry me."

"What's her name?"

"Valerie. But I don't see how that can affect anything."

"How old is she?"

"Twenty-nine. Just the same as…"

"Still young enough to have children then."

"Yes, of course. But that will depend on…"

"Do you really love her?"

"Yes. She's a member of the dramatic society. A very good actress."

In those days, divorces were long, messy, difficult affairs and the process would take eighteen months. The Knutsford house had to be sold and the profits divided between them. With her share, and a little more, Sara was able to put a deposit on a cottage in Wilmslow, where she moved with the two children, who remained in her custody. Alan moved back to Chester and he and Valerie were married. He still saw the children regularly, and quite often he saw Sara as well when he called for them. Valerie made him as happy as she could manage, although there were never any children. And Sara reached the rank of assistant inspector, loved her work and remained in post until she was compelled to retire.

Sara knew Wilmslow quite well. Its police station was the Divisional Headquarters of the Cheshire Constabulary where she had attended that first conference in the William Tudge case and where she first encountered Alan. Nowadays, Wilmslow is a prosperous 'commuter' suburb of Manchester, although actually it is in Cheshire. Once it had been just a small village with a well-proportioned ancient parish church, and surrounded by large areas of open land, which now has been swallowed up with good quality housing developments and commercial units. The town has an attractive main street, pedestrianized now, and other main thoroughfares with wide, 'airy' atmospheres. At one edge of the town, a lane branches from the main road which goes on to Manchester Airport and beyond. Another narrower lane branches from the first, and a number of small cottages, as well as some larger properties, front onto this lane. All the cottages have been modernised and extended, providing good homes, eagerly sought after. Sara had been able to purchase one of these.

When Jane phoned her from London, Sara remembered the little bridesmaid at the wedding in Clough Top all those years ago. Jane explained the reason for the call, and Sara willingly agreed to meet her. There are regular train services between London and Wilmslow, so it would be possible for them to meet, have lunch and the afternoon together, before the last train back in the evening. The meeting was arranged.

When they arrived at the station, they easily identified each other, for, although Wilmslow station is usually busy, it is not always so, particularly in the late mornings. Quite quickly, Sara's car was moving through the town and out towards the area of her home. "I thought you'd prefer to come home to talk, rather than go to a restaurant or something. So I've made lunch for us there," said Sara."

"That sounds fine. Thank you." Jane replied. In only a few minutes they were turning into the lane which sloped downhill until it reached the short row of cottages. Sarah parked and then led Jane into one of them. There was just an entrance lobby followed by a cosy lounge with a small, but very comfortable three piece suite, a sideboard, cupboards, a small table and a bookcase. The fireplace, which had a 'coal effect' gas fire, was extended with a slate ledge at one side, and on it there was a television set.

"Let me take your coat, Jane," said Sara, "Do sit down. We'll have some coffee in a minute. I set the percolator before I left. It should be ready."

"Lovely, thank you," said Jane. Soon they were settled with their cups of coffee, and for the first time, Jane was able to look at Sara properly. Her hair, no longer light brown and beautifully groomed, was grey, almost white and considerably shorter than how she remembered it from their previous encounters; it fell into her neck where the ends were curled. She still had an attractive figure, her bust accentuated today by a tight-fitting green dress, squared at the neck, still revealing the white skin of her throat and chest, under a small necklace. Jane thought that she seemed thinner than when they met at Jenny's wedding all those years ago, and she could certainly trace lines in her face, in spite of make-up expertly applied. "This is very cosy, Sara," said Jane. "Do you live here alone?"

"Yes, I do, now. Andrew, my son, married three years ago, and he and his wife live near Oxford, and my daughter, Lucy, lectures in Edinburgh. She gets home between terms, but even then, she only stays a day or two before she's off somewhere. There's no problem; it's just that she has so much to do, so many contacts to keep up with. But she's a poppet, really. That's her photograph above the fireplace." Jane had already noticed the photograph of a good-looking young girl wearing a mortar board and gown. "She graduated two years ago."

"What was her subject?"

"Modern History. She adores it." Then Sara changed tack. "Anyway, now then, you wanted to discuss the incident at Clough Top? It's a very long time ago, now, you know, my dear. I hope I can remember it all. What specifically....?"

"The boy, the one who drowned. Did you know him?"

"No, no I didn't. But I met his mother. She was a right bitch, I can tell you. Made him leave home and didn't want to know him. All because..." she broke off.

"Because?" Jane persisted.

"They said he was a bit – he had mental problems. Today they call it 'learning difficulties'.

"I got that impression from a photograph. It's in a newspaper cutting. Look." Jane produced the folder from Bella's scrap book, from a document case that she carried.

Sarah examined the cutting. "Yes, I remember this, now. But I don't know where the picture came from. His mother didn't have one, so it must have come from an album we left with Betty Marsh."

"Betty Marsh?"

"He was lodging with her, and she was very good to him. She treated him like a son."

"You said his mother didn't want to know."

"That's right. It upset me very much. It was as though the drowning actually relieved her of the responsibility. You know she didn't even attend his funeral. Betty arranged that and it was paid for out of some special church fund."

"But you did meet his mother?"

"Oh yes. She came for a day. We, the Constabulary, chauffeured her around, and paid for one night's stay at the inn there."

"The Huntsman?"

"That's right. She lived somewhere in Yorkshire. She came over for a day between the death and the funeral. Couldn't get back quickly enough and never even said thank you.   We weren't supposed to show much emotion in the force, but I couldn't help it. I wept afterwards."

"The fact that my mother kept that material so safely has made me wonder whether William was my father, Sara, and I need to know the truth. I need some certainty."

"I should think it's hardly possible now, Jane."

"Is there no way?   Forensic records or anything?"

"No. Nothing like that was ever held in those days. It might be different today, but we're talking forty years ago. And anyway, nothing is kept that long."

"But do you think....I mean, the way he was, would he have been..?"

"I think you should consider the matter more from your mother's side, Jane.   Is it likely that she would have wanted any relationship with a nineteen year old man, the way he was? You know your mother?"

"She had some strange ideas, strange emotions and they might just have 'hit it off', as they say, but...I don't know. Honestly I don't Sara.   There's one thing I am certain of, though. He would never have been able to take any advantage of her. My mother was strong, mentally and physically."

"I remember how this came about," said Sara. "There was another girl - only a schoolgirl - who said something about him. I think she told her friends that he'd made her pregnant. Actually, she wasn't pregnant at all, it was all fantasy."

"Dangerous though, for him. It would be rape, I presume?"

"Certainly it would. But it was nonsense. I interviewed the girl, and she admitted the lie. I gave her a good reprimand, I can tell you."

"So you don't think there was anything like that between them?"

"No. I'm certain. She said that the girls laughed at him."

"Do you remember her name?"

"I might, if I think hard enough. Mind you, she married later. There'll be someone who knows her name. In fact Eric Brewer will know, for sure."

"He's in Portugal for a month. What about his mobile phone?"

"I haven't got his number. But there's someone else. Jenny, Jenny Gregson. I'm sure she would have been at the girl's wedding."

"And she's running a pub, in Bristol. Mr. Brewer gave me the address, but I've lost it somewhere. Stupid me." Jane was stalling. There were reasons why she preferred not to confront Jenny on the matter at all at that time.

"Can you wait until Eric returns?"

"I'll have to. But I'd like to talk to that girl. She might know what he was really like. If he was aware of women, you know, that way. He was nineteen, after all"

"Yes, but...I don't know. That there was anything between them seems so unlikely. Your mother had intellect and integrity."

They went on discussing the matter for a while, until Sara decided that it was time for lunch. She went into the kitchen, finalised the cooking and invited Jane to use the downstairs cloakroom before coming into the small dining room for the meal. Afterwards, Sara tried to find any record of the young girl that she had interviewed and given a reprimand, but she could not. Late in the afternoon, she took Jane back to the station, in time to catch the train for London. They agreed to keep in touch and Sara wished Jane every success in her quest. As Jane boarded the train, she turned and the two women embraced. They would remain friends.

* * * * *

Eric and Mabel Brewer returned from Portugal in the middle of November, but it was many days later before Eric telephoned Jane: it was on the same day that Simon had to cross the Atlantic for a meeting in Washington. As a result, Jane was forced to postpone Eric's invitation to visit him in Malvern. She did, however, ask him if he remembered the incident with the young schoolgirl and William Tudge. "Oh yes," he said. "That was Karen Dinnet. Stupid little madam. Mind you, her father was a rum 'un, too. I'm sure she got it all from him."

"You don't know her married name, do you? Or where she is now?" There was a silence while Eric pondered.

"Well, I can see the lad, now, cheeky young sod. Always up to no good. I've probably got his name in one of my old note books, but I've stuck those away somewhere in our attic. I'll have to do a search. Take a day or two, though."

"That's all right. But if it's going to be a trouble…"

"No. None at all. Leave it with me and I'll get back to you, Jane." Then they terminated the call, and Jane waited for four days. Nevertheless, when Eric did phone again, after explaining that the delays had been caused by being unable to trace the appropriate box among the many that had been deposited in his attic, he was able to tell Jane that Karen had married Alf Gurteen – a surname that rang an immediate bell in Jane's mind, although she didn't just know what that bell was.

"I've heard that surname recently," she said. "But I can't think exactly where."

"At Clough Top?" he asked, trying to be helpful.

"Well, possibly."

"You don't hear it everyday, mind."

"No, you don't. 'Gurteen'," she pondered.

"You might try the Prison Service. I reckon he'll be on their books."

"You think so?"

"I'd be very surprised if he wasn't Did Sara mention the name, do you think?" Jane had told him that she'd been to see Sara.

"I can't recall her doing so But I'm certain it's popped up somewhere. Anyway, I'll have to think about it. And we're all going up to Clough Top sometime over Christmas, so something might jog my memory In any case, I can make some enquiries while I'm up there."

"Try the Phone Book," suggested Brewer.

"Of course. That's the first port of call," replied Jane, anxious not to appear foolish. But then she added, skittishly, "There might even be a number for him in prison."

"More than likely," agreed Brewer. "The way they're pampered in there, these days. Anyway, give my regards to the old place - Clough Top -. Did my apprenticeship there, you know, and I still remember it with affection."

"I'll do that," Jane promised. Brewer also renewed his invitation for her to visit him in Malvern. She said she'd love to, but it would have to be after the busyness of the Christmas season, by which time she might have other interesting things to report.

* * * * *

Shortly before Christmas, Simon had another conference to attend, which took him to Rome again for five days.   He returned in time for a church carol service – one that the family had gone to for many years, so that it had become a tradition.   The family spent Christmas Day together, although this year, for the very first time, they were joined by 'Rupe', Sally's boyfriend, Rupert.   On the day after Boxing Day, the family set off for Clough Top, although Rupe was unable to accompany them, in spite of a pressing and sincere invitation to do so.   Sally came reluctantly, but she determined in her own mind that this would be the last time that she would.   They arrived in the late afternoon, settled into the bungalow and were welcomed enthusiastically once more by Mavis and Stanley Fish, with whom, of course, the girls would be accommodated – Simon used the word 'billeted', but Jane implored him never to say it in anyone's hearing.

By the early evening, after they had settled, refreshed themselves and dressed suitably, the four set off walking across the 'backs' to Spring Street and the Huntsman Inn, where they had reserved a table for dinner. As soon as they entered the reception area, Jane remembered that the tall, 'leggy' girl at the desk on the day of her previous visit had been wearing a name badge with the surname 'Gurteen'. At that moment, there was no sign of the young woman, and they were shown to a table by a young waiter. As Jane always kept Simon abreast of developments, she told him about Miss Gurteen. "We can make some enquiries later, then," he said. "But come on now, love, I'm getting hungry, and so are the girls, I expect." When they were halfway through the meal, the handsome girl came into the room, and crossed to consult someone at a table on the far side. Even Simon's eyes grew wider as he noticed her.

"There she is," whispered Jane. "That's the lady I spoke to. I really must see her."

"We'll attract her attention when she's finished there," he said, eagerly anticipating the prospect of a closer encounter himself, and as she returned across the floor, he caught her eye and beckoned her to come over to them.

"Is everythin' all right, sir, madam?" she asked apprehensively, looking from one to the other. They could see the name badge pinned to her dress *'HEATHER GURTEEN'.*

"Oh yes, fine, thank you. It's just that my wife has noticed your name, and she has something she'd like to ask you. Do you mind?" They could see the look of bewilderment on the girl's face, for how could Jane have read the name badge from at least forty feet, which was the nearest she had been to their table.

"I came here a few months ago and we spoke then. I thought I remembered your name. It is Miss Gurteen?"

"Aye, that's correct, madam. 'Ow can I 'elp?"

"I'm rather anxious to find a Mrs. Karen Gurteen. She married a man called Alf."

"That's me mam an' dad. They only live a few doors down. Why d' yer want....?"

"I'd like to talk to your mother about something that happened here in Clough Top a long time ago. A young man was drowned." The girl eyed Jane suspiciously.

"I 'eard summat about that," she said. "It were a bit queer by all accounts. I'm sure me mam knaws nowt about it. Before 'er time, I think."

"Not quite," said Jane. "She was a schoolgirl. I'm certain she'll remember it."

"Well, yer can ask her, like. Bit late now, though. They'll be watchin' telly, an' then they'll be off to bed."

"No, that's all right. We're here for a few days. We're at the bungalow on Fell Lane."

"Yer mean Bella Warrington's old place?"

"Yes. Bella was my mother."

"Yer don't say? Well, yer can call to see me mam anytime termorrer. Number Thirty-two. I'll tell 'er."

"Well thank you so much, Miss Gurteen. I will certainly call tomorrow." Heather Gurteen moved away and Simon could find no legitimate excuse to detain her, although Jane sensed that he would have liked to try In a strange way she was interested to know that he still had an eye for a pretty girl.

* * * * *

" 'E were a reet daft little feller, were William," Karen Gurteen told Jane, as they sat together in the main room of the cottage. " 'E used ter live 'ere, yer knaw. In this 'ouse."

"Did he? So this was Betty Marsh's home?" Jane recalled that Sara had told her about Betty Marsh and that William had lodged with her.

"Aye, that's reet. We took eet over, rented eet laak, when she went into th'ome in Macclesfield. 'Course, she's bin dead now for...oh, Lord knows. Years, must be. Our 'Eather slept in th' same room as 'im. The one at the back."

"I think I can just remember Betty. But I've been away from the village for well over twenty years."

"I can remember yer, thaw. Aye, little Jane Warrington. Allus playin' around 'ere somewhere."

Karen Gurteen had grown fat, and she just slumped in a large, old, well-worn easy chair by the fire grate of her room. An open, coal fire burned, almost scorching her large, bare legs. She had moved a pile of papers from an upright chair so that Jane could sit down. The room was untidy, cluttered with books, papers, magazines, junk mail, ornaments, cheap-looking pictures, some family photographs – Jane recognised one of Heather in school uniform, and one of a much younger looking Karen and a little man with a bald head and gaps between his teeth, which were revealed by a somewhat awkward grin. 'No doubt that's Alf', she thought. Jane returned to her main subject. "How well did you know this William Tudge?" she enquired

"Aye well, no-one knew 'im much, laak, ya knaw what I mean? 'E kept 'iself to iself, like, ya know. Proper loner 'e were. Weird really."

"How did he get on with girls?"

"Girls? Na, 'e were frighted of 'em. We reckoned anything in a skirt an' 'e'd run a mile. 'Cept Betty Marsh, o' course. 'E loved 'er laak, an' she loved 'im – as a mother an' son, laak. Nothin' more of course. No 'anky panky' laak."

"Well, she was an older lady. wasn't she? You wouldn't expect anything improper. I wasn't suggesting…."

"An' she were a churchgoer, an' so were William. But I don't reckon 'e even knew much about women, not in that way, any road."

"You see," continued Jane, "I've heard it suggested that he could have been my father. I'm trying to get at the truth."

"Oh, luv, I've 'eard that one years ago. Bloody 'ell, don't you believe it. 'E wouldn't, and yer mam wouldn't, not wi' 'im. 'Ooever put that one around were dafter than 'e were. Don't believe it, luv. It's just not true."

"I need to be sure," said Jane.

"Look, some bloody stupid girl said she'd bin wi' William – yer know – 'ad sex like, an' she were in th' family way, yer knaw."

"She said she was having his child?"

"It were all made up; showin' off, bravado. She'd made it all up. Bloody little idiot."

"How old was the girl?" Of course, Jane had already heard the story from Sara, but she wanted to emphasise a point.

"Goin' on fifteen. Knew damn all about it at that age."

"She was under age. William would have been arrested."

"Aye. They would 'ave done 'im fer rape."

"Mind you, she would have been subjected to one or two very intrusive examinations as well, you know. She'd hardly enjoy those. But they'd need to prove it."

"Well, any road, it were all fantasy, laak I say. She were just tellin' lies."

"That still doesn't prove that he wasn't my father."

"Well, yer can think what yer like, luv. But yer've asked me what I think, and I think 'no'. An' if I'm wrong, well all I can say is yer mam must've bin stupid."

"Or compassionate," Jane suggested. "She had some pretty unorthodox views and ways."

"It still just don't seem right ter me, luv   I can't see it at all. Not yer mam an' 'im. Neh!"   Then Jane was just about to leave the matter when Karen completely surprised her. "Tell you what, though, luv. There was plenty of other fellers around 'oo it might've bin yer knaw. Even though me own dad swore 'e'd never bin near 'er – didn't even know 'er – me mam was never certin." Karen laughed, "Ee, luv," she said. "You an' me might be bloody sisters.   Me dad often said I might 'ave a siblin' somewhere."

Inside, Jane shuddered at the thought, but she asked: "Look. We might be able to prove or disprove that. Are your parents still living?"

"Not as yer'd know. Well, 'E drank 'iself ter death, two years since – well, drink an' smoke. Bloody cancer. An' me mum's in the sikey, sikey …"

"A psychiatric hospital?" Jane suggested.

"Well, I call it the 'Loony Ward', in Manchester. She's as daft as a brush now. 'Onestly she is."

"But I suppose you've got photographs of them?" Jane glanced around the room, but she couldn't see any that might be of either parent.

"There's one of me dad, somewhere. Upstairs, I think. 'Ang on, I'll 'ave a luke fer it."

"Are you sure it's no trouble?"

"No trouble at all, luv. Actually, there might be a better one, or one of 'em both. I'll 'ave a luke." Then Karen shuffled off upstairs, and Jane could hear movements, drawers being opened and closed, other noises, until, after a short time, Karen shuffled back into the room, holding several photographs. "'Ere we are, luv," she said, handing them to Jane before slumping back into her chair and raising a cushion, already covered in hairs, to the back of her head. "Now, that's me dad. 'E was quite tall an' 'mucsular' yer know. Quite a big feller." Jane looked at the picture and recognised the man.

"Oh, yes. I remember him, now. I used to see him in the street. I think I was frightened of him, a bit."

"Nay 'e'd never 'arm yer, luv. Belted me a time or two when I was young, an' I probly deserved it. But never anyone outside the famly. Not women, any road. An' that's me mam. She were better in them days."

"Yes, I remember her, too. She used to come into the shop, you know, Alice's."

"Blimey, aye. Yer remember Alice? She were a good un, she were. She used ter give me sweets, yer knaw."

"And me, too. You would wonder how she ever made a profit."

"She didn't out o' me, any road. But she were a good soul. Still livin' I think."

"Yes, somewhere in Wales." Jane looked at the other pictures that Karen had produced, but said she could see no resemblance between anyone and herself. Then she thanked Karen for the chat, handed the pictures back, and was soon saying 'Goodbye' at the cottage door. Then she set off back along the street and called in at the shop to make a few purchases. She chatted to the shopkeeper again, before making her way across the 'backs' to the bungalow once more.

oooooOooooo

CHAPTER NINETEEN

A number of weeks passed by before Jane was able to accept Eric Brewer's invitation to visit him at Malvern. Actually, the house was in the countryside, some miles from the town, and even outside the nearest village. It was the time of the year when a plethora of snowdrops and crocuses was infusing the first bright new colours into the banks and verges at the sides of the lanes, when the first green tracery could be distinguished in the hedgerows, and occasionally, the sun broke through the grey clouds to lighten the scene and add a little warmth to the chilly atmosphere. Jane's car sped along the M4 from London, crossed to the M5, and arrived at the nearest village. Here, despite Brewer's directions, she had to make enquiries, but finally she found the high, lane-side brick wall, and swung the car though the open gateway and into the enclosed cobbled courtyard, from which a few wide steps led up to the main door of the house. At one side of the courtyard, a stable block had been converted into garages. Mabel and Eric Brewer greeted her at the door, and took her through the wide hallway and into a large, bright, airy lounge, with windows that looked across the rear garden.

Mabel took Jane's coat and gloves and went out to prepare a pot of tea; they would collect her overnight luggage from the car a little later. Jane sank into a very restful armchair and closed her eyes for a few moments. Brewer stood near the window. He had aged now, put on weight and lost most of his hair. In fact his bald head was shiny and there were just small patches of hair on both sides and at the back above the line of his shirt collar. He could see that Jane was tired. "Difficult journey?" he asked.

"Difficult enough," said Jane. "No real problems, just traffic everywhere."

"And always in a hurry, too. I know what it's like. Some idiots drive as though there's no tomorrow. Well, you take it easy for a bit. Mabel will soon have some tea ready." And soon Mabel did return, pushing a serving trolley with tea pot, cups and saucers, milk, sugar, and plates for cake and biscuits. Mabel had become a stout little woman, her short hair was going grey now, and she dressed sensibly, though still quite stylishly. Gratefully,

Jane enjoyed the refreshments and afterwards she was conducted to a room, with en-suite bathroom that was reserved for guests, and Brewer carried her overnight case from the car. Finally, alone for a while, she admired the lovely view across a side garden and over open countryside: pastureland that seemed to roll out into the distance, beyond which, faintly, she could see a range of hills. She knew that these would be the Brecon Beacons and the Black Mountain range. Then she rested.

Dinner was at seven. Jane, suitably attired and quite refreshed, came down for the meal. Eventually, the conversation turned to Clough Top. "You went to see Mrs. Gurteen, then?" Brewer asked.

"Yes. She lives in the house where Betty Marsh was."

"They took that, did they? Did you see Alf?"

"No. She said he was out."

"Probably at the bookies. Unless he was 'helping the police with enquiries'. Rum little bugger."

"Eric!" Mabel was angry.

"Well, he was. Always up to something. The lead off Furness Bridge Parish Church went one night. He'd been down there, I knew he had. 'It wasn't me, Mr. Brewer, I've never bin near the Church', he said. A fortnight later we found them flogging it down in Birmingham. But no-one would say where it came from or who passed it on, but I knew. It had Alf Gurteen's name all over it."

"But you never proved that, did you, Eric?" Mabel remarked.

"No. But I knew it was him all right. I'd have liked to nail him there and then, that I would."

"He's produced a lovely daughter, anyway," said Jane. "She's the receptionist at the Huntsman. Even made my husband sit up and take notice – and that's saying something. Usually he doesn't show much interest, but she certainly got him going." Both Eric and Mabel Brewer raised their eyebrows at this – was Jane so naïve? – but they just smiled, and the conversation continued.

After the meal, they went into the lounge, where Mabel served coffee. Then Brewer asked Jane if she minded that he smoked a cigarette. Jane did not mind. "I wish to goodness he'd give that up though, Jane," Mabel said. "It's not doing him any good at all. I've told him often enough."

"Over fifty years I've been smoking now, love, and I'm still as healthy as ever. And look at Jim Gregson. He's probably smoked longer than me and still keeps going. It's just his eyesight, that's all. He'll be off down to Devon any time now, first of several holidays he has down there every summer, lucky old sod. And he'll be going on for ninety now, you know."

"Lucky? Devon?" Mabel interjected. "And you've just come back from a month in Portugal."

"Well, I wouldn't mind a few days in Devon as well, love," said Brewer, teasing her and winking at Jane.

"You're never satisfied. That's always been your trouble. You say it's a good thing in police work, but .... Anyway, Jim's not so well, Eric, either. You know that. It's not just his sight. He's having trouble walking; you said that yourself."

"Yes, but that's arthritis, that is. Nothing to do with smoking."

"Could be a contributory factor, though. He might be better off not smoking. And so would you be."

"Well, I've cut down. Used to be forty a day. Now it's about twenty."

"Still twenty too many," Mabel insisted.

"It's the best I can do at the moment, love. Sorry."

After coffee, both Mabel and Eric insisted that Jane continued to relax while they washed up   Eric quipped that they did have a dishwasher, and it was himself.   Then Mabel went to a separate room to watch a television serial that she was following and Eric returned to Jane.   "Now then," he said.   "What else has this investigation of yours thrown up, Jane? You saw Karen Gurteen. Then what?"

"Well, nothing else really, Eric. I think my next step will be to see Mr. Gregson.   He would know something about William. He employed him, didn't he?"

"In a manner, I suppose he did.   But the lad was very erratic, you see.   Never worked if he didn't feel like it, and Jim only paid him coppers.   He'd not get away with that today, mind.   Not with the minimum wage and all that."

"But do you honestly think William could have been having an affair with my mother?"

Brewer gesticulated, holding both his hands in the air. "I just can't say, Jane. With respect, your mother had some funny ways, you know."

"Yes, but intellectually at least, they must have been poles apart. She might have talked to him, helped him, even tried to educate him a bit – it seems he was pretty inadequate – but beyond that – no. She wasn't stupid."

"Certainly not. But perhaps, once, things went a bit too far. The story went round, you see, and it made sense, Jane. He'd even been talking to the Vicar about – that sort of thing. Vicar went to see your mother and tried to discover the truth, but she wouldn't say anything. She would hardly want to advertise a connection with the lad. That's what I think, anyway,"

"Sara told me about your encounter with William, when he talked about a leprechaun."

"Yes. Well, that was how he was. Simple."

"Exactly. Simple. Not really a man of the world?"

"It doesn't follow, Jane. That was a year or two earlier. He'd grown out of that, soon afterwards. I only christened him 'the Leprechaun' for fun. I'm sorry it stuck. Actually, I don't even know how he got the word into his head. Irish folklore or something, isn't it?"

"His father was Irish. Sara told me."

"Oh well, that explains it. He must have got it from his dad."

They went on discussing the subject for a while, and soon Brewer agreed that Jane should try to see Jim Gregson, who, he admitted, probably knew William best. "The trouble is, like Mabel says, Jim isn't very well these days, and he soon gets confused," he said. "But he might know something."

"I'd like to talk to him alone," said Jane. "I know he's with Jenny, in Bristol. You gave me the address, remember? It's a pub, isn't it?"

"That's right. In a bit of a rough area, but they seem to like it and they're doing well."

"You say he goes to the seaside quite a lot. The place in Devon?"

"Same one every time. A small hotel where they know him and look after him. He pays well, mind. But it seems to do him good. He'll be off down there in a week or two, I'll bet. So if you want to catch him in Bristol, you'd better ring Jenny, pronto."

"I might have to leave it for the moment, though. All sorts of things are happening with the family at home just now and Simon has to be abroad such a lot. I'll ring Jenny when I'm ready."

"Shall I tell her that? I usually ring her once a fortnight, unless she rings me first."

"No, say nothing yet, please, but if you hear that he's going away, you can let me know. Then I can regard that period as out. Ok?"

Eric Brewer agreed to this, although he was a little puzzled by Jane's hesitation. But he said nothing. Soon, Mabel returned, glasses of sherry were consumed until finally, it was time to go to bed. Jane gratefully went to her room and eventually enjoyed a good night's sleep.

After breakfast the next morning, Brewer insisted on showing Jane around his garden. At the rear of the house, a long lawn stretched right to the boundary, marked by a low hedge, and Jane noticed that, at the top end, near to the house, a small patch had been built up to form a teeing ground. A box of golf balls was close by and two or three clubs , or 'irons', were propped against the house wall. "My practice ground," said Brewer. And when they reached the other end of the lawn, Jane could see a small gate in the hedge, through which he could gain access to the open land beyond and so retrieve any balls that he managed to pitch so far.   The rest of the garden was traditional, with herbaceous borders, stocked with quality plants and bushes.

Jane's expertise in horticulture impressed Brewer, especially as she had learned many of the Latin names from her mother, and the pair discussed some of the plants knowledgeably She was rather surprised to learn that he had even risked 'smuggling' one or two cuttings of rare varieties from foreign countries, after golfing trips, but she told herself that, as a policeman, he knew what he was doing. When she ventured to ask for a few cuttings for her own garden, he willingly obliged.   There was an area at one side of the house devoted to growing vegetables and, on the other side, a less formal area where Mabel had a washing line and plants grew in pots and small tubs. Brewer also took Jane to see the outhouses across the entrance yard; these consisted of a garage for at least two cars, tool sheds, potting sheds, junk sheds and a small laundry fitted with washing machine, dryers and an ironing room.   Jane realised that the Brewers had quite a nice property here and it was of considerable value. From being a humble police constable of forty years ago, Eric Brewer had done well for himself.

Helpfully, Mabel served an early lunch, after which, Jane said her 'thanks' and 'goodbyes', and before long she was driving back along the motorway towards London and home. An addition to her overnight case was a small bag of plant cuttings.

* * * * *

It was only ten days later when Brewer phoned Jane. "Just thought you should know that Jim Gregson's going down to Devon next week.   Going for about a fortnight."

"Right," said Jane. "Thanks, I'll bear that in mind."

"Not been in touch with Jenny yet, then?"

"No, not yet.   Two teenage daughters and a husband have kept me pretty busy lately.   But I will get round to it when Mr. Gregson comes back."   Jane was actually telling a lie, but she wanted no-one, not even Eric

Brewer, to know what she was up to. Then she asked him, "Where did you say he's going to?"

"Devon. The place he always goes. I've got the details here somewhere." Jane could hear him searching through papers before he exclaimed, "Torbridge. That's the place, The Cliff Private Hotel, Torbridge. They know him there, and they look after him. He certainly enjoys it and it seems to do him good."

"Well, that's the main thing. By the way, you've not said anything to Jenny, have you? About my interest?"

"No. But you might do well to speak to her, Jane. She knew William as well."

"Yes, I will speak to her. Just leave it to me."

"Right," he said. Jane thanked him again, sent her love to Mabel, and the conversation ended. Immediately after receiving the information from Brewer, she booked a room at the Cliff Private Hotel, Torbridge, for three nights during the following week. She made arrangements for the girls and Simon to manage without her for those few days and, when the time arrived, she set off again, down to the little seaside village and the hotel on the cliff.

* * * * *

Old Jim Gregson accepted Jane's invitation to take a ride in her car. It took some time for him to get ready after lunch on the following day. Georgina brought him to the car in a wheelchair, with the whole operation being closely monitored by Mrs. Ponsonby herself. Finally, he was in the front seat, with the seat belt fastened, and Jane drove away, up the drive, onto the steep lane down to the village and off along the coast road. Soon she turned inland and, within half an hour, they were in the area of lush farmland that skirts the edge of Dartmoor.

Jane stopped at the side of a lane, suggesting that Jim should open the car door, so that he could smell the country air, the scent of new grass, almost ready for hay-making, the early hawthorn flowering in the hedgerows, nettles in the lane side bank, and other scents from the foliage. Birds were singing, twittering, coo-ing, there was the faint sound of a tractor from two or three fields away, and a gentle breeze freshening the springtime air. Jim could hardly see now, but he could smell and hear the familiar sounds of the countryside, sounds and smells he had not known for many years, and he was overwhelmed with the joy of it. Jane noticed that he felt for a handkerchief in this pocket and wiped tears from his eyes. "Eh, lass," he said. "This takes me back a good few yeer."

"I thought it would," said Jane. "They said you'd been a farmer."

"Aye. Many years since. I've bin wi' me daughter in Bristol for a long time now. Goin' on thirty yeer. In the city! Often I wonder if it were reet for me, but she needed money an' I promised it, laak."

"Well, at least you've been able to help her, and I'm sure she'll be very grateful."

"Aye," was all he said in reply.

After a little while, Jane asked him; "Now, how about afternoon tea? I'm sure we'll find a cafe, somewhere."

They found a country café with a tea garden, and Jane was able to park close enough for him to walk a few steps, with her aid, to a vacant table. They ordered tea with clotted cream and scones. Jim insisted on paying the bill. It was all enjoyable, but the poor old man had some difficulty with the scone, so Jane cut it small for him. The cream was difficult as well, so she assisted him again, using several extra serviettes for his mouth. At last, with all achieved and enjoyed, they returned to the car. When Jane headed back for the hotel, Jim fell asleep and remained so throughout the journey.

After breakfast the next morning, Jane was due to leave the hotel and return to London. Jim had already gone into the sun lounge by the time she was ready and when she had put her luggage in the car and paid her account, she went to say goodbye. Even then, he seemed a little confused as to who she was, but when Georgina explained that it was the lady who took him out in her car yesterday, he said, "Oh aye. We went t' th' farmland. I enjoyed tha'."

"Goodbye, Mr. Gregson," said Jane. She offered her hand. He took it and kissed it.

"Aye, luv. An' thanks." Jane walked away, and as she passed through the reception area, Mrs. Ponsonby met her. "Goodbye, Mrs. Lomax. And thank you for your kindness. I'm sure the little outing did Mr. Gregson a world of good. It was most thoughtful and kind."

"It was my pleasure, Mrs. Ponsonby. The old gentleman seemed so lonely."

"I shall tell his daughter, when she comes to take him home," said Mrs. Ponsonby.

"By all means," said Jane. "Although I would prefer to remain anonymous. Please don't disclose my name. The family might feel obliged in some way, and that is quite unnecessary."

"If that is your wish, madam, of course. Guest confidentiality is paramount. But thank you, again." Jane went to her car and began the long drive back to London.

* * * * *

Soon after her first meeting in Wilmslow with Sara Hardisty, Jane began to investigate the possible use of forensics in an attempt to identify her natural father by means of DNA profiling. She knew that this would be extremely difficult, probably impossible, in the case of William Tudge, but she felt that the elimination of other possibilities could increase the likelihood that it was him. Through a friend and near neighbour, she also made contact with a laboratory in London where a department was now dedicated to this type of research, often in conjunction with the Police Forensic Science Service. She visited the laboratory, met its Director, Dr. Cranston, and asked for their help in her investigation. Without any prompting, they agreed to assist and, in return, Jane promised a handsome donation to the laboratory funds. She insisted on, and received, assurances of complete confidentiality in the matter and that all material submitted for analysis, together the resulting compositions, would be destroyed immediately after the verification of results. She was instructed to submit samples for testing, labelled in accordance with any code she wished to invent, so that identities would be known to her alone. Dr. Mary Paschard was assigned to her, and this very nice, gentle, 'quiet' little girl was to be her permanent contact.

On her return to London, she took three samples to Mary. The first, which she labelled as 'Red 1', was a few small stands of hair, gathered from the head cushion that Karen Gurteen had used on the day of Jane's visit. She had obtained these while Karen was upstairs searching for her family photographs. Jane hoped that at least one of the strands would be of sufficient length and have enough of the root to be viable. The second, labelled 'Green 2', was the butt of a half smoked cigarette, discarded by Eric Brewer during that evening of her visit to Malvern. The third, 'Blue 3', was a paper serviette, soaked in spittle, which she retained from the afternoon tea with Jim Gregson. She had already submitted sufficient samples from her own body for easy comparison and possible matching. Mary took the samples and told Jane to expect the results in a few days.

To be truthful, Jane was not at all pleased that it had been necessary to be so devious. Karen, she imagined, and rightly so, could not have cared less and probably would have gladly submitted her own samples for analysis. After all, it was she who placed her own father in the frame, but Jane still considered secrecy to be the best option. As a former senior police officer, Eric Brewer might have objected, but Jane had a suspicion that, given an opportunity, an ex-marital liaison would not have been beyond him, in spite of his apparent devotion to Mabel. And Jim Gregson, a farmer with whom Bella would have had regular contact, was, she thought, worth testing, if only for the sake of a negative result. But it was for this reason that Jane avoided making contact with Jenny in Bristol. Awkward questions might have been asked, the answers would have needed to be lies, and lies were what she always preferred never to tell. For Jane, the need for some certainty outweighed any moral objection, and she had done everything possible to ensure absolute confidentiality and anonymity. The results would justify her devious means.

Dr. Mary Paschard phoned after several days. "Would you like to come to the lab? I've got the results."

"Would I like to come?" Jane always thought that such rhetorical questions were rather absurd. It really meant 'Will you come?' and, yes she was dying to come for the results. She went straight away.

Sitting in her little office, Mary passed an envelope across the desk to Jane, who opened it excitedly. "I feel like my daughters receiving their exam results," she declared.

She read. *'Sample one. Red. Negative. No match. Sample two. Green. Negative. No Match   Sample three. Blue. Positive. Absolute match. The person providing this sample and the person providing the main comparative sample will be closely related'.*

"Is there any margin for error?" Jane enquired.

"About three million to one.   There was a bit of a problem with the strands of hair, but we found enough to produce a definitive result," replied Mary.

"Then I know now the identity of my natural father."   Tears came into her eyes as the remembered him: struggling with the scone and cream in the garden café in Devon, sitting motionless in the sun lounge at the Cliff Private Hotel, and then kissing her hand, gratefully, on the morning of her departure.   Jane had hoped, that his age, physical condition, his deteriorating eyesight and the passage of years, meant that he really did not know who she was, then, yet there was still the possibility that the old chap was aware of her, but wisdom had taught him to keep the pretence.   Nevertheless, there was no doubt that the sample had identified Jim Gregson, and he had known Bella Warrington, her mother, more intimately than anyone in Clough Top had ever realised.

oooooOooooo

CHAPTER TWENTY

Mavis and Stanley Fish had gone out in their little car for the day. It was warm and sunny in late summer. They returned in time for tea and Stanley left the car on the track in front of their bungalow. He had built himself a garage at the far end of the property and the access from Fell Lane had been improved, partly by the Council and partly by Stanley himself - actually, the Council men had left a pile of stone and tarmac nearby and tipped the wink to him that it was 'surplus to requirements'. The couple watched television for a while in the evening, and then, while Mavis made supper, Stanley went out to put the car away. He returned with an expression that indicated bewilderment. "Mave" he said. "There's a light on next door."

"Is theer? At Jane's? Well that's strange. She allus phones first if they're coomin' up, just to let me knaw, laak. Are yer sure, Stan?"

"Well, you go an' look, then. I'm certain there is."

Mavis went to look and, yes, sure enough, there were lights on in both the sitting room and the bedroom.

The couple pondered over the situation.   Not wanting to intrude, they wondered if Jane had tried to phone while they were out, but then they found that there was no message on the answering service.   Still they were uneasy.   Suppose it was intruders?   Burglars?   They were responsible in a way, although Jane had never imposed any formal 'guardianship' upon them.   Finally, unable to settle, Stanley went round to Jane's bungalow and tapped on the front door.   It was opened by Sally.   "Oh, Sally," he said. "It's you.   We noticed th' light, an' …."

"Uncle Stanley, I'm so sorry.   Mum told me to phone you, and I forgot," Sally said, and she kissed him.   "We got here late this afternoon, and you were out.   We've been for a meal at the Huntsman."

"Well, now we know it's you, that's all…"

"Come in a minute, Uncle Stanley, I want you to meet someone."

She was wearing jeans and a blue and white striped top that had a V neck.   Her feet were bare.   She took Stanley by the hand and led him into the sitting room.   A young man sat there, similarly dressed to Sally in jeans and an open-necked shirt.   His feet were also bare.   "Now,

Uncle Stanley," said Sally. "This is Rupe, my boyfriend. We're here just for a couple of days." Rupe stood up and offered his hand, which Stanley shook.

"Hi," said Rupe.

" 'Ello son," Stanley just managed to say.

"Uncle Stanley, I really am sorry I forgot to phone. And as I said, you weren't in when we arrived."

"No, we've bin out for a run in th' car. Mavis enjoys that."

"I'm sure she does. Did you go somewhere nice?"

"Just round th' lanes a bit. The countryside's lovely at this time o't year."

"Yes, it is." said Sally. Then she added, "Oh, Uncle Stanley. Rupe's left his car on the verge at the end of the track – where Daddy usually parks. Will it be all right there?"

"Aye, we've all parked there up to lately, you know. But now there's proper access and I've got a garage. You can put it in front 'ere, if you want." He instinctively addressed Sally, rather than Rupe. Then he added, "So long as you leave room for me to get out if I need to. There's enough space."

"I'll look at that tomorrow, then," said Rupe. "Might as well stay where it is tonight."

"Aye, right. Well, anythin' else you want, Sally? I mean, em…"

"No, we're fine, thank you, Uncle Stanley. But do tell Aunt Mavis I'm sorry I didn't phone. And we'll see you tomorrow. Ok?"

"Aye. Night then. Both!" The pair said 'goodnight' and Stanley returned to his own bungalow.

Mavis had supper almost ready when he came in, and she was eager to know what he had found. "It's young Sally," he told her. "Come up this afternoon."

"Oh, that's nice. Is she all right?"

"Aye. Sends 'er apologies. Jane told 'er to phone us, and she said she forgot."

"Well, they don't allus remember things like that, at 'er age."

"She's not by 'erself."

"Oh, 'as Emma come as well? Lovely!"

"It isn't Emma. It's a young feller. 'Er boyfriend, she says." There was silence for a moment. Mavis handed a mug of hot milk to Stanley and placed some biscuits on a low table near the fire. She took her own mug and they both sat down.

"Well, she'll knaw 'er own mind. She's old enough."

"I thought as she might want our spare room again, but..."

"Yer didn't offer it?"

"No, but - I mean – there's not another room. The spare one is still Bella's office. It's not changed, 'as it?"

"They won't want no spare room or no spare bed, Stan, you daft 'apporth."

"You mean they'll be sharin' the same....?"

" 'Course. And it'll not be th' first time. Sally's almost twenty."

"But they're not wed."

"Were we, th' first time?"

"We were going to be married, though, weren't we? 'Ow long was our weddin' after? Six weeks?"

"Did you get 'is name?"

"Rupe. I spose that's short for Rupert. Do yer think Jane'll know?"

"Knaw what?"

"Well….you know."

"That Sally's wi' a lad? I should think so."

"But don't you think she'd mind? Worry?"

"If she did, I'm certin' that Jane would have enough gumption to keep quiet abart it.   Girls like Sally wouldn't want no interference in a matter of that sort."

"But she could give 'er advice on things. Like – you know?"

"Family plannin'? Eh, but I reckon Sally will 'ave sorted all that out already. She an' – what's 'is name? – Rupe."   But Mavis knew that in the year or so that Sally and Emma had been coming up and using their spare room, Stanley had regarded them as nieces, if not daughters, perhaps substitutes for the children that she herself had never been able to give him. So he never would have, consciously at least, envisaged the day when someone else, another man, would come between him and either of them. But now that day had arrived. Sally had fallen in love and she was in a relationship. The whole prospect for him had changed instantly.   Soon enough he would realise that even fathers cannot hold on to their daughters for always; life and nature itself sees to that.   But this was something new for Stanley and he would have to get used to it. Only in Stanley's case, it would take a little time.

Quite early the next morning, there was a knock on their front door and Mavis went to open it. Sally was standing there, holding hands with a young man whom Mavis assumed was 'Rupe'. Both wore shorts, Sally's turned up by about two inches, exposing even more of her beautifully proportioned and well shaped legs. Sally's soft, almost transparent blouse too, allowed glimpses of her cleavage, and the roundness of her breasts beneath. Her honey-coloured hair hung loosely onto her shoulders and there was only the slightest evidence of the application of lipstick. Rupe wore a sports shirt; he had black hair, cropped very short, and, like Sally, he wore trainer shoes.

"My, Sally, 'ello luv. 'Ow are ya? Come in, both of ya. Do." The couple entered the bungalow. "Yer Uncle Stanley's still shavin' in th' bathroom, but I don't expect 'e'll be that long."

"Hello, Aunt Mavis," said Sally, as she kissed her.

"I've brought my boyfriend to meet you. This is Rupe." Mavis held out her hand, which Rupe shook.

"'Ello, Rupe," she said.

"Hi," the young man responded. "Pleased to meet you. Sally's told me a lot about you."

"Well I 'ope at least some of it were good," said Mavis.

"All of it. Nothing but praise. And no doubt richly deserved."

"Oh, I don't know abart that," Mavis said coyly. Then she added "Rupe? Is that short for 'Rupert?"

"Of course," replied Sally

"Then I shall call 'im Rupert, if ya don't mind. I might seem old fashioned, but... "

"Not at all," said Rupe. "Whatever you prefer. Call me 'Don Juan,' if you like. I'll not be offended"

"Now don't be silly, darling," said Sally. "You'll give Aunt Mavis quite the wrong impression. He's such a softy, Aunt Mavis, really he is."

"I'm sure," said Mavis.

"Oh, Auntie, I'm really sorry about yesterday. Mum told me to phone you, and I forgot. I'm so busy and it's all been such a rush."

"That's all right, dear. Only yer Uncle Stanley saw th' light on in th' bungalow, and we thawt it might be burglars, laak 'E couldn't rest until 'e'd bin round."

"Of course. I really should have phoned. Mum will be angry. I suppose Uncle Stanley was surprised to see us?"

"'E was relieved. If it 'ad bin burglars.... Any road, it weren't, so that's all right, luv. Now, are ya both sittin' down for a few minutes? 'E'll not be long, an' I'm sure 'e'd want to see ya. Come into th' sittin' room." They went into the room, and the couple sat together on a sofa. Mavis went to the bathroom door and called, "Stan!"

"What?" he answered back.

"It's Sally and Rupert come round. Will ya be long?"

"No. Out in a jiffy. 'Ang on."

Mavis returned to the sitting room. Sally and Rupe were holding hands again Sally asked, "When Uncle Stanley came round last night, Aunt Mavis, I expect he was quite surprised."

"'E didn't know as ya were courtin', luv."

"Yes, me and Rupe have been together for nearly a year, now. We're very much in love, aren't we, darling?" Rupe nodded enthusiastically.

"And that's all as matters, in't it, dear? Trouble us, thaw, Uncle Stanley still thinks of yer as a little girl. 'E just doesn' proply understand that ya've grown up. You're a young woman naa, and a lovely un at that."

"Thank you, Aunt Mavis." Stanley came into the room and greeted them. He kissed Sally enthusiastically, but he was a little distant with Rupe, who quite understood the older man's difficulties with the situation. In answer to their enquiries, Sally told them that she was training to be an accountant in the City of London, Rupe was a junior partner in a firm of architects, and Emma had been accepted for a degree course at Warwick University. Then Mavis asked,

"And 'ow's yer mam? 'Ow's our Jane?"

"Oh, she's very well. Recently, she discovered who her real father was. She's been trying to find that out for a long time. She's 'over the moon'."

"We thought she knew about that. We 'eard 'e were drowned in a tragic accident – 'ere, in the river below

Fell Lane End. 'Appened before she were born. That's what we 'eard," said Stanley.

"No, it wasn't him at all, Uncle Stanley. It was a local farmer. She's proved it with a D.N.A. match." Both Mavis and Stanley had heard of D.N.A., but neither of them knew exactly what it was and they were too embarrassed to ask. "But Mum's still curious about something. The drowning incident."

"But if the lad weren't 'er father?" asked Mavis.

"There was still something odd about it. No-one knows exactly how the accident happened. But Mum thinks that Grandma kept journals, year after year, and they might give some clues. She's only found one, though. The one Grandma was writing just before she died."

"As she's not found th' rest, then?" asked Stanley.

"No. But they must be somewhere, Uncle Stanley. Mum thinks they're probably in a newspaper archive somewhere. But where?"

"How about your grandma's loft?"

"Loft!" exclaimed Sally.

"Your grandma had a loft put in th' bungalow roof, several years back. Didn't your mother know about that?"

"She's never mentioned it, Uncle Stanley, and she can't have known. Otherwise.... But how do you get to the loft?"

"A trap door above th' back porch. You have to lower a step ladder down from th' inside. She stored everything up there. I'll show you, if you like."

"Oh, yes please," said Sally, excitedly. "Can we do it right away?"

"'Course we can. Come on."

"You don't mind, do you, Rupe, darling?"

"No, of course I don't, Sal," he said. "Come on, let's go."

Excitement surged through Sally's veins as she walked hand-in-hand with Rupe, and alongside Stanley, back to Bella's bungalow. They went straight through to open the back door. The rear porch was closed in now by an outer door that gave access to the garden and in the small ceiling there was a trap door. Stanley found a long pole with which he pushed the trap door open. It was hinged inward: a hook on the end of the pole engaged a slot in the step ladder, which he was able to pull down to the floor with considerable ease at a steep, but not too steep, an angle. He motioned to Sally. "Want to go up first, young lady?" he asked. "Oh, there's a light switch 'ere. 'Ang on."

But even before he could press the switch, Sally's pretty young legs were climbing the ladder, and then she was there, peering through the opening in the ceiling into a long, narrow room that seemed to stretch the full length of the bungalow. It was just high enough for a person of average height to stand upright and it was lined with wooden shelves. Halfway along the room, skylight windows were set at both sides of the roof ridge, but they were rather small and the additional fluorescent tube light was very necessary. The shelves contained rows of box files, ring files and binders, books, ledgers, boxes of stationery, bound copies of several different magazines, and much other office paraphernalia. On one length of shelf there was a row of loose-leaf binders, each bearing an identical label 'Journal', and numbered 1 to 33, consecutively, without a break. Sally knew instantly that this was what Jane had been looking for. Rupe had climbed up to join her, while Stanley stayed below, somewhat anxiously watching the steps to ensure there were no accidents.   But none of them had bargained for the fact that Rupe was slightly taller than average.   As Sally reached into the pocket of her shorts to extract her mobile phone and declared, - "Darling, I must phone Mum right away.   She'll be ecstatic," - Rupe straightened himself to full height and banged his head on the roof.

"Oh, bugger!" he exclaimed.

"Darling, are you all right?" shouted Sally.

Rupe swayed a little, put his hands to his head, took a deep inhalation of breath, and replied, "Yes, I think so. But God, that hurt."

"Come on, we'll get you down. I can phone Mum later."   She went down first, allowing Stanley the pleasurable sight of her bare legs coming warily down the ladder backwards, followed slowly by poor Rupe.   Finally, when they both reached the floor, Sally said, "Go and lie on the bed for a while, darling. Go on, and I'll bring you a cup of tea."

"I'm all right, really," said Rupe, although Stanley thought he looked far from all right.

"I still think you'd better have a rest, my love. Maybe just half an hour? Go on, for me."

"All right, then," Rupe acquiesced, and as he went into the bedroom, Stanley glimpsed for a moment at the bed, with double pillows, and he was angry with himself for the twinge of disquiet that he felt then. This wasn't jealousy: he didn't love Sally in any romantic way, nor was it judgemental; he had no personal qualifications to make any judgement on grounds of morality, and anyway, Mavis's acceptance of the situation was sufficient for him. It was simply that he felt that he had lost an important part of Sally, and lost it forever.

Neither had he got anything against Rupe. The poor lad obviously had received a nasty bang on the head and he appeared to be a good, honest young man with a career in architecture in front of him. It was simply the knowledge that, as Mavis had tried to explain to him, Sally was grown up now, she had fallen in love with this man and she was having a relationship. However good that was, however natural, however delightful and acceptable it seemed, it still meant that he could no longer regard her as anything special to himself. And he had to admit, even reluctantly, that it hurt him. So he made his excuses to get back to Mavis – there was nothing more he could do there

– and left Sally to make a cup of tea for Rupe, and then phone her mother. "Well, thanks so much, Uncle Stanley. This will make the day for Mum, you know. I'll phone her in a minute. Just let me get this tea to my beloved."

Stanley just said, "Right o! Sally."

"I'll bet Mum will be up here in no time. Just wait and see."

"We'll look forward to seeing 'er, then. 'Bye for now, love." Somehow he felt that he should not kiss her this time, and he just wandered off to his own bungalow.

Rupe looked a little better when Sally delivered his tea. He did kiss her and remarked, "That was a stupid thing for me to do. I knew the damn roof was low. I just didn't think, Sal."

"Easily done, darling. But you'd better rest up for a while. Go on, now. And I'll phone Mum."

* * * * *

Although Sally's phone call thrilled Jane exceedingly, and the time when she would get up into that loft in the bungalow roof to explore the treasures that might be hidden there could not come soon enough, she did not rush up to Clough Top right away. On the phone, she gave her daughter strict instructions to leave everything in the loft room exactly as she had found them. Nothing must be moved an inch and Sally obeyed. She had several commitments at home; Simon needed her for a day or two, and then he was off to Brussels for at least a couple of nights. Emma needed further help in her preparations for university, and Jane herself had agreed to speak at a meeting of the local Women's Institute on her objections to a major local development that was now at the planning stage, and she was reluctant to cause them problems by backing out at short notice. But even beyond these considerations, there was something more. There is a part of human nature that enjoys a challenge, enjoys the process of solving problems, so that once the problem is solved, it is no longer there and one can feel bereft, alone, abandoned, and perhaps sub-consciously, Jane felt this now. She knew that once she was able to read whatever her mother had recorded in those journals, probably all would be resolved, over, finished. Her problem would not be there any longer. Desperate though she was to know what actually happened – assuming of course that Bella had recorded it all – there was a small part of her that wanted to cling on to the problem. It was like having an old friend, and knowing that soon the friend will go, and will be gone forever. She found herself almost wanting to postpone the inevitable. But there was something else, too, something unidentifiable, telling her not to go up yet, although she hardly knew it was there, and even less clearly could she define it. Still, problem or not, bereavement following its resolution or not, the unidentifiable something telling her to delay or not, the day came when all was ready. Emma was having a few days of rest and relaxation, Simon was home, though still going to his office each day, and Sally was spending most of her time with Rupe, even sleeping at his flat on many nights each week, a fact that Jane had given up worrying about many months ago. So Jane prepared for her departure on a particular day. All was ready when, on the evening before, Eric Brewer phoned. "Just had news from Bristol. Jim Gregson passed away this morning. There'll be the funeral at Clough Top next week." This, Jane knew, was the unidentifiable something that had told her to delay her departure She would now arrange matters and be in Clough Top in order to say 'goodbye' to her father.

"Strangely enough," she said, "I was planning to go up there, tomorrow.   But this might change things. Whatever I do, I'll go up for the funeral. I'd like to attend it. Thanks for letting me know."

"Spoilt your hopes of seeing him alive, though, hasn't it, love?" said Brewer.

"No.   I've seen him.   But I couldn't ask him anything. He was too confused."

"When was that, then.   And where?   Does Jenny know?"

"I'm afraid I had to be rather devious.   But it was for the best.   And Jenny doesn't know."

"But, but...how the devil?"

"Shall I see you at the funeral?"

"Yes, of course I'll be there."

"I'll tell you about it then," she told him.

"Right,. See you at Clough Top."

"Yes. And meanwhile, not a word. All right?"

"If you say so. 'Bye for now, then."   Jane replaced the receiver. She had bought some time and would invent a story that would satisfy Eric Brewer, and it would be partially true at least.   Then she postponed her journey to the bungalow at Clough Top for a few more days.

oooooOooooo

CHAPTER TWENTY-ONE

It was a dismal, grey day in early autumn. The Parish Church at Clough Top was dark, cold and uninviting. A solitary candle burned on the altar, but otherwise, everything was black. Only a few people sat in the wooden pews, huddled in overcoats and scarves, and most of the ladies wore dark hats. Jane sat alone in a pew towards the back. After what seemed like an eternity, a movement was heard in the porch outside and the voice of a lady – the new Vicar – was heard intoning those inevitable phrases, "I am the Resurrection and the Life, saith the Lord. He that believeth on Me, though he die, yet he shall live:" and the words, more familiar now, continued as the procession moved to the front of the church. Six men carried the large coffin and with due reverence, placed it near the altar steps, bowed, and retreated. They were followed in by a middle aged couple, dressed plainly in black, obviously Jenny and her husband, Thomas; two or three other younger people came as well and there was a tall, distinguished man, accompanied by a lady, presumably his wife. Last of all came Mabel and Eric

Brewer.   Just as the service was about to start, Sara Hardisty tip-toed in and sat at another pew, almost across the centre aisle from Jane.   The two women gestured to each other and then returned their attentions to the rituals of the service.

When it was over, the small family party followed the coffin to a graveside in the churchyard, but as neither Jane nor Sara were inclined to go so far, they stood together, at a distance.   There had been an invitation given for anyone who wished to do so, to take refreshments at the Huntsman afterwards,   and although Jane felt some reluctance, she thought better of it and decided to put in an appearance, just for as long as necessary.   But while they were waiting, feeling cold, and with a few drops of rain spotting on their faces, Jane asked Sara, "Can you come back to the bungalow, afterwards?   I've got something to show you."

"Yes, of course," agreed Sara. "Is it something interesting?"

"Very," Jane emphasised.   "I think you'll be amazed."

At the Huntsman, Jenny, supported by Thomas, greeted each person as they arrived. No longer was she the little schoolgirl that Jane remembered seeing as she walked with her father behind her mother's coffin, nor even the beautiful young bride, to whom Jane had been bridesmaid almost thirty five years ago. Now she was a mature woman, not very tall and not very good-looking, but Jane still remembered her face. Obviously she had put on some weight and not made any effort to lose it again, or to maintain any glamour that once she might have possessed. Jane thought she had become a typical pub landlady. Thomas still seemed to want to help her and please her, and he stood beside her now, shaking hands with each person, and responding to her explanations, This is Mr. so-and-so, you remember he was ..." with "Yes, dear," or "Of course, dear" as might be appropriate.

At first, Jenny looked hard at Sara, and Sara had to respond. "Hello, Jenny. Sara Hardisty. I was W.P.C. Sara Dawson "

"Sara, of course! You dealt with the accident when William Tudge was drowned. I didn't know you had married."

"Married and divorced, I'm afraid. But we had two children. They're grown up, now, of course." The two women embraced.

"My, how time flies. Tom, this lady was a police woman. She was very supportive at the time of dad's accident with the tractor."

"Yes, dear. I remember you telling me..." But then Jenny looked at Jane, whom she recognised almost at once.

"It's Jane, isn't it?" she said, taking Jane's hand and kissing her warmly, as well. "How good of you to come. Where are you living now?"

"South London. But we still have my mother's bungalow here, you know. We often come up for a few days."

"Oh, that's wonderful. Yes, now I remember reading your mother's description of your lovely garden. I knew she was 'Country Girl', you know, and I always read her articles. They were lovely."

"Thank you. She'd have been delighted."

"And your husband?"

"Simon? Yes, he's in the Foreign Office. He's actually abroad today. He had to go off to Strasburg, last night. Otherwise he would have been here. He sends his apologies."

"Thank you. Obviously, he's a busy man. Now, Jane, you know Tom, my husband? Tom dear, Jane was one of my bridesmaids. You remember?"

"Yes, I do. Hello, Jane," said Thomas, and he kissed her.

"Your other bridesmaid was a girl called 'Wendy'. Wendy Mason? Is she here?" Jane enquired.

"No, I'm afraid we lost touch with her. She married, but I don't know where she is, Jane. But you will remember Philip, Tom's best man? He's here."

"Is he? Where?" And Jenny pointed out the tall, grey-haired distinguished gentleman, whom Jane had noticed at the church service. "Oh," she said. "I'll introduce myself. You know he was the first boy who ever kissed me."

"Well, be careful," said Jenny, playfully. "He's got his wife with him now." Jane went over the room to where Philip and his wife were standing. She introduced herself and Philip shook her hand, politely. He introduced Barbara, his wife, and she too, took Jane's hand limply and shook it. But there was no warmth, and after only a minute or two of stilted conversation, Jane thought of Simon, made an excuse, and moved away. Refreshments were served from a buffet, and there was some wine.

It was then that Jane noticed the frail little old lady seated in a comfy side chair, and being assisted by a younger lady. Instinctively, Jane knew her, and crossed to her seat. "Alice," she asked. The old lady looked up, and smiled.

"That's right," she said.

"I'm Jane. You'll remember my mother, Bella Warrington." The old lady clasped Jane in her scrawny arms, and just wept.

"Oh, Jane, love, of course I remember you. Our little Jane." Jane turned to the younger lady.

"I knew Alice when I was a child. She was always very good to me."

"Oh, she's still like that, m' dear," said the lady, in a lovely lilting Welsh accent. "Looks out for every one of us in the home, you know   Though it's us - who - ought to be look-in' out for yer, really."

"I can believe that," said Jane.

Alice said: "Sorry I never managed to get to your mother's funeral, my love.   I 'eard about it, but I was having trouble with me hips, just then, and I just couldn't make it. Not that I didn't want to, mind. But...."

"That's all right, Alice, really. Don't worry about that.   But it's good that you've been able to make Mr. Gregson's."

"Well, he were such a good man, you know, love. Proper decent he were. Never did anything bad. So when Megan offered to bring me over in her car, I really couldn't refuse, could I?"

"You did right, Alice. And it's so good to see you. Lovely."

At this point, Megan looked at her watch. "Well, Alice. I think it's time we were get-ting away, now. It's a fair drive back, you know, and we mustn't - let you get too tired - love, must we, now?"

"Aye, all right, Meg. You've been so kind, and we'll not delay. Ee, but it's been great to see you again, little Jane, really great." Then Alice and Jane embraced each other warmly, before parting. Jane watched as Alice was helped away, said her farewells to Jenny and Thomas, then finally and slowly made her way to the exit. Held with Megan's strong arm, she left the room.

Jane shed some tears, but soon, Sara rejoined her.

"A difficult goodbye?" she asked.

"Very," Jane replied. "You know, that old lady...oh, it's a long story. I'll tell you sometime."

"Perhaps you're ready for an early departure as well?" Sara suggested.

"Yes, but I'd better have a word with Eric and Mabel Brewer. I'll do that, and then we'll go, if you like."

"Suits me. And I'm dying to know what you've got for me, back at the bungalow." At that moment, Eric and Jane achieved eye contact, and Jane went to them.

"Wondered where you'd got to. You're with our Sara, I see," Brewer greeted her.

"Yes. Well, two women on their own, you know."

"I saw you talking to Jenny."

"Yes, but not about – anything important.. This is hardly the right time."

"On the phone you said something about talking to Jim, but he was confused. When was that, then? I told you to get a move on, love. Too late altogether now."

"It doesn't actually matter any more," said Jane. "I've made other discoveries."

"Oh?" Brewer was very curious.

"My mother left some writings. I've learnt everything I needed to know."

"Who your father was?"

"Possibly." She wanted to be cautious, still.

"Jane, please. For God's sake!"

"The writings are private, Eric. But I'll think about it. I'll be in touch, I promise."

"It's over forty years, Jane. Surely...?"

"I said I'll think about it. Please let me do that."

"If that's your wish, of course. But it's been a mystery all this time, I think we have a right to know. Private or not."

"But if it's private, Eric," put in Mabel, "Perhaps it should stay private."

"I don't see why," said Brewer.

"The truth might be hurtful to someone, dear. You must let Jane decide about that. And she's promised to phone you, when she's ready."

"I will be in touch, Eric, honestly. I just need to think."

"All right then, love. But please, let us know something. It's only fair."

With that, Jane kissed them both and walked away. Soon afterwards, she was in Sara's car and they were on the way back to the bungalow.

* * * * *

After Jane received the call from Eric Brewer, telling her of Jim Gregson's death, she did not travel to Clough Top until a couple of days before the funeral. This was not deliberate, except for the fact that she did not want a very long absence from home. As it was, Simon was called away on the same day, Emma had departed for university and, with Sally more or less living at Rupe's flat now, Jane felt that it was important for her to be at home for at least some of the time.

Jane had pondered the reason why Bella had never told her about the room in her loft. She had never even said that work was in progress, or that any extra storage space was required. "Mother might have told me," she remarked to Simon.

"Come to think of it, she did, you know. I remember now," said Simon,

"You remember 'now'!"

"You were very busy with something else at the time, love. It slipped your mind. And mine as well. I admit that. But she did tell us, I'm sure of it. And anyway, at least Mavis and Stanley knew." Jane was unsure as to whether or not Simon was simply employing his skills of diplomacy, for she had no recollection of being told anything about the loft conversion, but she decided not to argue, and just said: "Yes, fortunately. Otherwise we might never have known for many years. Perhaps never at all."

But now they did know about it and she was on her way, at last, to make what she hoped would be some important discoveries. Any desire to postpone the inevitable had gone from her now. This was it: the time when she would find the answers to at least some of her questions. She was ready.

She arrived at Clough Top late in the afternoon. Sally had told her that she could park in front of the bungalow this time, and she did so. She had also phoned Mavis beforehand and she and Stanley were watching for her. Stanley came to the car immediately. "Mavis 'as got tea brewed and biscuits, if you'd like to come to us first," he said, putting his arms around her as they embraced.

"That's very kind," said Jane. "I'll just pop into ours' with my bags and powder my nose, if you don't mind. Then I'll come round, right away All right, Stanley?"

" 'Course, love. D'yer need any 'elp with the bags?"

"No, I'm all right, honestly."

"Well then, just come when you're ready."

From the moment that Sally and Rupe first asked if they could spend that week-end at the bungalow, Jane had an apprehension about how Mavis and Stanley would react, and so, as soon as the initial greetings were over, and they had settled down to the tea and biscuits, she remarked, "I expect you were surprised to see our two love-birds here, the other week?"

"We were worried when we saw th' light on, that's all. We thought someone might've broken in, laak, ya see Jane." said Mavis. "Stanley couldn't rest 'til 'e knew. 'E felt 'e oughta go round."

"Of course. I told Sally to phone you, and she forgot. You know what these young folk can be like. I am so sorry. And I'm very grateful, Stanley. Really I am."

"Well, you can't be sure of anythin', these days," Stanley said.

"It's very kind and reassuring to know you're here. Thank you. But that's not entirely what I meant," Jane went on. "You must have been surprised to find them together? I hope you weren't shocked."

"Nay, luv," Mavis said kindly. "Course, we didn't knaw that young Sally were courtin', laak That were a bit of a surprise, but..."

"Courting - and sleeping together?"

"It's what they do, nowadays, in't it? Gone are the days of waitin'. That's what I said to Stan. But if they're 'appy, so what?"

"What does yer husband think about it?" asked Stanley.

"He's not said a lot. But we think it's pointless trying to interfere. They're obviously well suited to each other, and they say they're very much in love. So we just have to stand back and let it all happen. And he's a nice lad, very trustworthy and honest. I'm sure it's a good match."

They sipped the tea in silence for a few moments. Then Stanley asked, "I suppose you'll be wantin' to see th' loft. then. Seems you didn't know nowt about it?"

"No," said Jane. "Simon's sure that Mother mentioned it some time ago, but I don't remember. It's very strange."

"Likely slipped yer mind, then," said Mavis, trying to be diplomatic.

"Oh yes. Sometimes I just wonder about my own mental state."

"Yer just forgot, luv," Mavis added. "Anybody can do that, yer knaw."

"I simply don't have any recollection. But never mind that now." Jane wanted to see the loft. "Yes please, Stanley", she said. "Will you show me the ropes?"

So Stanley went with Jane, back to her bungalow, and, in the same way as with Sally and Rupe, he showed her the loft and made the access ready. Jane went up the ladder, but compared to her daughter, she was more appropriately dressed in trousers. "Mind yer 'ead on th' roof, luv. You know what happened to the young gentleman."

"Oh yes, I heard all about that. Poor Rupe."

"How is 'e? Got over it all right?"

"Yes. There were no ill effects".

Jane was in the loft at last. She saw the files, binders, boxes and books, which were lined on the shelves, as well as covering parts of the floor and being scattered on a small table. Most importantly of all she saw the row of binders, labelled 'Journal' and numbered consecutively. What secrets, she wondered, would they reveal? She would spend the whole of the following day, the day before Jim Gregson's funeral, sifting through it all. She would see what material could go, either to a newspaper archive or a local heritage library. She would decide if any material should, or could, be assigned to the waste paper bin and she would sift through the journals. For the moment, she searched for the one covering the time of the drowning of William Tudge, and she felt hairs standing up on the back of her neck as she read the entries. She would have to be extremely careful choosing whom, if anyone, she would show what Bella had written.

* * * * *

The body of Jim Gregson was interred with that of Edith in the churchyard. Eric and Mabel Brewer went to the graveside and, with Jenny and her husband and others, threw ceremoniously, small handfuls of soil onto the coffin. Afterwards, they stayed a short while to look at names on some other headstones. They soon found William Tudge, forlorn and lonely now, and somewhat set apart. Then they noticed too, ones for Annie and Brian Halstead, Steve Dinnet alone - so Mavis was still alive - Joe and Martha Hodges, and Trevor Marsh, indicating that Betty, too, lived on. There were residents and trades people – in fact four graves for the Benson family – and other names remembered, but faces forgotten. Before they left Clough Top, they took a walk around the village, noting the improvements that had been made, the re-surfacing of Spring Street and the provision of pavements and kerbs. Alice's old shop was the mini-supermarket, as Jane had discovered, and other business premises had been converted, modernised or replaced by more up-to-date buildings. The 'police house' was still there, but it looked very shabby and, although the little office was also there, that was locked, and there was a free telephone facility on the outside for use in emergencies. The couple had, of course, already seen the improvements at the Huntsman when the funeral refreshments were being served and Eric even caught a glimpse of Heather Gurteen. He understood quite well the interest she would have aroused in Jane's Simon.

* * * * *

Sara and Jane arrived back at the bungalow after the funeral. Jane had left a portable radiator on in the hall – there never had been central heating – and a gas fire was burning low in the sitting room. As they drove down the hill from Spring Street, Jane said to Sara, "I'm afraid I've been quite devious. If he knew, I don't think Eric Brewer would ever forgive me."

"So what have you been up to?" Sara asked. Jane told her of the samples she had managed to obtain for the

DNA testing, and then the result – Jim Gregson was her father. By this time they were inside the bungalow, and Sara sat down by the gas fire. "Good Lord," she said. "That is a surprise."

"But there's more," said Jane. "A lot more." Then she told Sara about Sally and Rupe's stay at the bungalow. "I don't think Mavis and Stanley quite approve of that situation, but they're trying not to show it. Mavis whispered to me that Stanley still regards Sally as a little girl."

"Little girls grow up, don't they?" remarked Sara. "And they discover boys. How do you feel about it, Jane?"

"My only problem is that she doesn't stymie her career, that they don't start a family too soon. She's clever, Sara, and in a good job. A baby would ruin everything for her at the moment. Mind you, there's child care, and I could help out as well, but.... Anyway, we're getting away from the main point." She then told Sara of the discovery of the loft, and all its contents. She had brought the journals down and there they were on a side table. "I went through them all yesterday and I've flagged up the relevant entries. Have a look, starting with the earliest. You'll be very interested."

The first binder into which Jane had inserted a tag of coloured paper, covered the year prior to Jane's own birth. The first flagged entry was for a day in the summer.

'Cheshire Agricultural Show - Hooton. During the afternoon a tall, thin man came to me and introduced himself. He was Mr. Gregson, who farms Moorside, above Clough Top. He said he'd seen me around the village. He keeps pigs, and has sheep on the moors, mainly. A bit rough, but nice enough, I suppose.'

The next entry was for only a few days later. *'Met Mr. Gregson in the village. Talked about farming in general, and he said if I wanted any information, tips or just general gossip, I could always ask him. He'd be glad to help.'* A further entry was for the following day: *'Mr. Gregson came to the bungalow and offered me a small quantity of freshly cured bacon. It was 'spare', he said. I accepted it.'*

Several days then passed before Bella wrote. *'I was anxious to discover the current MAFF Regulations concerning the dipping of sheep. I called at Moorside, and*

Jim Gregson gladly obliged with copies only recently issued. I was able to borrow them – very helpful. Met his wife and daughter. Jenny is a lovely little schoolgirl His wife was a bit tricky. Rather stiff and reserved, I thought. Oh well!' Entries for several intermittent, subsequent days, though mainly concerned with her journalistic activities, which, in fact, always formed the main text of the day, were endorsed with short abbreviated notes – *'Saw Jim;'* *' J. called in;'* and one admitted, *'With J. at Chelford C.M. A few drinks at a local place afterwards.'* - Jane soon realised that C.M. stood for Cattle Market -.

The entries went on, but early in the New Year the contacts were becoming more frequent. Then one said, *'He stayed for the afternoon, and we made love. But this is getting ridiculous. This man thinks he loves me, and I…what can I do?'* The most revealing of all the entries came on the day that William Tudge drowned:

'I had sent a message via Willy Tudge, for J. to call, urgently. Soon after breakfast he came. He was in a great hurry, saying that he'd left the tractor and trailer on the lane side at the track end, with Willy on. Willy was prone to ignore instructions and tamper with things. But I

needed to tell him the news. I was going to have his child! He was shattered. Would I have an abortion? Of course I wouldn't! We argued a while and he left, abruptly, angrily. He returned only a few moments later. The tractor had gone! It had descended the hill and crashed through the river wall. I think he panicked He told me to say nothing, and went off across the Common.'

Further entries described the aftermath, Gregson's remorse at running away, and leaving the scene. But William would surely have drowned – his fate was sealed from the moment the handbrake on the tractor was released. And the stories Gregson told the police, and maintained forever afterwards. That he had left the tractor parked safely on the croft at the bottom of the hill, and that he had been away on the moors, all day. There were notes about the police enquiries – he even lied to his friend, Eric Brewer – and at the inquest. The story about the Council lorry having to reverse downhill was one lie. But Gregson knew that scars had been left on the roadside, tracing back to the end of the bungalow track from where the tractor had descended, and an explanation might be needed. So he told Brewer first, and Brewer accepted it as the truth. There was one final, relevant entry. *'Finally, he agreed that I should have the baby, but on condition that a father would never be identified. Further, he said, that the responsibility might be placed on someone else, and I was to agree never to affirm, or deny, any rumours that might emerge. I agreed to it.'* But to this, a further note was added, squashed in between the first and a later entry. It read, *'If I had known what was intended - the rumour put around – I would not have agreed so readily. It turns out that J planted the rumour in a chat with EB, and obligingly, EB opened his mouth. But I had given my word, my child was soon to be born - it was too late. At least I have kept my side of the bargain.'*

Sara read, and re-read the entries several times, and Jane noticed tears in her eyes. Finally, she said, "There's so much humanity here, don't you think, Jane?"

"Human weakness, for a start," said Jane. "Apart from the matter of the infidelity, there was his fear of prosecution over the tractor business."

"If we, the police, had known that he'd left that lad in that situation for a second, we'd have prosecuted. I'm sure of that. He might have got time for it, you know.

Obviously, the lad couldn't be trusted not to mess around with the tractor controls, and Jim knew it."

"So he ran away and then denied all knowledge of the incident"

"A deceit he's managed to maintain ever since. That's remarkable."

"But my mother had delayed him." Jane observed.

"It might have already happened. Almost as soon as Jim had turned his back and walked away from the vehicle. A few seconds would've been long enough."

"So they let William take the blame for everything. How convenient. "

"Your mother kept her word. She had little option. The Vicar tried to get at the truth, William was a member of his church. But she kept quiet. She never even put his mind at ease. He told me that at the time. And another thing: Edith Gregson, like Betty Marsh, was a strong churchgoer. If it had got around that Jim was having an affair with your mother, or indeed, anyone else, there would've been ructions. Might even have been a divorce."

"I hardly think so," said Jane. Look, there's one more important entry, but it's much earlier." She indicated a tag in another journal, and it covered the time of Edith's death from breast cancer.   Bella recorded taking Jane to Moorside Farm shortly after the funeral, and while the little girl went out to see the rabbits with Jenny, Jim Gregson had cried.   It wasn't only grief at the loss of his wife, whom he truly loved, as the text disclosed, but it was remorse as well:

'He had been unfaithful to her.   We had deceived her, and now he felt unbearable pain.   For my part, I sometimes felt that Edith knew, but she saw no gain in exposure – for what good would that have done?   Now we must both live with the knowledge of what we did then and hope that the day might dawn when the pain is less severe.'

When Sara had read this, she said, "It's like I say, so much humanity."   Then she added,   "E.B.   Eric Brewer.   Don't let him see this, Jane.   It would hurt him terribly."

"Yes, I know."

"Just think, too," Sara went on.   "Your mother and Jim Gregson could never have married. That would have told Eric much.   He would have realised some of the truth and that would have been very dangerous."

"Yes, of course it would." Jane agreed. "But who's to say that either of them ever wanted to be wed anyway?"

"No. Probably it was something they never considered," Sara concluded. "But that little path across the 'backs' was useful for them. Secluded and a short cut between the farm and the bungalow. Jim's visits would be unobserved."

"Very useful," Jane agreed. "Now let me show you something else," she said, going to a cardboard box at the side of the room. She extracted the little bridesmaid's dress. "I was a bridesmaid to Jenny. I wore this dress."

"Yes, so you did. I was there, remember. I saw you, and you looked gorgeous."

"I think he organised that, you know. After all, Jenny is my half sister."

"He wasn't going to leave you out."

"No. And Mother kept the dress. Doesn't that say something?"

"It says volumes," said Sara.

Jane made a snack meal, and they sat discussing the issues as they ate. They agreed that the journals should be kept under lock and key forever. Jane would take them home, along with the scrap book and some other personal material. The remaining items would be deposited in an appropriate archive. She would attend to all that as well. Sara also then remembered her encounter with Alec Tozer on the Heath, at Knutsford. 'He was right, all along,' she thought. But she knew as well that Tozer had died only recently. If he hadn't, might she have tried to inform him? A rhetorical question that she was unable to answer.

Sara and Jane considered what they should tell Eric Brewer. In a fortnight, Sara knew that he and Mabel were off on another golfing holiday – several weeks in Spain. They would stall matters until then, and perhaps his curiosity might wane after the holiday. Sara would talk to him.

But now, Sara and Jane knew the truth, for there it was, written down in Bella's hand. Jim Gregson had been an utter rascal, if not an outright criminal. Nevertheless, Jenny had remained happily ignorant of it all and she was long established in her chosen occupation as a pub landlady. Hopefully the blissful ignorance of her mother, Edith, to the end of her shortened life, had been preserved as well. It had been a child for Bella, wonderful Jane, now an adored wife and mother herself, and two beautiful and talented daughters just embarking on exciting lives of their own. True or false, not a bad legacy for the 'Leprechaun'.

Two weeks later, the Brewers went off on the Spanish golfing holiday. They stayed at a top class hotel at Alicante, linked directly to a golf course. Eric enjoyed some good rounds. On one day, he felt a little off colour. He went out and played five holes in spite of everything. There he had a heart attack. He was rushed to hospital, but did not survive. He died within an hour.

oooooOooooo

The Author

David Huxley has been interested in writing ever since a poem won him a school prize. He has written plays for the amateur theatre, several of which have won competition prizes, been performed, or published (one in the U.S.A.). *Legacy of the Leprechaun* is David's first novel in adulthood. It was written in his retirement, following a career in local government, small publishing, and as a second-hand bookseller. He has also researched the history of Manchester's theatres and is preparing a text for publication.

oooooOooooo